WICKED SINNER

"*Wicked Sinner* has sexy suspense, banter, friendships, and a second chance at the one. Ms. Kennedy provided a good balance between the romance, suspense, heat, and humor. Fans of J.S. Scott and Stefanie London will enjoy *Wicked Sinner*."

—Harlequin Junkie

"A tantalizing mix of thrills, fierce friendships, and second-chance sexiness!"

—Fresh Fiction

"Second chance romance, small town, ruined wedding: *Wicked Sinner* delivers all of it."

—The Book Disciple

"A lovely romantic suspense that is sure to leave you wanting more."

—Lovely Love Day

"A powerful small-town love story about second chances and forgiveness. Asher and Remy's story is heartbreaking and magical."

—Cocktails and Books

"A great story about two people who get a second chance at love. Sweet and sexy."

—Guilty Pleasures Book Reviews

Ruthless Bastard

Ruthless Bastard

Dangerous Love #3

USA Today Bestselling Author

STACEY KENNEDY

New York   Boston

Forever Yours
Hachette Book Group
1290 Avenue of the Americas, New York, NY 10104
read-forever.com
twitter.com/readforeverpub

First published as an ebook and as a print on demand: April 2020

Forever Yours is an imprint of Grand Central Publishing. The Forever Yours name and logo are trademarks of Hachette Book Group, Inc.

The publisher is not responsible for websites (or their content) that are not owned by the publisher.

The Hachette Speakers Bureau provides a wide range of authors for speaking events. To find out more, go to www.hachettespeakersbureau.com or call (866) 376-6591.

ISBNs: 978-1-5387-4697-4 (ebook), 978-1-5387-4699-8 (print on demand)

For anyone who hit a few detours in life,
but always found their way home.

Ruthless Bastard

Prologue

Kinsley Knight's lush body was temptation. Her pouty lips, pure seduction. And the lust in her eyes pulled Rhett West in until she left him dizzy.

She was also totally off limits.

The blistering heat on the tropical island remained, even though the sun had gone down hours ago. Rhett's entire inner circle of friends were celebrating tonight. His two childhood friends, and fellow detectives, Boone Knight and Asher Sullivan, were standing at the bar ordering up another round of drinks. On the beach, twirling on the makeshift dance floor, was Asher's wife, and Kinsley's best friend, the vivacious Remy, with her bright green eyes and sunny blond hair. The gorgeous blonde with hazel eyes full of happiness, and wearing the white wedding dress, was Peyton, Boone's new wife. And among them were all of Boone and Peyton's family, as they'd all come to witness the intimate ceremony, which also included a week-long trip in the tropics. Tomorrow they'd all leave, while Boone and Peyton stayed for another week to enjoy their honeymoon. Rhett was counting down the hours. All week long, Kinsley was getting in his head, making him want things he shouldn't.

With the bulb lights twinkling off the trees they were hung in, Kinsley spun, her arms in the air, when suddenly she caught him looking at her. A slight smile curved her lips. The temptress knew exactly what she did to him and played on that, and the fun way she danced shifted. She held his gaze, slowing rolling her hips, her dress flowing with the curves of her body, hardening Rhett to steel.

He shouldn't take the bait, but he couldn't help himself either. He leaned back in his chair and sipped his scotch, watching every sexy move she made. She spun around, her gorgeous ass moving slowly, the satiny dress revealing every perfect curve. When she turned back again, and gave him a little smile, he groaned and polished off his second glass of scotch.

For the past three years, after retiring from the military, he'd worked as a detective for the Stoney Creek Police Department, and he took pleasure where he could find it, ensuring he kept Kinsley at arm's length. But it was this damn tropical island. Seeing her strutting around in a string bikini with barely anything covering her had fueled his desire for her. He wanted a taste of her sun-kissed skin.

And she knew it.

"Something caught your eye?"

"Shut up." Rhett snorted, glancing at Asher. His friend's light green eyes were all but twinkling as he took a seat beside him. No one except Asher knew that Rhett had a soft spot for Kinsley. Rhett had never told him, but Asher always had a way of reading people. Those people skills made him a damn good detective. Luckily, Asher only hinted that he knew; he never came outright and said the truth Rhett wanted to avoid. "Shouldn't you be dancing with your wife?" Rhett asked, giving him a shove to go away.

Asher grinned. "And miss this fine show happening over here?"

Rhett scowled, lips parting to spew a few choice words when Boone dropped down in the chair on Rhett's other side. Both Kinsley and Boone shared their father's brown hair and blue eyes.

"She's handling this well," Boone said before taking a swig of his beer.

Rhett's chest tightened, heat flushing his already warm skin beneath his white button-up. "Handling what well?"

"Our mother being here." Boone gestured toward the bar.

Rosemary, along with her husband, were talking to her ex-husband, Hank. Rosemary looked a lot like Kinsley, just an older version with a bob instead of long hair, and dark eyes instead of blue. But the biggest difference between them was on the inside, not their physical appearance. Kinsley was loyal and kind, whereas Rosemary was a horrible person, who'd walked out on her family, leaving them behind. She should not even be there as far as Rhett was concerned, but Boone had made peace with his mother, something that Kinsley never wanted.

Rhett wondered if that's why their inner circle of friends was always so tight. Boone, Asher, and Rhett's friendship had been born from hard times. Boone's mother left. Then Asher's mother died. It brought them together in a way that forever bonded them, leaving no room for anyone to break them apart. Until Rhett returned from the military and found Kinsley all grown up. No longer was she the kid that drove them crazy;

she was a beautiful woman who drove him crazy with desire. And she was certainly the one person who could break their friendships apart.

Laughter from the beach drew Rhett's gaze. The women were now sitting in the sand, obviously having fallen over in their dancing.

Boone chuckled and rose. "And that's my cue to take my wife to bed."

Rhett got to his feet as well, pulling Boone into a rough hug. "Congrats, man. Couldn't have been a better day."

"You're right about that." Boone smiled before making his way toward his wife.

Rhett vaguely watched Asher go and collect Remy. The night was wrapping up and the few remaining guests began leaving, but something else caught Rhett's eye. Rosemary was no longer at the bar; she was approaching Kinsley. Rhett felt himself take a step forward before he forced that foot back down.

Seconds passed like long minutes as Rosemary touched Kinsley's arm, garnering her attention. Kinsley turned around, facing her mother with the bravery he'd come to expect from her. Rosemary's mouth moved. Kinsley simply blinked and then walked away. The hurt crossing Rosemary's face made Rhett's blood turn red-hot.

He strode forward. Now that Boone had left, he finally felt free to say his piece. He stopped next to Rosemary. "You're lucky that one child forgives you," he told her. "Respect her wishes not to talk to you." Rosemary's tears only enraged him more. He stood with Kinsley on this. Her leaving them as children and barely even keeping in touch with them now were unforgivable.

His head screamed at him to stay put, but his feet were

moving, almost against his will. A minute later, he found Kinsley standing on a rock, her high heels dangling from her hand. The warm breeze fluttered in the night. "All right?" he asked, slowly approaching her.

Kinsley glanced over her shoulder, tears in her eyes. She eventually nodded and turned her gaze back to the dark water.

Rhett settled in next to her, staying quiet, not even knowing what to say.

Kinsley finally filled the silence. "It's funny, you know. I wasn't sure what I'd feel seeing that woman."

"It's understandable if seeing her upsets you."

She looked up at him with those crystal blue eyes that pierced right through him. "Seeing her only upsets me because it reminds me that my grandmother isn't here. The people who really loved Boone should be here, not the one who never mattered."

An unusual rush of warmth washed over him. His fingers twitched to reach out to her, as a tear brushed down her cheek. Her strength blindsided him and her beauty engulfed him with an intensity he couldn't extinguish. But her emotion, seeing those eyes fill with sadness, broke down any wall he had up against her.

He wasn't thinking about repercussions when he reached out and brought her into his arms, only that he needed her close. She wrapped her arms around him, and he heard her high heels fall against the rock as her chin lifted. He looked into those eyes that penetrated places no one had before and he turned his mind off. His lips met hers, and there was no thought anymore. There was only her and him and the perfection of a long-awaited kiss that made him only want *more*.

So much more that somewhere between kissing her on the

beach, finding their way back to his suite, he'd thrown caution to wind, forgetting why he should stay away from her.

Up until the next morning when he stood over her, while she lay sleeping in his bed, her dark hair curtaining the white pillow.

Stark naked, he glanced at the floor, finding three open condom wrappers.

Fuck.

"Why are you staring at me?" Kinsley groaned, her face buried in the pillow. She turned her head a little and peeked open an eye. "Ugh. There's two of you, and both of you look really pissed off."

Rhett thrust his hands into his hair. "Please tell me this is a nightmare and we actually didn't sleep together last night." But every moan, every hot kiss, was burned in his memory. He remembered just how she tasted while his tongue trailed over her flesh, the amazing floral scent of her stuck in his nostrils.

She rolled over then and Rhett caught a full view of her incredible breasts. *You're so goddamn beautiful…* he'd practically purred at her last night after she'd bared herself to him. The lustful eyes she gave him after that comment had him quickly turning around now, as he desperately tried to scrub the memory from his mind. "Get dressed," he told her.

"You're naked too, you know," she said with a smile in her voice. "And it's quite clear you still want me."

He frowned at her over his shoulder and then scowled at his hard cock. "Get dressed. Right now." He went to his suitcase, took out a pair of shorts, and slipped into them. When he turned back around, he found her sitting up in bed with the blankets covering her chest. His mind stuttered at the sight of her. Long, dark tousled hair and gorgeous blue eyes, both of which were a stark contrast against the white pillows and sheets. "Jesus Christ," he said aloud, moving to the chair, wanting to be as far away from her as possible, considering he was contemplating climbing back into bed with her. "What the fuck have I done?"

"Me," she said with a laugh. "And damn, it was good."

He dropped his hands and frowned at her. "Kinsley," he said in a warning tone.

Instead of responding, which was what he'd expected, she pushed away the sheets and rose from the bed. Rhett's cock went from hard to rock hard so fast, he grunted.

Harder...faster...God, yes, Rhett...more... Her husky voice echoed in his head. No, hell, in his goddamn soul. She was perfect last night. And she was perfect now. Every single inch of her. Curves in all the right places. Her skin smooth and creamy. But those eyes of hers—filled with heat and sass and something he couldn't put a name on—unraveled him. "What are you doing to me?" he grumbled.

"Making this as painful as possible." She grinned and reached for her bra and panties on the floor, turning her heart-shaped ass to him as she bent over.

He groaned. Every stroke inside her body still burned against his flesh. "It's working."

She quickly dressed in her sexy thong panties and black lace bra, then slid into her slinky bridesmaid dress, reminding Rhett that they were there at the resort for her brother's wedding. He was a fucking terrible friend.

Kinsley finally turned around and gave him a sexy smile. "You can relax. Boone will never know about this." She walked over to Rhett and stared down at him, her pretty hair curtaining the soft lines of her cheekbones.

Rhett clenched his fists, fighting against his desire to tangle his fingers in their strands and pull her right back onto his lap. "This shouldn't have fucking happened." He stood up abruptly. And as he did, he saw the way her pupils dilated. The same way they always did when he got close. It was why he kept his distance. She deserved better than him. Kinsley was sunshine and light; she radiated warmth. She deserved a man that had his shit together and knew how to commit to a woman. Rhett was not that man.

Bold as ever, she took a step forward, closing the distance between them. "We both knew this eventually would happen. Now it has, and we can finally get over this push and pull thing we've been ignoring for years." She gave him a smile that didn't quite reach her eyes. "Don't worry, West, you can go back home and let everyone keep thinking you're a ruthless bastard." She made her way to the door.

He balked. "I am a ruthless bastard," he called out to her.

Her hand froze on the door handle and she glanced over her shoulder. She didn't need to say a word. With just that warm and soft look, she slayed him. "Rhett," she said slowly. "We both know that I could never think that." Then she walked out, shutting the door behind her, and all that was left was a breathless, weightless feeling deep in Rhett's gut that whatever they'd done last night wasn't going to change just them; it was going to change everything.

Chapter 1

Two months later...

"Gimme another whiskey, tits!"

Kinsley let the drunk's rude remark roll off her back. He'd never been in her jazz club, Whiskey Blues, until tonight, and since today was her twenty-ninth birthday, the last thing she wanted was to deal with this jerk. As the owner of one of only two bars in Stoney Creek, a small town hugging the coastline in Maine, she was used to a rowdy customer every now and again. She'd purchased the dive bar with the inheritance her grandparents had left her right after college, and she had redecorated right away. She'd left the bar's original flagstone walls, but she'd brought in burgundy velvet chairs and added an abundance of gold accents to the space, as well as four large crystal chandeliers to bring warmth and class to the bar. It had taken more than a few years to get the bar off the ground and running, but now she had a waitlist of jazz singers to play on the shiny black stage set in front of the round tables. Every single part of this bar was her heart project, and she'd never been prouder of what she'd built there and the success the bar had seen in these last six years. Therefore, a few vulgar slurs and drunken fools she could handle.

"Hey, blue eyes, did ya hear me?"

Kinsley finally sighed and acknowledged the man. She took in his lost dark eyes, the deep wrinkles set in his face. It didn't take much to see that the man had been through hard times. It looked like he'd lived three lives already. She swallowed back the verbal lashing sitting on the tip of her tongue and met the gaze of the head bartender, Benji. He stood at the far side of the bar, wearing jeans and a black T-shirt with WHISKEY BLUES written across his chest. Benji obviously caught the conversation, his mouth set in a tight line, and his sharp green eyes locked on to Kinsley. She gave a quick nod, and Benji disappeared into the back, only to return a few moments later with Justin, the cook, who did MMA fighting as his hobby.

As the sweet and tender voice of Annabella, a new singer to Whiskey Blues, filled the room, entertaining the crowd, Justin approached with a powerful stride and a body packed full of hard muscle. "Problem?" he asked, sidling up to Kinsley, his stern gaze roaming over the man sitting on the stool.

"This gentleman needs to go home now," she said. "He's not using his nice words."

Justin's mouth twitched but any and all amusement fled when he looked at the drunken man again. "Do I need to help you leave, sir?" His voice was polite but also laced with a warning. "Or can I stay here and watch you leave?"

The unruly man gave Justin a hard look, taking in the corded muscles on his forearms and the size of his biceps, then cursed and stumbled toward the door, giving them a rude gesture on the way out.

"His nice words?" Justin laughed, turning back to Kinsley.

She shrugged and grabbed a rag near the sink. "It must be a full moon or something; that's the third rude person tonight." She'd seen it time and time again. Full moons made people act…*wild*.

"Well, let's hope that's the last," Justin said.

She nodded. The shadow beneath his eye was a reminder of the tourist from last weekend who had decided Justin was his mortal enemy. Luckily, Boone had been in the bar that night, stepping in when Justin took the powerful punch. "Thanks for coming to get him on his way."

Justin saluted her. "It's what you pay me the big bucks for."

She laughed. He wasn't lying. She did pay him more than she would a short order cook, but she was glad to have the extra muscle on staff.

While Justin headed back to the kitchen, she took away the man's empty glass and wiped down the bar.

"If that's not your cue to get out of here," Benji said, stepping in next to her, "I don't know what is." He leaned a hip against the side of the ice bucket and folded his arms. Being a few inches taller than her, Benji could certainly hold his own. "Do I need to remind you that you own this bar? You make the rules. Why the hell are you working on your birthday?"

Why, indeed?

Lately, all Kinsley had been doing was keeping herself busy. She didn't even try and pretend she didn't know why…*Rhett*. "What can I say, I just love you so much, Benji. Why would I be anywhere else but here with you?"

Benji flashed his charming grin, his unruly blond hair falling down over his brow. "I am pretty lovable, aren't I?" He nudged her in the playful way they were accustomed to ever since they'd spent two hot weeks together—long before she hired him as head bartender.

"Truly." She smiled.

Benji's grin fell. "Seriously, though, get out of here. Lola and I've got the bar tonight." Lola was the other bartender on staff, whom Kinsley had hired after Remy quit to open up her own New Age magic shop next door.

She knew she needed to face tonight. Another birthday...*alone*. "I'll help until Lola comes then I'm outta here," she said.

"Good." Benji flashed her his cute grin that always won over the ladies. It had made an impact on Kinsley too, until the lust died between them and all that remained was a good, solid friendship. "Any big plans for tonight?" he asked.

Kinsley tried not to flinch. And failed. "Does watching reruns of *Friends* and eating a bag of chips count as big?"

Benji frowned. "Kinsley, you're twenty-nine, not dead."

She certainly wasn't dead, but she wasn't sure what she was anymore. Bored, lonely, and everything in between. She tried not to feel emotional that no one had dropped in today to greet her—not her brother or Peyton or her father or Remy. They'd all been so busy with their lives, it seemed they'd forgotten her birthday. "I'm sure we'll end up doing something next weekend."

"You better," Benji said, right as the bar's front door opened.

Three men entered. All tall and wide in the shoulders. The one leading the group held Kinsley's gaze as he approached. Shaggy brown hair, dark eyes that held little warmth, and lips that curled at the corners like he had some wicked insight. "I'll grab these guys," she told Benji. "Wanna make sure we're all stocked up before things get busy tonight?" In two hours, the bar would be packed full because of the headline singer coming in from Nashville.

Benji's attention stayed with the men entering the bar before he looked at her and nodded. "Yeah, sure."

When he disappeared into the back room, Kinsley closed in on the three men sliding onto the stools at the bar, catching the RED DRAGON crest on the arms of their leather jackets. The biker gang hailed from Whitby Falls, the larger neighboring city to the north. They were bad news, a ruthless, dangerous motorcycle gang, who killed often, and never asked questions. Her dad, brother, and late grandfather were all cops, and growing up, Kinsley had heard stories of these guys. Terrible stories of murder, greed, and more murder.

"Welcome to Whiskey Blues," she greeted them, placing three circular coasters down on the bar with the club's logo of a guitar in neon blue and WHISKEY BLUES written in a bold yellow. "What can I get ya?"

The man who'd led the group inside ignored her question. Instead, he said, "Cute place."

"Thanks." She forced a smile, even though his tone made it clear that he meant to insult, not praise. "What can I get for you?" she repeated.

"Whiskey. Neat. All around."

She turned away, fighting against the slight tremble of her fingers before she forced herself to get it together. Men like these got off on scaring the public. She'd never give them that satisfaction. She reached for three shot glasses then grabbed the whiskey bottle behind her bar, feeling their gazes examining her every move.

She poured the shots. "Enjoy."

The same man grinned darkly, sending a chill straight into her bones. With his gaze set on hers, he lifted the shot glass in salute then downed it. There was something disconcerting in the way he watched her. A little too closely, knowingly almost. Though what truly worried her was the gun she saw resting beneath his leather coat.

After a lifetime around cops, Kinsley knew to trust her instincts, and her inner alarms screamed at her. While the other two men polished off their shots, she quickly moved to the other side of the bar, the hairs on the back of her neck rising with every step. She grabbed her cell phone from her back pocket and dialed her brother.

No answer.

"Dammit," she spat.

She tried Asher.

Again, no answer.

The room began to swallow her up. A quick look back, and the leader smiled at her again. Not a nice smile, but more of a I'm-going-to-eat-you-my-dear grin. She *really* didn't want to make the next call. For two weeks she'd been trying to get in touch with Rhett. He'd never returned her call. Not once. She'd even showed up at his house one night. He didn't answer the door, even though she knew he was inside.

But the tightness in her gut and the steady thumping of her heart had her texting Rhett: 911. That was their code for call immediately.

Her phone rang a second later. "What's wrong?"

Rhett's low smooth voice sent goose bumps racing across her arms. "Wow. You actually called me back."

There was a pause. A long pause. One that went on and

on, with all the awkwardness that had been present between them ever since that hot night in the tropics. And yet…*and yet*…Kinsley wouldn't go back and change a thing. It didn't matter that Rhett could barely look her in the eye anymore, or that he never came into the bar, that night had changed her life. In good ways that she'd never regret.

"Are you in trouble?" he finally asked, breaking the heavy silence.

"Maybe. Are you busy right now? There's some guys that just came into the bar—"

"I'm on my way." The call ended.

She released a breath and slid her cell phone into her pocket then shuffled back to the bar. Neither of the three men had moved, still watching her with their creepy eyes.

"Sweetheart," the leader said in a voice that stole any warmth from the word. "Another shot for me and my guys here."

She avoided the coldness in his stare and grabbed the whiskey bottle on the back wall then refilled the shot glasses. "Let me know if you need anything else," she told them.

"Oh, I definitely need something else," he purred, a scary edge rising in his gaze.

Kinsley sighed heavily, making sure he heard. There was one thing she hated more than drunk rudeness, and that was arrogant cockiness. "Listen, I've already kicked out one person tonight. Wanna be number two?"

The guy's wink sent off warning bells in her mind. "Now *that* sounds like an interesting night."

And just like that, she'd had enough of men tonight. She craved her bed and some peace and quiet to have her pity party over her terrible birthday. But right as she went to turn away, the man latched on to her wrist. Hard. She whirled back to him, but any insults she planned on yelling at him died. His stare penetrated her, practically stripping her skin off and peeling back the layers until he found her weak spots.

"Remove your hand."

The sharp order snapped her attention up. She released a shuddering breath, both in relief to find Rhett had arrived and surprise at the venom in his voice. But too soon all she felt was a heady warmth brought on by his closeness and the dangerous glint in his rich chocolate brown eyes and black hair. Rhett *was* intimidating. He'd left for the military as a kid and come back home stronger and all grown up. Now thirty-three years old, Rhett's body was made up of solid muscle from dedication to being in top form. He was a bit too rough to be called handsome, but Rhett was pure masculine perfection, and Kinsley was there for all of it.

The man's fingers only tightened on Kinsley's wrist. "We got a problem here, West?" he asked.

Rhett slowly gestured toward her wrist, those eyes now blazing. "Do you need assistance removing your hand, Dalton?"

The fact that Rhett knew him only made Kinsley feel better about calling. The man squeezing her wrist was a well-known criminal. She sensed the bar go quiet, the customers at their tables slowly turning to watch them. She stood frozen, her free hand moving to her belly as her earlier dinner went leaden in her stomach. No sounds crept in except the quickening of her heartbeat in her ears. Until the guy squeezed her wrist again. Hard. She flinched against the pain, and then everything happened so fast.

Rhett took Dalton to the ground, which nearly pulled her onto the bar since the biker fought against letting go. The other two men jumped to their feet, their stools kicked to the side, but Rhett was ready with his weapon aimed in their direction.

A beat passed.

"Do not toy with me, Dalton," Rhett growled, his attention on the standing men.

Kinsley blinked.

"You can leave," Rhett went on, "or I can take you down to the station." He dug his knee into Dalton's back, easily pinning him with a fierce hold on his neck.

It was the absolute worst time for Kinsley's attention to roam over Rhett's bulging biceps and the corded muscles on his forearms. Heat rolled over her. Outnumbered, Rhett looked bold and brave and damn near the sexiest thing Kinsley had ever seen in her life.

Dalton laughed gruffly. "Ah, West, I didn't know she was your girl. My apologies. We'll go."

Rhett was off him a second later. Both his hands were on his weapon now, not aiming at anyone specifically, but Kinsley knew that if he needed to take them out, he'd do so in a second, without a blink of an eye. The trained soldier was coiled, ready.

Dalton jumped to his feet and brushed off his jeans. "Still a quick bastard, I see," he said, grinning at Rhett. Then his gaze swept over Kinsley, roaming from head to toe. "Didn't realize you were a claimed woman. Too bad, princess. We could've had fun."

"Go home, Dalton," Rhett warned. "Last chance."

It occurred to Kinsley why Rhett didn't correct Dalton's assumption that they were together, and it had nothing to do with caring for her. If Dalton thought she was with Rhett, a Stoney Creek detective, he likely wouldn't come back.

Which was fine by her. She didn't want Dalton to come back. Ever.

Dalton gave Rhett a slow smile before returning those cold, hard eyes to Kinsley. She found something so unsettling about him but couldn't quite pinpoint the reason.

Before she could figure it out, he was gone, his men following behind him, and finally, Kinsley could breathe again.

"Are you all right?"

Kinsley forced a nod. "Yeah. Yeah, I'm okay."

But she wasn't okay. She was anything but okay. It had been two months since she'd seen Rhett. Everything she felt for him hit her like a punch to the gut. And she realized the greatest threat to her hadn't left the bar but was standing right in front of her.

Chapter 2

Kinsley was all warmth, affection, and so much…brightness. Rhett could barely breathe as they stared into each other's eyes, reminded of all the ways she wrecked him. Two months had gone by since he'd touched her, and every minute, every second, had been a struggle to stay away from her.

She quickly regained her composure like she always did, but he had to force himself to look away first. If he stared too long, he got lost in the intensity between them. Rhett couldn't allow that. For her sake. He was a soldier, not a civilian. He belonged on the battlefield, not living in a small town or playing house with anyone. And through the years of watching Kinsley grow up, he knew she wanted the husband, the 2.2 kids, the walks in the park, the movie nights. Rhett could barely sit in one place for longer than twenty minutes before he got edgy.

The rumble of motorcycles roared on the other side of the door and Rhett gritted his teeth. Dalton Greeves, and the others with him, belonged to the notoriously dangerous RED DRAGONS motorcycle club. It wasn't often that Dalton and his men came into Stoney Creek. They had no business there. And Rhett hoped this wasn't a start to something, especially considering Dalton had put his focus on Kinsley.

When the motorcycles were all but a soft rumble now, Rhett noticed the silence in the bar. He took in the customers, all sitting at their tables looking in his direction. Most were pale. Some looked ready to bolt. "It's all right," he told the crowd. "I'm police. You're all safe, and they won't be coming back tonight." He glanced at the pretty singer onstage and nodded her on.

She quickly moved toward the microphone and got right back into the song that obviously had been interrupted, filling the bar with her velvety voice.

To settle the crowd, Rhett holstered his weapon and slid onto the stool. When his gaze met Kinsley's again, he found that the connection they'd had a minute ago was now gone. "Any idea why they were here?" he asked her.

She shrugged. "Being aggressive pricks is my guess."

The slight movement of her shoulder drew his attention to her body. Her beauty stunned him, every damn time. Her blue eyes were like no other color he had seen in his life. Bright against her chocolate brown hair. But what he liked most about Kinsley was her strength. She had her shit together.

Just then, Benji, the guy Rhett still could never get a read on, sidled up next to Kinsley. "I leave for one second to stock the fridges and all hell breaks loose." He examined her, a little too intimately if Rhett had anything to say about it, before sliding his arm around her. "Are you okay?"

She nodded, her face ashen.

Rhett stared at Benji's arm, willing it to burst into flames. Benji's affection only reminded Rhett how bad he was with people. He should have comforted her. Christ, he should have done a lot of things, but getting anything right aside from being a soldier and a detective wasn't in his nature. He stayed put, arms resting on the bar, not getting any closer to Kinsley than was absolutely necessary. He did not trust himself to keep his hands to himself. "They won't come back," he told her, hoping to reassure her. "This is what the gang does. They come in, rattle people up, and leave."

"They better not come back," she said, stepping out of Benji's arms. "The last thing I need is a bunch of hooligans scaring off my customers." She placed her hands on the ice bin in front of her and drew in a long, deep breath, and with that single breath, she seemed to shed the remainder of worry shadowing her.

She looked very much like the in-control, sexy woman that Rhett had found when he came home from the military. Kinsley had always just been Boone's younger sister. The cute, feisty kid who stood up to bullies on the playground and got into more trouble than her older brother did. Rhett had once pulled her off one of the biggest guys in high school as she clawed out to hurt him for spreading lies about one of her friends. She'd always been a spitfire, but when Rhett left for the military, she'd still been a kid. When he came home, he discovered that she'd become a woman, a gorgeous one at that, and she drew him right in. For years, he fought his attraction to her, but she was simply unforgettable. And yet, he couldn't be more wrong for her.

Rhett knew how to hunt and how to kill. He knew how to make sure a woman left his bed satisfied. But he didn't know how to love her. Not in the way she should be loved. And even if he wanted to, which he wasn't sure he did, he was too far gone.

To make the boundary between them as clear as ever, he slid off the stool and said, "If they come back, let Boone know."

He wasn't lost to the tightening of her lips before she said to Benji, "If anything comes up, just call, okay?"

Benji nodded then gave her a quick hug. "Go and enjoy the rest of your birthday."

Her birthday. Yeah, Rhett knew all about it. He'd spent the last week trying to avoid all the conversations regarding today that Remy and Peyton kept trying to get him involved in.

"Thanks for coming," she finally said to Rhett after Benji strode away. "I tried Boone and Asher, but no one answered their phone."

Rhett shoved his hands into his pockets. "It's fine."

The way she flinched at his dry voice made him hate himself even more. But that was minuscule compared to the emotion in her eyes. "Were you at the station?" she asked, grabbing her purse from underneath the bar.

He shook his head and let his silence be the answer. He'd done everything he could for the last two months to try to forget about how good Kinsley smelled, felt, how incredible she tasted. He'd failed miserably to forget her, but even though he wanted to, he couldn't find it in himself to be with anyone else.

"Oh." She cringed, obviously assuming he'd been with someone else tonight.

He hadn't, but he let her believe that since it was far better than the hurt he'd give her if he let her in. If he let *anyone* in. And Benji's thoughtfulness toward Kinsley only cemented Rhett's choice to keep his distance.

"Well, sorry I dragged you away." She barely gave him another look as she hurried into her winter jacket, and matching scarf and winter beanie, and walked out the front door.

Rhett cursed. He rushed after her, the door slamming shut behind him as the brisk winter wind bit his face. Tension sank deep into Rhett's muscles as he sidled up to her.

She glanced over at him. "What are you doing?"

"Walking you home."

"Don't bother," she snapped. "Your date is waiting for you."

Whatever punch she threw at him, he'd take it. A thousand times. As long as it kept her safe. "Your brother will kill me if I don't walk you home after Dalton's appearance," Rhett countered.

"Fine," she grumbled. "Whatever."

Silence fell between them that was as cold as the bitter air. Stoney Creek's Main Street was the height of excitement for the small town known for its fresh seafood and gorgeous views of the Atlantic Ocean. The sun had long ago set, the cool east wind cutting through the town as Rhett shoved his hands into the pockets of his jacket. Christmas was still a month away, but the townsfolk had already begun decorating with wreaths on their shop doors and twinkling lights on their signs. The beams of the streetlights caught any snowflakes fluttering to the ground to melt away.

They strolled past Black Cat's Cauldron, Remy's magic shop, walking beneath the wooden sign. The lights were on in the storefront, showing off jars and candles and a broomstick, along with a stuffed cat animal. By the time they passed by Peyton's lingerie shop, Uptown Girl, Rhett began counting the minutes until he could get away from Kinsley. He liked being near her. Too much. It felt too…*good*.

Ten minutes. That's all he needed to keep this silence going and keep things as casual as possible before he had her home and safe.

Obviously, Kinsley had other ideas. "I've been calling you."

"I know." He'd been dodging her ever since they came home from the tropics.

He felt her stare on him, but he kept looking straight ahead, hurrying his steps.

Of course, she didn't let him off easy. "Is there a reason why you're not returning my calls, or are you just really milking this asshole vibe?"

"You know why I'm not indulging this," he said. Damn, why couldn't her house be closer?

"So that's your plan then?" she asked, quickly catching up to him. "Just ignoring me until I go away?"

He glanced at her and found that she was scowling at him. Good. Scowling was better than when she looked at him with those sweet eyes that ruined him. "I'm not ignoring you," he told her. "I'm stopping whatever you think may or may not be there between us."

She froze right there on the sidewalk, as the cold air bit Rhett's skin.

A beat passed.

Then, "You're honestly unbelievable," she said with a dry snort. She brushed past him and snapped, "Don't give yourself that much credit, West. You're not as memorable as you think you are. I haven't thought about that night once."

"Liar," he mumbled beneath his breath, staring after her. She was all fire blazing down the street, leaving a path of flames behind her. He shouldn't indulge this, but he couldn't help himself. "If I'm so forgettable, then why call?"

"I had to talk to you." She turned down her street and moved quickly toward her two-story house on the corner.

The charming yellow brick house had once belonged to her

grandparents. When they passed, they left the house to Kinsley's father, who then gave it to Boone and Kinsley. Boone eventually moved out, leaving it to Kinsley.

She reached the front porch with black pedestal posts that Rhett had helped paint last year. Before she got to the door, he called out, "Then talk now." He felt like a dick. He *was* a dick.

"The next time I want your opinion of what you think *I* should do," she shot back at him, "how about you go fuck yourself first."

Dammit. Pissing her off hadn't been what he wanted. When she reached for the door handle, he raced up the steps and grabbed her arm. "Listen, I'm not good at this shit."

"Ya think?" she growled, ripping her arm away. She turned to her door, opened it, then whirled back around. "By the way, Mr. Big Shot, I'm not this teenage girl chasing after you with stars in her eyes."

As she was yelling at him, Rhett caught movement in her bay window. He saw more than one shadow, and a sudden realization had him lurching forward to place a hand over Kinsley's mouth to keep the conversation private.

He instantly realized his mistake.

Her eyes were wild with a fury he suddenly feared, and before he had the chance to tell her they were not alone, she bit his hand and sacked him in the nuts with her knee. Light flashed before his eyes as he bent over, wheezing against the pain.

"I wanted to do this another way," she yelled at him. "Any other way but how you're making me do it." He forced his eyes open and brought his gaze up to hers. The world suddenly stopped moving at the emotion paired with the seriousness in her expression. "I'm pregnant. The baby is yours. That's why I've been calling, you stupid ass!"

Gasps of shock came from inside the house, and he nearly emptied his guts on her snow-covered porch. He dropped to one knee and placed his hands in the icy snow, easing the cold sweat washing over him that had nothing to do with his testicles being lodged up into his throat.

A few seconds passed before Kinsley's eyes slowly widened with awareness. She stepped into her house, flicked on the light.

A long awkward pause followed.

Until the bubbly Remy yelled, "Surprise!" And then blew her party horn.

Still hunched over, now sucking in gulps of air for another reason, Rhett took in the streamers, the HAPPY BIRTHDAY sign strung up in Kinsley's living room, and the birthday cake on the coffee table. He'd known they were throwing her a surprise party tonight. He'd been told the party was at Boone's. Plans must have changed. He glanced at Asher, finding his friend's mouth wide open. Peyton's hazel eyes flickered between him and Kinsley. And then Rhett felt the weight of two gazes on him burning with anger that suddenly made his skin flush *hot*. Boone and Hank, Kinsley's father, glared at Rhett like they were coming up with all the ways to kill him. But that was the least of his worries.

Kinsley was pregnant. A baby...*his* baby.

Chapter 3

Kinsley could sum up the last two weeks in two words: *shit show*.

The day the doctor confirmed she was pregnant, she had resorted to calling Rhett, since he'd gone into hiding ever since Boone's wedding. He'd dodged her calls, so she'd even gone into the police station to talk to him, but he'd avoided her every time. Never, not once, in her life had she ever chased after a guy, especially one that had landed himself at the top of the epic douche bag list. A minute ago, she thought her life couldn't get any worse. But *this*, seeing the shock on her brother and her father's faces, was worse. Her stomach somersaulted, nearly emptying itself all over the floor. Rhett was still on his knees outside, but instead of groaning, he was silent and motionless to the truth she'd hit him with.

She swallowed the emotion crawling up her throat. This was not how she'd wanted the news to come out. Tension made the air heavy, and the passing silence grew more formidable as the seconds went on. With no way out, she faced her daunting reality, noting the controlled rage simmering beneath the surface on

Boone's and her father's expressions. They all shared the same quick to smile demeanor, but of course, those smiles were nowhere in sight now. Dad was a bit shorter than Boone, but the air of command he carried always made him seem taller, more authoritative somehow. Especially when he wasn't happy. Like now. To break through the silence, she forced a smile and asked no one in particular, "You planned a surprise party for me?"

Peyton finally nodded and broke the ice. "We thought you could use a good surprise."

And now, everyone knew why—she was *pregnant* with Rhett's baby. Both Remy and Peyton had known about her pregnancy from day one. They had been there when Kinsley had taken the test. "You're right, I did need a good surprise." She quickly entered her house, leaving the door open for when Rhett finally picked himself up off the porch. "I actually thought you all forgot today was my birthday."

"Never in a million years," said Remy, glancing between Kinsley and Rhett.

"I'm so lucky to have you all. Thank you," Kinsley exclaimed, throwing her arms around Peyton, spying the horribly decorated cake on the coffee table in her living room that resembled nothing in particular. A mouse? A cat? A purse? Who knew? "Did you make the cake?"

Peyton gave a proud nod. "I think it's my best one yet."

"I bet it's scrumptious." Peyton's cakes always tasted great. They just looked terrible. No one ever had the heart to tell Peyton that, though. "You know I'm going to eat half of that all by myself, right?" Not a lie. She couldn't stop eating lately.

"As you should." Peyton smiled.

Kinsley turned back to Remy. "And let me guess, you provided all the good juju?" The hints of gingerbread incense were enough to know that Remy was pulling out all her magical guns for this party. She probably had some orange peel tea around somewhere for luck for the year ahead.

Remy smiled, bright and tight, obviously trying to salvage the party she'd planned. "Girl, your house is now stuffed full of so much positive energy."

Kinsley *almost* snorted. Right now, the energy in the room lingered between shock and confusion, with a strong undercurrent of anger. But Remy was a ball of sunshine—who was Kinsley to say that she was wrong and dampen all that warmth. Now, armed and ready to face the music, she glanced at the men in her living room, and immediately gave a dry laugh. "By the looks of all of you, I think we need the biggest dose of positivity we can get right now."

No response. Not any movement.

Kinsley lifted her brows. "Anyone got anything to say?"

Silence.

She loosened a breath. "All right, so here's the thing. I'm beyond grateful that you planned this party for me, and I love you all like crazy, but honestly, this day has been absolute shit. And since you all know that I'm pregnant, I can tell you that I've barfed my brains out ten times today. What I need more than anything else right now is my bed." She glanced back at Remy and let her guard down, showing Remy everything she was feeling. Everything felt raw. Most of all, her heart. "Would you hate me if I went and crawled into bed?"

Remy's eyes saddened but she shook her head. "Totally fine. We'll do a dinner together another night. No worries."

"Dinner sounds really, really nice." She gave Peyton and Remy quick kisses on their cheeks, then turned toward Remy's husband, Asher. His soft eyes held hers, radiating the warmth she'd grown to expect from him. He was a good friend not only to her brother, but to her. "Thanks for coming tonight," she told him.

"Happy Birthday, Kins." His hair fell over his brow when he reached down and took her into his embrace. When he released her, he added with a smile, "And congratulations."

"Thanks." She smiled back, and that smile felt a little more real.

Before she could even get to Boone, her brother grabbed her hand, tugging her into his arms. "I thought there was something different about you these last couple of weeks, but I couldn't figure it out. I thought you had your hair done differently or something." His laugh brushed over her as he released her, his smile tender. "I'm gonna be an uncle, huh?"

She nodded.

He winked at her. "Surprising news, but you always do seem to keep us on our toes. You know we're here for you."

Emotion climbed up her throat again. She clamped down against it and the tears welling in her eyes. "I know, thank you."

"You'll let me know if you need me?"

"Always do," she told him.

"Good." He stepped away.

Then she found herself under her dad's wise gaze. He pulled her into his strong and comforting arms. Any control she had over her emotions vanished. The day had been too much. Holding on to this news had been too much. There was all this love around her and yet all this uncertainty. She broke, a whimper spilling out as tears rolled down her hot cheeks in the safety of his father's hold.

She was on the pill. Rhett had worn condoms every time. They'd taken every precaution for this not to happen, but somehow, it did. Of all the dreams she had of becoming a mother, none of them included having a man at her side that didn't want to be there. She was far past hoping Rhett would come around. After the first time he dodged her call, she was more than annoyed with him. From that day on, her attention turned to finding a way to tell him about the baby. What happened tonight, it hadn't been how she'd wanted him to find out, but his arrogance, and his belief that she couldn't control herself around him, made her blood burn. The jerk.

"Ah, kiddo, none of that now." Dad's rumbly voice spilled over. "Everything's gonna be all right."

She stayed put, letting him hold her and make this all better for a minute. She had never been an emotional person, but pregnancy had done strange things to her hormones. Lately, she cried over commercials.

Dad eventually pressed his lips to her forehead then gave her a level look. "We always get through, don't we?"

She wiped her tears. "Yeah, we do." Because they had to. Mom left Dad when Kinsley was six years old. In every one of Kinsley's memories, her mother didn't want the small-town life Stoney Creek offered. So she left them and moved to California. There, within a handful of years, she found herself a new husband and had two more kids, and Boone and Kinsley no longer mattered. Boone had made peace with their mother, but even when her mother had tapped her on the shoulder at Boone and Peyton's wedding like she had the right to and then said, *"Kinsley, please stop shutting me out,"* Kinsley did not want to talk to her. Ever. That would never change. Mothers shouldn't abandon their kids. Some things were unforgivable.

When Dad finally stepped away, Kinsley felt a small measure of relief rush over her. Everyone knew about the baby now, but

the heaviness at her back told her that things were more complicated than ever. "Now if you'll excuse me," she said, picking up
the cake, along with a plastic fork, before heading for the foyer.
"I'll be in bed, eating my emotions."

* * *

War, Rhett could handle. But a baby?

The world had shaken beneath him the moment Kinsley hit
him with the news. He'd replayed the words in his head over and
over: *I'm pregnant. The baby is yours.* He had seen the condom
wrappers on the resort room floor, and yet he also didn't doubt
her. She wouldn't dream of having a child with him; no one
would. He eventually pushed up from the porch and stared into
the fury in Hank and Boone's faces. Then with his balls still
lodged in his throat, he walked away. Anything he said then
would have been wrong. He'd seen the pain in Kinsley's eyes.
Pain he'd caused. He strode back to his truck at the police station
on Main Street, the brisk east wind cutting through him. Once
in his truck, he drove to the one place that grounded him.

Home.

He'd bought his parents' house from them when they moved
away to Wisconsin for his father's new job. They'd inherited
the property from his maternal grandparents and they'd given
it to him for a steal. The twelve-hundred-square-foot bungalow
wasn't anything spectacular, but the view was what made the
property priceless. He pulled into his driveway then immediately stepped on the breaks. Hard. In the middle of his gravel
driveway stood a doe, her eyes glowing under the beam of his
headlights. Yeah, he felt a little like that too. Dazed, for sure.

He slowly lifted his foot off the break, inching his way forward, and the doe quickly took off into the forest. He parked his truck in the circular driveway and headed for the back door. The night was still and silent around him. Once inside, he flicked on the lights as he entered through the small kitchen and dropped his keys on the worn oak counter. By the time he grabbed the whiskey bottle from his grandfather's old liquor cabinet in the living room and headed outside, he was barely thinking anymore, only needing air and alcohol to numb the raging rawness in his chest.

The property sat atop a cliff, and Rhett headed straight for the left side, going down the staircase lit up with solar lights that led to the beach. When he hit the sand, the half-frozen water and starry sky greeted him, and he quickly built himself a campfire before plopping his ass in the Adirondack chair that he kept there. He took two big gulps of the whiskey, the warmth of the liquid burning in his gut. Only then could he breathe fully.

A baby? With Kinsley?

When he raised the bottle to his lips again, his mind drifted and went back to the place that made sense.

The sun began to set over the forbidding mountains, giving a slight reprieve to the brutal heat soaking Rhett in sweat, but the constant screaming and echoing of gunfire remained. As part of the Army Rangers, they'd been deployed on a top-secret mission to capture a high-value target, though upon arriving at the town tucked away in the treacherous mountains, they were surrounded by enemy forces and immediately under rapid gunfire. Rhett kept his gun aimed, his focus steady, and fired bullets, watching bodies drop. He never looked at their faces. Never made it personal. This was a job.

His fellow Rangers stayed close, tucked safely behind boulders while they fired.

Rhett felt a body fall next to him, heard the roar of pain. He reached out, grabbing his buddy Matthews by the vest and yanking him back behind the boulder. After a quick assessment, he grabbed Matthews's hand. "Got shot in the thigh." He squeezed his hand around Matthews's leg. "Don't let go."

Matthews nodded quickly. "Yeah. Fuck. Yeah."

Rhett took aim again and saw the enemy forces moving higher up the mountain. Hundreds of them, compared to the ten in Rhett's crew. He shut his eyes, knowing perhaps this time, death had come calling.

Until he heard the sound of fighter jets overhead, followed by explosions rocking the ground beneath him.

Rhett blinked, staring into the crackling fire. After serving in the Army Rangers for twelve years, he'd retired with a medical discharge after an M60 machine gun, 7.62 NATO caliber, tore into his shoulder. He ran his hands through his hair and drew a deep breath. Pride filled him. He'd kept his brothers safe, but war was war, and it wasn't pretty. The things he saw came home with him, and there was no fixing that, but that life, that purpose, made sense.

A baby?

He raised the whiskey bottle to his lips again when he realized he wasn't alone. He didn't bother looking up from the fire, knowing exactly who'd come. The *only* person who would show up tonight to demand answers and put Rhett firmly in his place.

"Brought out the good stuff, huh?" Boone asked, pulling the other chair closer to Rhett before taking a seat.

"Just preparing myself for either the punch or the lecture

coming my way," Rhett replied. He deserved both, and worse. For years, he'd kept his control. He never slipped up with Kinsley, knowing she was off limits. And now his one moment of weakness had cost Kinsley her very happiness. He deserved to rot in hell.

Rhett offered Boone the bottle. He took a big swig then handed it back. "Hate to break it to you, but neither of those things are going to happen tonight," Boone said quietly.

Rhett slowly looked at his longtime childhood friend. He couldn't find a hint of anger in Boone's expression.

The orange hues from the fire flickered across Boone's face, showing only warmth on his expression. "How about just stating the truth."

"What truth?" Rhett asked.

"This isn't some chick you don't care about. It's Kinsley."

Rhett dropped his head back against the chair and stared up at the stars, the Milky Way visible tonight. Caring for her was precisely the problem. She deserved better and he knew it. Had always known it.

Boone added gently, "I stayed out of whatever's been going on with you two when I knew you'd been together at the wedding."

That was news to Rhett. "Did Kinsley tell you?" he asked.

Boone snorted. "Yeah, right. She's loyal to her bones. You know that." He gave Rhett a knowing look. "I'd be a shit detective if I didn't notice that you two came back from the tropics barely able to look at each other."

But Boone knowing he'd slept with Kinsley wasn't a problem. Rhett never thought it would be. As long as Rhett's intentions were good, Boone would support him, as much as he'd support Kinsley. It had always been in Boone's nature to stand by those he cared about. But Kinsley deserved a man who had his feet firmly planted on the ground. Rhett was barely treading water lately, nearly drowning in this civilian life he'd returned to after the Army. He dropped his head and threaded his fingers in his hair, stating *his* truth. "I can't fucking do this. I'm not good for her."

Boone hesitated a moment before he said, his voice firm, "What you can, and can't, do isn't really up for debate anymore. Kinsley's pregnant. You can't run from this." He turned to Rhett fully, looking him right in the eyes. "I've got one thing to say on this, and then that'll be the end of my involvement." His gaze went steely, coiled frustration simmering just beneath the surface. "Whatever you've gotta do from now until you see her next to pull your shit together, that's exactly what you're gonna do. You won't make this harder for her. Do you hear me?"

The point was clear enough. The fire crackled, drawing Rhett's attention again. He considered what either Boone or Asher would do in this situation. Finally, he got his answer. "I'll do right by her, if that's what she wants," he finally said.

There was along pause. Then Boone burst out laughing.

Rhett frowned. "This is somehow funny to you?"

"Oh, shit, yeah, that's hilarious," Boone said with another booming laugh. "We're talking about Kinsley here. Do you really think she's going to let you"—he made quotation marks with his fingers—"make an honest woman of her?"

Rhett considered this then shook his head. "No, she won't." Kinsley was tough as hell. She didn't need him and, apparently, didn't want him as she so proved tonight. But she wanted to tell him the truth, and that was Kinsley. She always gave it straight. Never played games.

Rhett was her polar opposite. It occurred to him then that

he was a gigantic asshole. She'd called him, and he'd dodged her call, thinking she was chasing his tail. He should have known she'd never come running after him. That wasn't her style.

Whatever Boone saw on his face couldn't have been good. He cupped Rhett's shoulder, offering the warm comfort he always gave when things got bad. "All of this, whatever happens between you and Kinsley, it's gonna be all right, man." With a friendship that spanned thirty years, they'd seen each other at their worst.

"I'm not as sure about that as you are," Rhett admitted before taking another swig of the whiskey.

Boone accept the bottle again and drank back a shot. "Just let this storm ride out and settle. Not all surprises are bad. And a baby can't ever be a bad thing."

Rhett's gut churned as he set his gaze on the water. It was barely moving tonight, almost as if the world knew Rhett needed everything to be still. Before the military, he might've been able to give Kinsley everything she needed and more, but once he'd joined, his priorties changed, *he* changed, and he couldn't ever go back. And he didn't think he wanted to. Besides, he couldn't even picture himself as a father. He worked, all the time. That was his life. Boone and Asher gave him a life outside that, but without them, he'd spend his time either at the station or at a bar to find himself a woman for the night. But Rhett couldn't run from the blame that he'd caused all this. He turned to Boone. "I never meant to—"

Boone raised his hand, giving Rhett a hard look. "Passion is passion. Let's not have that conversation. Kinsley is her own person. She's been that way since she was two years old. I know you would have done your best to avoid her out of respect for me, but I also have no doubt in my mind that if Kinsley wished it, she would have made it near impossible for you to ignore her." He gave a kind smile. "You're as close as a brother to me, Rhett. I trust you."

Rhett envied Boone's solidness. He had it all together and then some. Rhett knew how to fuck, how to hunt, how to kill, and even how to protect. Beyond that, he was a ghost, floating through life, unsure exactly how to interact with his world. And that wasn't fair to someone like Kinsley.

Again, Boone frowned at Rhett's expression. "You don't need to be perfect for her. You don't need to be anything you're not. She knows who you are. She won't expect anything from you that you can't give."

God. All these people were so fucking good. Rhett never should have come back to Stoney Creek.

The flames danced around the logs in the firepit. The warm alcohol coursed through his veins, stealing the weight on his chest. With every ember that sparked up into the air, the reality of the situation sank in. He needed to take this one step at a time, until he managed to pull his way through it, like he'd done with every mission. And with that settled, the truth hit him. Hard. "I'm going to be a father," Rhett finally said aloud.

Boone grinned. "Let's hope it's a girl. Another Rhett running around town is the very last thing anyone needs."

Rhett laughed. A full belly laugh.

* * *

The sugary icing melted on Kinsley's tongue as she dug into the cake. It was a banana cake, her absolute favorite. She sat on her queen-size bed with fluffy pillows at her back and vintage linen wrapped around her. Her room wasn't anything special. She had a bed, an oak dresser beneath a window that was covered in long white curtains, and an old cedar blanket chest at the foot of the bed. But this room had been her home since her mother left them and her father moved them all into her grandparents' house. That time in their lives had been confusing for everyone, but there was so much love in this house, it eased the absence of her mother.

She wondered what her grandmother would say about all this. The thought had her reaching into her bedside drawer and taking out the box there. She opened the lid, revealing her grandmother's handmade cards. She passed over a birthday and a Christmas card and found the one she was looking for. The card had a drawing of a wineglass in the rain. She flipped the card open and brushed her fingers over her grandmother's handwriting that read: *Life isn't fun if it isn't messy, my darling. Some days are terrible, but those days are few and far between. Chin up. Tomorrow will be a brand-new day. Love you dearly, Grams.*

Kinsley couldn't remember what happened for her grandmother to write that card, but it seemed fitting for today. Her grandmother always seemed to know what to do and what to say, to make everything that seemed bad so much better. She'd been the mom when her mother left them. She'd kissed the scratches, read the stories at night when her dad had to work, and tucked her in tight.

She missed her grandparents and their love terribly. She shoved another bite of cake into her mouth, nearly purring at how delicious it was, and slowly, she began to feel better. Her twenty-ninth birthday…*sucked*.

A part of her lit up at the idea that she would have a baby before she turned thirty. She'd long ago given up on that idea, considering she'd fallen for Rhett, a man who had become entirely unavailable. The truth was, she wanted it all—the guy who adored her, the hot romance, and the happily-ever-after. And she wanted Rhett to be that guy.

A hopeless wish. Nonetheless, it was one she couldn't ignore.

Right as she shoved another large bite of cake into her mouth, there was a knock on her closed bedroom door. She hurried to put the box of cards away then called out with a full mouth, "Come in."

It came as no surprise when Remy and Peyton hurried inside and shut the door behind them.

"I gotta give it to you, Kins," said Remy, plopping down at the end of the bed, "that was one spectacular way of breaking the news."

"Well, had I known that everyone was waiting in my living room, I wouldn't have said anything." Kinsley finished her bite then added, "But he just pissed me off so much."

"That was pretty clear. What did he do?" Peyton asked.

"Oh, well, you both know he's been refusing to answer my calls, and tonight he told me that apparently he's been avoiding me because he was trying to ensure nothing further happens between us. You know, because I just can't control myself and keep my hands off him."

Peyton's mouth dropped open. "He seriously said that?"

"He seriously said that." Kinsley stuck her fork back into the cake.

Remy rolled her eyes. "What an idiot."

Kinsley shoved another huge bite into her mouth. "He's Rhett. I shouldn't have expected anything different. But I just got so…"

"Ragey?" Remy offered.

Kinsley nodded. "Exactly. His level of prick went to new heights tonight."

She handed Peyton the fork. As Peyton stabbed a piece, she said, "Boone and your dad seemed okay about it all, though."

"I can guarantee neither are okay with this, but they love me," Kinsley countered. "They'll support me, no matter what." That's what her brother and father did for her. Probably since they'd had to band together after her mom left. She knew she and the baby would be okay, with or without Rhett. It was only her heart that needed to get that memo.

After Peyton ate a small bite of the cake, she handed the fork to Remy, who dug in and said, "I'm sure they'll have some words for Rhett when they see him next."

Kinsley accepted the fork back and cut off an even bigger bite for herself. "They're not talking to him now?"

There was a long pause. Then, "He just took off," Peyton said solemnly. "Your dad told Boone to go find him."

Of course her father would want someone to go after Rhett. Everyone knew that Rhett didn't want the family, the kids, or the happily-ever-after. He wanted the military and his life as a soldier that had been stripped from him. It didn't take much to know that this would affect Rhett; the only lingering question was how he would respond to it. Truth was, as a teenager, Kinsley had thought that she and Rhett were a possibility. But once he came back from the Army, Kinsley knew Rhett couldn't love her, not in the way she needed or deserved. Being a soldier had changed him, and he came back distant and noncommittal. In the tropics, she just wanted one taste. *This*, having his child, was never part of the plan.

But one thing was certain—she hoped this news wouldn't send him to the dark place he'd been in when he first came home. That day she'd looked into his vacant eyes, and her heart shattered at the emptiness there. It took months for Rhett to even spend time with anyone. Slowly, he'd come back to them, piece by piece, but she still missed the old Rhett. The guy with the cute smile, the bright eyes, and all the charm in the world. The one she'd fallen in love with during high school. The guy she could still see sometimes...even now.

Silence again settled in the room as they shared the cake, until a good dent had been made.

Remy finally groaned, waving off another bite, and said, "If I can put in my two cents, I just hope Rhett does the right thing and thinks of you and the baby in all this before himself."

Kinsley's stomach churned and she placed the cake on her bedside table. "We'll see what happens." Because that was all she could hope for. This was complicated. Rhett didn't do serious anything. In fact, since he'd come home, she'd never seen him with a girlfriend, only lovers. And those lovers never lasted longer than a night.

Peyton slowly cocked her head, seeing the certainty on Kinsley's face. "What do you think he'll do next?"

Kinsley didn't even have to consider her words. "He'll sleep his way through every pretty tourist in a miniskirt that crosses into Stoney Creek like he always does."

Remy reached for Kinsley's hand. "And you're okay with that?"

She paused to mull it over then shrugged. "Rhett is who he is. I knew that the night I slept with him. I knew waking up after that night, everything would be different. I knew we would never be a couple. I was perfectly fine with just a fling."

Both her friends just stared at her.

Until Remy said, "Okay, I'm gonna say it. If you're good with Rhett being Rhett, then why do you look so sad?"

Peyton took Kinsley's other hand. Kinsley stared down at their entwined fingers. "Having a baby this way, it's just not the dream, you know." She swallowed the emotions rising in her throat, making her voice squeaky. "With my mother…the way she was and how she left us…I wanted to do everything right when I became a mom." Her voice hitched on the last word.

Remy's arms wrapped around her tightly, followed very quickly by Peyton's. "Just stop that right now," Remy said sternly, her head resting on Kinsley's shoulder. "You're going to make an amazing mother, whether Rhett steps up or not."

Peyton squeezed tighter, with emotion raw in her voice. "She's right. Your baby is going to be so lucky to have you."

"And," Remy added, holding on just a bit tighter, "you've got us, Kins. That's like having two nannies around to help you whenever you need it."

"Plus, you have Boone and your dad too," Peyton added.

Remy finally let go and took Kinsley's face in her hands. "You've got this."

Peyton gave a firm nod. "One hundred percent got this."

Kinsley smiled, and the smile felt more honest now. "You say that now, but will you both have my back like this if I murder Rhett and bury him in the backyard?"

"I'll bring the shovel." Peyton grinned.

"You know I'm really good with gardens," Remy added. "We can make it so no one will suspect anything."

Kinsley laughed and sank back against her pillows, Remy and Peyton snuggling into her. "Well, if that's the case, I *do* totally have this."

Chapter 4

The next morning, Kinsley exited her house to start her day, wishing she had a hangover. That would have at least dulled her runaway emotions. Rhett stayed heavily on her mind all night and she barely slept. Part of her still wanted to throttle him for being such an arrogant idiot. The other part of her wanted to see him to make sure he was okay. None of this could have been easy. Rhett...wasn't an easy guy. And coming to terms with both those sides of herself left her head spinning and her heart bleeding. Because her problem now wasn't that she loved a guy she shouldn't love. Her problem was that that guy was the father of her baby.

She sighed heavily, her breath a fog in front of her, as she locked her front door.

"Morning, kiddo."

She whirled around, warmth instantly touching the tension in her chest. Dad stood at the bottom of the steps, wearing jeans and his dark leather winter coat. "Guess I shouldn't be surprised you're here this morning," she mused, even though Dad never showed up unannounced. Or hardly ever.

He gave his comforting smile and gestured at the road behind him. "Thought I could walk you to work this morning."

"Sure, I'd love that." She carefully headed down the porch steps and fell into step next to him.

The sunny day was most welcome, considering lately gray winter skies had taken over. The heat against her face was in full contrast to the crisp air biting her cheeks.

She grabbed her chunky mittens from her pockets and slid into them as Dad asked, "Is today a better day than yesterday?"

She shrugged, looking down at the sidewalk, as they passed by the biggest oak tree in the neighborhood. "I'm not sure what I am today other than happy that everyone knows." That was the simple answer.

Dad laughed softly. "That was a grand way to tell everyone. Very much your style."

She gave him a sidelong glance, staring into the sparkling pride in his eyes, and she laughed too. "I suppose you're right. I can't do anything small, can I?"

"Nope," Dad said.

She took note of her father's easy gait, both hands shoved into his pockets. It didn't add up. "Okay, what gives. Why are you not surprised about me and Rhett?"

"Well," he said, staring out in front of him to the snow-covered sidewalk before addressing her again. "We all knew something was up a long time ago. I'm a bit surprised you two didn't happen sooner, if I'm being honest."

While she'd had her very loving grandmother when growing up, who had been the nurturing maternal figure Kinsley needed, she and her father had always had this easy way of talking. He'd been the solid rock she could depend on. The one who gave her the talks about periods and sex and all the embarrassing stuff that no kid wanted to hear their parents talk about. From those talks, she knew what that tight set of his jawline meant. "But you don't approve?"

"Whether I approve or not really isn't for me to say," Dad replied after a long moment of deep consideration. "You're having Rhett's child. He's always been a part of the family; now he's simply more so."

Kinsley let that sink in for in a minute. If she boiled it down to simple terms, that's all this really was. Rhett had always been there for as long as she could remember. He, Boone, and Asher had been inseparable since their first day of school. But if she were honest with herself, her heart hurt knowing that all they'd ever be were co-parents, only involved in each other's lives because of their child. She wanted more, but those were her emotions talking. She knew what she deserved, and she knew that Rhett couldn't give it to her. "I suppose you're right," she said with a smile that seemed more genuine than anything she'd felt since the motorcycle gang had sauntered into her bar. "We just gotta take this one day at a time."

"That's right, kiddo." Dad nudged her shoulder. "You've got this handled."

She slid her arm through his. "Did you have any doubt?"

"Never," he said with a firm shake of his head. "You're my girl."

Silence and a whole lot of love drifted between them as they walked along her quiet neighborhood and took the next left, which led them toward downtown. When they hit Main Street, Dad stopped walking and turned to face her. "The traditional way of life isn't always the right way," he said. He must have overheard her conversation with the girls last night in her bedroom. "I did things right. I married your mother young. Provided for her. And that, as you know, didn't have a great ending."

Kinsley heart somersaulted in her chest. "You were an amazing father."

He gave her a small smile that hinted at a long life filled with his own worries and pain. "Thank you for that, Kinsley." That smile faded as he went on. "All I'm saying is, you're going to be an incredible mother. And as for Rhett, it might take him a bit, but he'll either get this right or he won't, but that's his situation to deal with, not yours." Dad took her in his arms and hugged her tight. "I don't need to remind you what you're worth, right?"

He'd always said the same thing to her through every heartbreak. *There's no one in the world like you, Kinsley. Don't ever forget that. Any man you accept into your life needs to realize how lucky he is. You should never need to remind him of that.*

She leaned her cheek against the comforting warmth of his chest. "I remember."

"Good." He placed a kiss on her forehead then she laced her arm with his again, and they continued on toward Main Street. "By the way, in case I didn't say it last night, you've made me very happy. A grandfather. What a beautiful thing."

"You'll be a good one too."

He beamed as he patted her hand against his arm.

She hated the world for how it treated her father. It was the very same reason she felt nothing toward her mother. Dad never deserved the hardships her mother had hand-delivered to him. He deserved love and happiness. And she hoped one day a woman saw her dad how she viewed him. The goodness and kindness in him. How much he sacrificed to make others happy.

When they finally turned onto Main Street, she found the town already busy, with most of the shops open and tourists walking along the treelined street, taking in the eclectic shops.

Vintage streetlights hugged the road, with benches and flowers adding to the picturesque scene, and there was no garbage littering the streets. The town kept good care of their downtown. Everything was freshly painted, and the shop signs were all a mix of cute and unique. Small towns had their quirks, but Stoney Creek had oodles of charm. When they got closer to Peyton's lingerie shop, Kinsley spotted Boone leaning against her bar's door, scrolling through his phone.

Dad must've seen him too and chuckled. "I guess I wasn't the only one who couldn't sleep much last night."

Kinsley's heart swelled as they passed Black Cat's Cauldron. "Boone," she called.

Her brother glanced up, took in their father, and smiled, tucking his phone into his pocket. "Morning."

"Apparently, a busy morning," Kinsley said, glancing between the two protective, loving men in her life.

Boone shrugged, shoving his hands into his pockets, looking like a younger version of their father.

"I better get off to the station." Dad dropped another kiss on her forehead. "I'll check in on ya later, kiddo."

"Thanks, Dad. Love you."

His smile was his reply. Dad didn't say those three little words, but he showed them his love all the time. The words didn't matter much. He cupped Boone's shoulder as he strode by, obviously leaving her and Boone alone to talk. She turned to her brother. "Is Rhett okay?"

Boone frowned, pushing away from the door. "Let's not make worrying about Rhett a habit, but yes, he's fine. I talked with him last night."

She'd never learn about that conversation either. Boone was a vault when it came to his brothers, as was Rhett and Asher. The three men were so in sync with each other, Kinsley knew that bond would never break. Not even when one of them knocked up the other's sister.

"Just be patient with him, Kins," Boone added gently. "This…"

"Is hard for him," she finished, waving at Doris, the lady who worked at the pharmacy, as she crossed the road. "You don't have to tell me that," she said, looking back at Boone. "I know he's going to struggle with all this, and with any type of relationship, even if it's a co-parenting one."

Boone gave her a leveled look. "Which begs the question, why would you let anything happen between you?"

She deserved the question, as well as the reprimand in his gaze. Expected it even. She was smarter than to get mixed up with a guy with ginormous commitment issues and a whole laundry list of other emotional issues. "It wasn't meant to be a *thing*. You know, it was just meant…"

Boone's mouth twitched. "To scratch the long itch that you've had for years."

She narrowed her eyes at him. "You knew?"

"Of course I knew," he stated gruffly, nodding hello at an elderly couple who passed by before he addressed her again. "When Rhett came home, he looked at you differently, and you certainly didn't look at him the same either."

"Then why didn't you just say something?"

Boone's brow arched. "Give my approval, you mean?"

"Yes. Exactly."

Her brother watched her for a long moment then said softly, "You know why."

She swallowed back the sudden emotion rising up in her throat. "Because you wouldn't pick him for me."

"He's not solid enough for you, Kins," Boone said gently.

"Regardless if there's something there between you two, you don't deserve to take on the weight of his shit. It's heavy."

But didn't everyone have something heavy? The thing she had always liked about Rhett was that he didn't hide it. She'd met a few guys over the years that seemed like these great, put-together people, and then suddenly, they weren't that at all. There was no hidden agenda with Rhett. The cards were all laid out on the table. She knew it was just sex, and anything more than that with Rhett was a gigantic mess that no sane woman wanted to take on. "You don't need to worry about me," she told Boone. "I've got my head on straight, no matter how emotional I am right now."

Boone examined her intently then gave a firm nod. "I wouldn't expect otherwise. You'll let me know what you need from me?"

Not *if* but *what*. That was Boone, supportive through and through. "I will, thank you." She gave him a tight hug. "And thanks for coming to check in on me this morning. I love you."

He dropped a kiss on the top of her head, much like Dad had done. "Love you back."

Reminded of how lucky she was to have all the love she did, she asked, "Are you working today?"

"After I grab a coffee, I am," he said from behind her.

She unlocked the door. Boone often came to the bar in the morning. Not only to say hello, but also to order the butter pecan coffee he loved. Sure, opening in the morning was odd for most bars, but Kinsley knew bad stuff happened at all times of the day and she wanted to be there for people when all they needed was a drink, some quiet, and maybe a bartender to listen to them. Most days, no one came in, and she worked on the books while she sat at the bar. But every once in a while, the bar was exactly what someone needed, and that felt good. Important.

Once she got inside, she flicked the light on. Suddenly, everything slowed down, and all that she knew spiraled away as she glanced around her beloved bar. Nothing looked like it had when she'd left the place last night. Tables were overturned and destroyed. Chairs were smashed. The mirrors behind the bar were shattered into a million pieces. The liquor bottles were broken into shards of glass.

"What the fuck?"

Reeling, and cold, so very cold, Kinsley whirled around to find Rhett standing in the doorway.

He surveyed the damage, eyes wild. "I've got the back," he growled at Boone, then rushed forward with his weapon in his hand. He vanished into the back room a second later.

"Do not move from this spot," Boone snapped, his weapon now in his hand too, while he took off toward the bathrooms.

My bar.

Kinsley scanned every piece of broken wood, every shard of glass, and her breakfast did terrible things in her stomach. Her skin flushed red-hot. Sweat coated her flesh.

Oh no.

She quickly looked left and right then dove toward the garbage can, her hand burning on something as she hurled her guts out.

* * *

Rhett had cleared the back room and Kinsley's office before he found the entry point. The back door was wide open. He looked at her security system on the wall by the door, finding it had been turned off. Whoever broke into her bar obviously had the equipment and the skill to disable the alarm and open the door, or this was an inside job. Rhett didn't like either of those possibilities.

He ground his teeth as he returned to the main bar, then breathed past the clenching of his muscles as he found Kinsley throwing up into the garbage can by the front door. If that reaction was the result of stress, rather than morning sickness, someone would pay.

Rhett decided to stay back to give her privacy, when Boone strode out from the women's washroom. He wove his way around the broken furniture, his face a mask of controlled rage. "Clear."

"In the back too," Rhett confirmed, reholstering his weapon. "Any idea what happened here?"

Boone tucked his weapon away as well. "Not a fucking clue. We just walked through the door seconds before you did."

A feeling pulsed through Rhett that he couldn't quite identify. Urgent, wary, whatever it was, he didn't like it. His gaze fell on Kinsley again, and he felt a deeper lick of fury course through his veins as he spotted blood sliding down the side of the garbage can from her hand.

"We need to get the team in here," Boone said.

Rhett glanced back at him with a nod then gestured Boone toward the door. "Give me fifteen before you call them in."

Boone's gaze turned probing before he eventually nodded, with what Rhett thought looked close to approval on his face. "If you need more time, let me know." He gave Kinsley one last look then headed for the door.

Rhett had barely slept, and he'd ended up going for a run

in the middle of the night. He had no idea what steps to take forward, but he'd decided this morning that talking to Kinsley was a good start. He waited for her to stand up before he drew closer to her. She reached down to tie up the garbage bag, but he quickly intervened, gently pushing her hands away. "I'll get that. You need water."

She slowly looked up at him with surprise in her eyes, which admittedly, only made him feel more like shit. She thought the very worst of him, thought him unable to offer a gentle hand when needed. "I need crackers," she said.

"You got those in the back?"

She nodded, guarded in the way she watched him.

"Let's get those," he offered, reaching for a few napkins by the cash register. "And we can deal with the cut on your hand too."

She glanced down, her eyes going wide. "Oh, shit." She quickly accepted the napkins, placing them against her wound.

He tied the garbage bag then pulled it from the can. She followed him into the back room, and he headed out the back door, where he knew the Dumpsters were for all three shops that belonged to Kinsley, Peyton, and Remy. He tossed the bag inside the Dumpster then glanced up, spotting the security camera. He needed to see what was on there, but first, he needed to fix leaving last night in the way that he did. When he returned inside, he found Kinsley at the metal kitchen sink, water running over the cut on her hand.

"I must have cut myself on a piece of glass when I dove for the garbage can," she explained.

"Let me take a look." He held her hand under the light, noticing she'd grabbed a first aid kit and left it on the metal table. His blood heated as he got close to her, electricity brushing across his flesh as those fiery eyes held his intently. "You get sick like that often?"

She nodded, as breathless as him. "At really weird unexpected times too."

He acknowledged that with a nod. Her breath hitched when he took her soft hand in his callused ones to examine the wound, and heat spiraled through him. "It doesn't need stitches." Using his free hand, he patted the table. "Let me clean it up."

"Where did Boone go?" she asked, pulling her hand from his and inching closer to the table.

"I imagine to go get your father and call in a forensic unit," Rhett answered, watching her awkwardly try to hop up. His hands found her waist and he hoisted her up onto the table, the world immediately drifting away. One touch, and he was right back to their incredible night together. She smelled so good, like a fragrant garden made especially for him. He vividly remembered kissing those hips he'd just touched when he explored every inch of her. His groin tightened and his cock swelled as he recalled how she'd laughed so freely when he kissed along her rib cage. And as he looked into her lust-filled eyes, he knew he wasn't the only one remembering that night.

He loosened a breath and opened the first aid kit. Then he got to work, forcing his mind to clear away those memories. He cleaned the wound, her hiss haunting him. "How long have you known about the baby?" he asked, reaching for the small flashlight in the kit.

"Two weeks," she said.

Two goddamn weeks. He felt the tremble of her hand in his, and dark shame rolled over him. "I should have been there," he said, putting a voice to the realizations he'd come to last night on his run. He looked up into her eyes, finding them even wider than before. "You should not have had to deal with this alone."

She shrugged. "I'm okay about it now."

Her answer suggested she hadn't been okay. She'd been scared and alone, and Rhett had done that to her. He'd sworn to himself that his messy life would never touch her, but it did. The only way forward now was to ensure it never happened again. He shifted her hand from side to side. "I don't see any glass in there."

"Thank God," she drawled and gave him a quick smile. "I imagine this is going to suck enough without you digging in there with tweezers."

He hastily pulled out the gauze and antiseptic cream from the kit to avoid her. She always had a way of lightening the mood.

Silence settled in between them. But what was once an easy, comfortable silence now seemed strained while he tended to her wound.

When he'd finished up by placing a large bandage over the gauze, he braced both hands on either side of her legs. Only then did he look into her eyes again. The intensity there sent a hard-hitting blow to his chest, but he pushed through the iciness that trickled into his veins and the alarms in his head telling him to run. "You always say that you know me. Do you really?" he asked her.

She gave a soft nod. "Yes, I know you."

Her quick answer startled him. "Then you know being a father, having a baby, was so far down on my list of what I wanted for my life." Hurt crossed her face, so he swiftly continued, "I'm here for you, Kinsley, whatever you need, whenever you need it, but"—he pushed past the tightness of his throat—"I can't promise…I can't promise that I'm going to get this all right, and I want to be up front about that."

Her eyes softened and her sweet touch landed on his arm, easing the ache in his chest. "I don't expect you to promise me anything. I also don't expect you to swoop in and become overjoyed about this news. I know this is a gigantic shock. I've had weeks to process it all. And I'm still not even sure how all of this is going to work, or what really happens now, or if I'm being honest, if I can even believe that this is happening. You deserve time to figure this out, and I'm okay with giving you that time."

Most times, her strength totally blindsided him. Today even more so. "We'll take it day by day," he clarified. "One step at a time." That's all he could do right now. "You tell me what you need, whatever it is, and I'll do that, okay?"

She nodded and grinned. "That works but get ready for late-night calls for egg salad sandwiches and ice cream sundaes."

She meant it as a joke, but he took a mental note. He couldn't be what Asher was to Remy, or what Boone was to Peyton, but he could make her egg salad sandwiches and bring her ice cream sundaes.

Feeling like he had taken at least a small step forward with her, he helped her off the table. She all but slid down his body, dragging her round breasts down his chest. They both knew the move was entirely unnecessary. She was playing with him, like she always played with him. Teased him, tormented him madly. He should back away, and yet his feet weren't moving. Her cheeks flushed deep in color, and the memory of those stained cheeks when she orgasmed blasted across his mind. She nibbled her bottom lip, and he recalled how those pouty lips tasted and felt, especially when they slid across the hardest part of him.

And when her breathing grew rough, he forced himself to take a full step back in fear of what he'd do next if he didn't.

She smiled, like she knew she had him wrapped around her finger, and held up her bandaged hand. "Thanks for fixing this." He was saved by sudden loud voices from the main bar area. "That must be the Cavalry."

She moved around him, and he let out a long breath, calling after her, "Kinsley."

"Yeah?" she asked, turning back to him.

"You're not alone anymore in this," he told her. "I'm here."

Her brows drew together, the heat gone from her pretty eyes. "You mean that?"

"I mean that."

She inhaled slowly and blew it out even slower, regarding him intently. "Well then, as long as you continue to want that, then okay, but let me be entirely clear. You're in this because you want to be, and if that changes, you need to man-up and make that decision before the baby gets here. I know what it's like to have a parent jump in and out of your life. I won't have that. Do you understand me?"

The air sucked out of the room. "Yes, ma'am."

Chapter 5

Everything felt different when Kinsley returned to the main bar. She hoped Rhett meant what he said, but she knew better than to blindly believe him. He couldn't commit to anyone, maybe not even his own child. One day at a time. That was the only way she could move forward with all this, and the first step was finding out who had destroyed her bar. Glass crunched beneath her winter boots as she stopped in the middle of the room. She scanned the damage again, wishing her eyes had betrayed her. Sure, she had insurance to cover some of this, but the entire place was in shambles. Every single item she'd spent weeks picking out and placing had been ruined.

Back when she was a child, her dad would bring her into the pub where all the cops went after their shift to let go of their day before going home. Those memories were full of laughter and football games and friendships. She'd realized at a very young age the importance of having a place for people to go when they needed that feeling of home and comfort. She'd known ever since she was eighteen years old that she wanted to own such a place, so she'd gone to college to get her business degree. And now, here she stood, in the middle of the ruins of her dream, thinking that a month ago, life had been normal, and now it was as if every day brought a new change and challenge.

Boone waited near the front door with two guys Kinsley had met before. They were the forensic unit. The room wavered a little, wanting to swallow her up. Maybe that would help her wake up from this nightmare.

"I'll find who did this."

Kinsley glanced at Rhett, not realizing he'd joined her. "Do you think the motorcycle gang from last night would be capable of this?" she asked.

He paused to consider her question then finally acknowledged her thought with a nod. "Capable? Definitely. It's easy to go to that conclusion, but at the same time, what could possibly drive them to do this?" He gestured toward her ruined bar.

She snorted. "You pulled a gun on them last night. Isn't that enough of a reason?"

"To come after me, hell, yeah," he answered, shoving his hands into his pockets. "But why would they take what I had done out on you?"

"Because they're pricks," she offered.

Last night had proved that enough. And she didn't blame Rhett's strong reaction. There were three of them, and Dalton had squeezed her wrist hard enough that she was surprised she didn't have a bruise this morning.

Rhett nodded again, obviously to appease her, considering he didn't look convinced. But suddenly, something caught his gaze and he abruptly left her side. Kinsley followed him to the bar. There, two words were carved into the wood: SHUT DOWN.

"Okay, that's an odd warning," she stated.

Rhett stood eerily still before he gave her a sidelong glance. "Got any enemies you need to tell me about?"

The answer was all too easy. "Nearly every weekend, we end up having to kick people out of here if they're too drunk or something, but we haven't had any big incidents until the one last night."

The door suddenly slammed open, and her father strode in, a deep frown on his face. "Christ sakes, look at this place." He scanned the room from left to right then quickly walked over to Kinsley, taking a brief look at the wood carving before addressing her. "Who have you pissed off lately?"

She rolled her eyes. "Why do you both think this has something to do with me? Rhett's the one who pulled the gun last night."

Dad's nostrils flared before his face went flat. "Explain," he barked at Rhett.

"Red Dragons showed up here last night," Rhett reported, arms folded over his chest. "Can't speak as to their motive, but Dalton latched on to Kinsley's wrist and refused to let go." He hesitated, seeming to consider his words, then added, "He may have resisted letting go because I told him to, though I can't be sure what would have happened had I not arrived."

Dad studied Rhett for a long moment then gave a firm nod. Rhett wouldn't have acted without being provoked. Even Kinsley knew that.

Her father crossed his arms, turning his focus wholly on Kinsley. "Did you say anything that might have rubbed them wrong?"

Kinsley didn't take offense. Her loud mouth could, and often did, get her in trouble. "A couple months ago, you know I totally would have probably lipped off to them." She placed her hand on her belly. "Now, definitely not."

She sensed Rhett go unnaturally still. She looked over to him and found him staring at her hand on her belly. For a split second, his expression went utterly soft and melted her bones, but then all emotion was erased from his face when his gaze met hers.

"All right," Dad drawled, bringing her attention back to the hard lines of his mouth. "Let forensics do their thing and we'll go from there."

"I'll need to call the insurance company," Kinsley said, again staring at the disaster around her. She wasn't even sure where to start.

Dad nodded, enveloping her into his warm hug. "So sorry about this, kid. It's the last thing you need right now."

"You're right, it is," she agreed, clamping down on the emotion threatening to rise, letting the rage and fury burn in her belly instead.

"They're going to do what they can," Boone said, sidling up to them as Dad let her go, "but Tony doubted they'd get much, considering there are thousands of fingerprints here."

"We've got the security footage," Rhett injected. Boone nodded, and then a dark shadow crossed over Rhett's expression. "We should consider that this may be King."

Kinsley gulped. That name registered and scared her.

"What about King?"

Asher's voice was hard and hinted at unsettled business. He wore a mask of boredom, but beneath that lay controlled rage. She didn't blame him for that one bit. A few months back, Remy got a personal introduction to Joaquin King, the son of the incarcerated crime boss, Stefano King from Whitby Falls, when she'd unknowingly spent King's money and he wanted repayment. Remy had paid King back his money, which seemed to conclude the bad business between them, and everyone hoped that was the last time they'd see King.

But maybe not?

Heaviness sank into the room, and Kinsley wasn't sure what was worse, having a motorcycle gang break into her business, or King. Both were bad, but she quickly realized King was worse. That last name had been uttered many times over the dinner table while she was growing up. She had been born into generations of cops, and her grandfather was one of the detectives that had taken Joaquin's father down. Stefano was serving one hundred and thirty-nine years for murder, racketeering, and a laundry list of other charges, without any possibility of parole. In his absence, Joaquin had taken over his father's empire, only he was a smarter criminal than his father. Joaquin remained untouchable. She turned to Boone. "Would King do this"—she waved out at her bar—"as retribution?"

"I wouldn't put anything past him," Boone replied without hesitation.

Rhett made a disgruntled noise then moved closer to the bar, studying the carving again. "If we take this for what it says, someone wants this bar closed down." He turned around, and asked Kinsley, "Do you know of anyone who would want that?"

"Not that I can think of," she said, then shrugged. "I mean, I've been open since I finished college. No one's made a peep, and my only competitor is Merlots." The other bar in town was a swanky night club, and she knew the owner, Bernie, really well. "Bernie wouldn't do this to me."

Dad considered that before nodding in agreement. "Let's keep King and the Red Dragons as possible suspects for now. I doubt Bernie has any part in this."

Boone added, "Until we've got a better understanding of what's going on here, stay with me and Peyton." His gaze settled on the wood carving, his brow furrowing. "This is an odd enough warning that we don't want to take chances that this isn't a serious threat against you."

"No."

The hard snap of Rhett's voice had Kinsley whirling around toward him. His jaw was tight, eyes narrowed. "You're with me until we get to the bottom of this." She parted her lips to point out that was a terrible idea, but Rhett added with an arched brow, "*Our* child. Mine to also protect."

The primal glint in his eyes shut her mouth tight. Her heart flipped a few times in her chest, but she also hastily reminded herself not to get overly excited. Rhett didn't do love. He protected. "Okay," she finally said.

Thick, intense silence followed, and the room pulsated with the very loud statement Rhett had made, filling the space between them. Until Dad cut through all the unsaid things. "Good. We've got a plan." He closed the distance and kissed Kinsley's forehead. "Give us some time on this, kid, we'll get it figured out."

"Thanks, I know you will." She couldn't bring herself to look at Rhett, afraid he'd see right through her. The emotion oozing from her threatened to wash over and break down all the walls that she built up to protect her heart from him.

Dad added to Boone, "Keep me updated as the case develops."

"Will do," Boone replied.

While her dad headed for the front door, Kinsley faced her

shattered dream again. "I need to call my staff and let them know we'll be closed for a while. Fixing all this isn't a quick job."

Boone sighed heavily. "Yeah, you go do that. I'll send one of the rookies to keep an eye on things here—and on you."

"Is that really necessary?" she asked.

Of course, Boone ignored her in full protective mode, and added to Rhett and Asher, "Let's get back to the station and see what the security footage shows us."

"Good plan," Asher agreed, and obviously realizing it was going to be a long day, he added, "I'll grab coffees and meet you there."

Both Boone and Asher glanced at Rhett, before hastily walking away. Only then did Kinsley turn toward him, feeling fully back in control of herself. But one look into his face and she immediately wished she'd kept her gaze averted.

Rhett's intense dark eyes held hers, staring right through her, which he didn't do very often. Under that potent stare, heat rolled around in her belly, setting off fireworks that she wanted to explode. She cleared her throat, putting that fire out. "Should I just meet you at your house later then?"

"Let's see how the day plays out," he answered, staying true to form about never offering anything he couldn't deliver on. "I suspect I'll drop by later to pick you up."

She forced her heart not to pitter-patter at the idea of sleeping in the same house as him. Of maybe sharing dinner together. It was a teenage dream, the one she'd longed for, for so long, even now. "Okay." She smiled and whirled away to bring herself back to reality.

"Oh, and Kinsley…" She turned back to him, and he added, "The next time you call, I'll answer."

* * *

When Rhett returned to the station, he was still questioning his choices. Having Kinsley sleep at his place had to top the stupidest idea he'd ever come up with, but when Boone suggested that he would protect the woman carrying *his* baby, Rhett's mouth opened, and words fell out without thought. He strode through the station, shaking off the snow from his hair, and was greeted by the scent of stale coffee. He shut the door behind him and passed the receptionist, the frosty morning still nipping at his ears. The station was quiet around him, apart from a rookie's fingers banging away on the computer, writing up a report. The few other officers there were sitting behind their desks at their cubicles in the center of the station. The offices lining the wall belonged to the detectives, with Rhett's being in the middle, between Asher and Boone's offices. The station's walls were a pale blue and lacked any warmth. In the back of the station were two small jail cells, mainly used to house drunks who needed time to either sober up or cool off. The jail in Whitby Falls held any criminals waiting for their court date before being shipped off to one of the federal prisons.

Rhett skipped past his office, which contained only the bare necessities: a desk with his computer and a leather chair, and not much else, and headed straight for the command center. This space typically was used for morning roll call, but during big cases, the briefing room was the center of the evidence. When Rhett drew closer, he saw through the glass window that Boone had already gotten a case file started and had the file number written on the white board, with pins in the corkboard, ready to hang up the photographic evidence the forensic team gave them.

"West."

At Hank's sharp command, Rhett exhaled slowly then faced the chief. Hank never showed much emotion on the job, but growing up with Boone gave Rhett the understanding that when Hank used Rhett's last name, it meant his mood was strung tight. "I'll be driving Kinsley to your place later," Hank said by way of greeting, "and I'll wait until you get home."

I want to talk to you was what he'd left off. "Yes, sir."

"What time would you like her there?"

Mistake. Big fucking mistake. "Whenever she'd like to go home. I'll drop off a key to her in a bit. Just shoot me a text when you're on your way."

"Can do," said Hank, then gestured to the room. "Get this solved. Nice and quick."

"Yes, sir." Rhett's gaze followed Hank as he headed back to his large corner office in the station, then Rhett entered the command center, finding Boone grinning at him. "What?"

"I used to shake in my boots whenever he would tell me he'd wait for me to get home," Boone answered.

Rhett snorted, taking a seat at the meeting room table, not indulging the conversation. He didn't shake in his boots. He'd made his mess and was prepared to clean it up. He took his cell phone out from his pocket and placed it on the table, noting the large computer screen that was attached to Boone's laptop set up next to the white board. "Get anything from the security footage?"

"Haven't had a chance to look yet." Boone hit a button on his keyboard to wake up the monitor screen.

"If you hoped the town didn't get wind of this, I come bearing bad news," Asher said, entering the room carrying a tray of coffees. "Ms. Abbott just stopped me in the street and already knew about the break-in."

Mary Jane Abbott was a meddling, nosy woman who created more problems with her gossip than not. "Let's get a look at the footage," Rhett said, keeping the focus where it needed to stay.

Boone clicked on a few things on his laptop. Before long, the security footage flickered to life on the monitor. When Kinsley had purchased the bar, Rhett and Asher both helped Boone install the security equipment. Rhett snagged his black coffee from the tray, muttering a quick thanks as Boone fast-forwarded through the timestamped video. The hours of the day went by rapidly, showing Kinsley working the bar and then her employee, Benji, coming in. They saw the Red Dragons coming into the bar, Dalton grabbing Kinsley, and Rhett pulling the gun on him. Then the Red Dragons leaving. From there on, nothing appeared out of the ordinary, until early in the morning. The timestamp read 2:17 a.m. when a group of five men, all wearing plain black clothes and ski masks covering their faces, appeared at the back door of her bar.

"How many Red Dragons were at the bar last night?" Boone asked.

"Three." Rhett's eyes narrowed on the man that picked the lock. The security cameras didn't detect sound, but in seconds, they'd gained entry. "They either had the skill to disable her security system, or one of her employees gave away the code."

"I vet any employee she hires," Boone said. "Unless all of a sudden they have gotten into crime, it's highly unlikely this is an inside job."

"Let's check them out again." Rhett didn't want to miss anything. He rose with his coffee in hand and settled near the screen, careful not to block the way. "I'm not seeing their leathers."

Red Dragons never took the pride of their club's name off their bodies, and they never feared the police. "Am I missing it?"

"No," Asher said, sidling up to Rhett, eyes narrowed on the screen. "This doesn't look like the Red Dragons."

Their arrogance was their signature move. They thought they were untouchable, above the law. If they wanted to make a threat, they'd stand behind that threat, not fear the repercussions. Rhett sipped his coffee to control the fury sliding through his veins as the group began smashing the bar to pieces. Every chair gone, every table destroyed, every bottle of booze in shards on the ground. For Kinsley, Rhett would make whoever was behind this pay. The tension in the room shifted, becoming thick and filled with the fury to protect one of theirs. Rhett's chest tightened as one of the men took a switch blade from his pocket and settled in front of the bar. Rhett watched every second of the man carving those words into the wood.

Once finished, the man glanced up, looked right at the camera, then made the gesture of cutting his neck with his knife.

"Fucker," Rhett growled. Boone froze the video on the man, zooming in on his eyes. The lack of light in the bar made making out shape or color impossible beneath the ski mask. Not getting any further by examining the footage, Rhett returned to his seat next to Asher. "He knew exactly where the camera was."

"It's gotta be King," Asher offered, taking the lid off his coffee cup, steam spiraling out.

"But the question begs to be asked, why target Kinsley's bar?" Rhett asked. "What could that possibly serve King?"

Silence was met with hard frowns. As a trio, they had a perfect record solving cases. No one liked not having an answer, and in most cases, that usually meant trouble was on the horizon.

Rhett took another quick sip of his piping hot coffee, tasting the hazelnuts in the flavor, before he studied the man on the monitor again. He took in every single detail of the man, the way he stood and his mannerisms, imprinting them in his mind. "All of these men are fit and well built; they don't look like a motorcycle gang." Some in the Red Dragons had that description, like Dalton, but most of the men in the club didn't spend hours in the gym to keep in top shape. "These men look like soldiers or special ops."

Boone frowned.

"King's men are retired Navy SEALs and Army Rangers," Asher pointed out, obviously already convinced. "They fit the description."

Rhett wasn't so easily swayed. "But it still doesn't explain why King would do this to Kinsley's bar. He's been quiet for months since Remy's troubles with him. It doesn't add up. Besides, he'd come after us, or Remy." He saw the flare in Asher's gaze but went on, "Logically, that's what make sense here. This, destroying Kinsley's bar, someone either wants her to shut down or they're sending us a warning."

Heavier silence descended on the room. No one liked being in the dark, especially when it involved someone in their inner circle.

Boone finally rose and pushed his chair back under the table, frustration etched in his face. "We're not going to get any answers from the footage. I'll give the chief a report on this and get in touch with Whitby Falls to see if they've had any similar vandalisms." He unplugged his laptop then reached for his coffee. "Perhaps we've got a new gang in town and they're just making their presence known."

That felt wrong to Rhett, but he kept the thought to himself.

"I'll check out Kinsley's employees again and see where that takes me."

"Can't hurt to have another look," Boone said.

Asher rose. "I'll contact the surveillance team trailing King." Surveillance on the crime lord never stopped. A team in Whitby Falls was dedicated to taking King down and had kept eyes on him ever since he'd stepped into his father's footsteps. "Maybe he's got some new men on his payroll. If he does, I'll see if I can get some photographs."

"It's a start," Rhett agreed. He reached for his coffee, suddenly aware of the stillness in the room.

He looked up, and Boone asked with raised brows, "Care to tell us what you're planning?"

"Who says I'm planning anything?" Rhett asked.

Asher leaned against the door frame and barked a laugh.

Boone merely gave him a knowing look.

Rhett snorted, giving his head a slow shake. "If you both know me well enough to know I'm planning something, then you also know that I'd never tell you what I was planning." And with the men he considered his brothers chuckling behind him, Rhett strode out of the command center. His only plan was not waiting for that group of bastards to act again. This next move belonged to him.

* * *

Two hours had gone by since Rhett left the bar this morning, and Kinsley was still reeling from their talk earlier. He'd rattled her then, and she still felt rattled. She could stay strong against jerkish Rhett, but when faced with the sweet, caring, and tender

Rhett who fixed her hand and offered his house up to her, she felt the strands of her strength waver. She chugged the cold water in her glass and set it back onto the bar when she heard Remy say, "Oh, my God, Kinsley, I'm so sorry."

A quick look at the front door revealed that not only had Remy arrived but so had Peyton. Both were ashen faced. Remy took two big steps in and spun in a slow circle. "Who would do this?" she gasped.

"First guess would be the Red Dragons," Kinsley explained, feeling the dull headache building behind her eyes. She'd spent an hour calling her staff and explaining what had happened then another hour with the insurance adjuster when he came by the bar. He told her that he had what he needed to get the claim rolling. She moved to the stage, which luckily hadn't been smashed in, and took a seat on the edge. "But my dad called a bit ago and said that the guys didn't think it was them."

Peyton picked up a chair leg before tossing it back into the pile of broken wood. "Did he say anything more than that?" she asked.

"Nope, just that." Kinsley hesitated. Then, and fully aware of the reaction she was going to get, she added, "Well, not exactly just that. He did say that he'll be picking me up later to drive me home to grab my stuff before taking me to Rhett's." At her best friends' bewildered expressions, she gave a laugh that sounded empty even to her ears. "Surprised?"

"Yes," they said in unison.

She laughed again. A little more honest this time. "I was surprised too, believe me. Rhett showed up this morning, and we had a talk."

"Which obviously went well," Peyton said.

Kinsley nodded. "Things are moving forward, and right now,

I think that's about as good as I'm going to get. I mean, this is a shock. For everyone, I'm sure. We all just need to catch up, and luckily we've got time to do it." She noticed the tightness in Remy's mouth. "All right, out with it. I know you've got feelings on this."

Remy's voice came out in hyperspeed. "Staying with him is a terrible idea. I mean, there's just a lot going on right now. You can stay with me and Asher, where there's absolutely no one that's going to upset you."

She only loved Remy more. "It's sweet for you to offer, thank you. Boone already offered, but Rhett's trying to do the right thing. I need to let him." She paused, trying to get this right. "I know it doesn't really make sense, but it feels like I'm making the right move here. At this point, I just gotta trust what I feel and hope to hell this is all going to work out okay."

Remy didn't look convinced.

Peyton glanced between them then, being her ever-sweet self, smiled. "Boone told me about Rhett stepping up this morning. I think this will be good for him. Just might help him accept that this is happening, you know. Seeing what you go through and stuff."

"Like barfing my brains out at totally random times and wanting really weird food combinations," Kinsley offered.

"Exactly." Peyton laughed.

Remy didn't laugh. Her eyes narrowed on Kinsley. "Well, if I can't talk you out of this, then you can't go into his house without backup." She marched out of the bar to no doubt go to her magic shop to bring back every candle, incense, good luck charm, and whatever else she had to bring positivity and light to Kinsley.

"It's good Rhett came by to talk to you," Peyton said as the door shut. She turned to Kinsley. "To be honest, considering how his talk with Boone went last night, I think it's great he's already stepping up."

"It went that well, huh?"

Peyton lifted a shoulder. "Boone said he was just…torn up a bit."

Kinsley didn't have a reply, so she simply nodded. Yeah, and that was because Rhett wasn't the guy you had a kid with. Hell, he wasn't even the guy a woman should date. He had always been that hot-as-hell tough guy that gave a woman the best sex of her life. Rhett had been that for many women. He'd been that for Kinsley too in the tropics, but she also had something no other woman had with Rhett. A long-standing friendship. She'd known him as a boy, as a teenager, and known him right before he went off to the military. Sometimes, every so often, in his smile she could still see the kid who wasn't so…*torn up*.

"Shit, man."

Kinsley whirled around right as Benji stormed through the front door. He scanned the space, looking probably like she did this morning. Tormented.

Benji's sad eyes finally met hers. "Kinsley, I'm so sorry." He rushed toward her and, in mere seconds, had her in his arms.

She wasn't quite sure why her emotional dam broke when he hugged her, but maybe it was just the buildup of everything from the past couple days. Besides, her emotions lately never made any sense. She cried watching a commercial about a puppy last night but felt nothing during a sad movie the other day. She fell into Benji's comforting embrace and shut her eyes, tears rolling down her cheeks.

"Kinsley."

She heard the restrained control in Rhett's voice even before she opened her eyes. He stood right in front of her, but he was not looking at her. His attention was absolutely fixed on Benji's arms around Kinsley.

He closed the distance between them quickly, his eyes now wholly on her face. On her tears. "Why are you crying?" he asked through clenched teeth.

Benji slowly slid his arm off Kinsley's shoulders and took a step back, as if sensing the threat in front of him.

Even she felt the intensity rolling off Rhett in waves, and she chalked that up to his being in full protective mode because of the break-in. He'd trust no one and suspect everyone. She moved away from the others to put some distance between them to keep the conversation private. She saw Peyton draw Benji over to the stage to help her begin cleaning that area up. "I'm just overwhelmed," she said, wiping her face. "It's just…today…it's been…a lot."

Rhett released a breath like all the plans he'd had to take out his frustrations on Benji had vanished. "What can I do to make that better for you?" he asked sincerely.

She watched him for a moment, sensing his struggle. She'd met so many men over the years working behind the bar. Arrogant men. Cocky men. Sad men. Pathetic men. But Rhett was a different kind of man. An honorable lost man. One who had no idea how to retransition into civilian life. "I'm okay. Honestly. Just emotional."

He didn't look convinced, but he reached into his pocket and handed her a key. "Your dad's going to drive you back to my place after his shift."

Her heart flipped in her chest at the idea of staying the night with him. "Where are you going?" she asked, accepting the key.

"Got a couple stops to make before calling it a day."

The bar's door opened again, and Remy walked through with a grocery bag full of her magical help. She took one look at Rhett and cringed, before reaching into the bag and closing the distance.

She sprayed him twice with something that carried a floral scent. "There, that'll at least get us started," she said.

Rhett frowned.

"Oh, this is bad!" Remy looked outright horrified and then sprayed him five more times before shaking her head at his deeper scowl.

Rhett didn't so much as move, but the authority in his voice filled the room. "Spray me again, Remy, and you're not going to like what I do to that bottle."

She watched him intently for a long moment then shoved the bag at Kinsley. "This is no good at all. I'll be back."

Rhett watched her as she scurried away.

Kinsley laughed. "You better get out of here. I've seen that look. Not only is she determined to fix your mood, but she told me she made a new drink that could battle any negative emotion."

Rhett shuddered. "I'll see you later then."

"See ya," she said.

With a final stern look at Benji, Rhett vanished out the back door.

Remy ran back through the front, holding up a glass filled with a liquid that looked like vomit. "Where'd Rhett go?" she asked.

"To run from that," Kinsley said, pointing at the glass. "Seriously, Remy, no one is going to drink that."

"Oh, please, it's fine." She took a sip then gagged. "Okay, you're right, no one should drink this."

Chapter 6

Rhett booked it around the building and headed toward his truck parked at the curb. He liked Remy, but there was no magic to cure him. Especially now, when confusing jealousy cut through him as Benji's arms around Kinsley filled his mind, and he hated himself for it. She deserved a guy like Benji. A man who could love her right and be that perfect guy she needed. And yet the thought of Benji's body anywhere near Kinsley burned Rhett's blood red-hot.

When he reached his truck, a low snort escaped him when he saw someone sitting in the passenger seat. He got into the driver's seat and said, "I guess I shouldn't be surprised to see you. How did you know I was on my way to see King?"

"Because it's exactly what I would have done," Asher replied, his seatbelt already buckled. He hesitated, his nose scrunching. "Do I even want to know why you smell like flowers?"

"Blame your wife," Rhett growled.

Asher's deep laugh filled the truck as Rhett turned on the ignition, and soon, they left the small town behind for the country roads heading toward Whitby Falls. Traffic was typical along the coastline, with most driving slow to take in the scenery. Rhett passed two cars before he settled into the open road.

When the town faded behind them, Asher broke the silence. "Have you given King a heads-up on this meeting?" he asked.

Rhett nodded. "I thought surprising him wasn't in my best interests." King was a smart criminal, so smart that he had people believing he'd gone straight. "He's expecting me."

"Smart call," Asher said, taking out his cell phone. He laughed a moment later. "Remy has instructed me to bring you back to her shop when we're done."

"You can try," Rhett warned, grinning at Asher, all teeth.

Asher chuckled and fired off a text.

Not that Rhett blamed Remy for trying to make the situation better. She and Kinsley were connected in ways Rhett couldn't even fathom. If Kinsley was feeling off, Remy would feel the same way too. But that didn't mean Rhett would indulge Remy. If he did, she'd unleash the full force of her New Age magic on him.

Outside his window, the bright sun glistened along the ice on the water, and on any other day, Rhett would've sunk back into his seat and enjoyed the ride. While on tour in the Afghan mountains, he'd often dreamed of the ocean, of the coast, even in wintertime. Nothing was as beautiful…well, he could think of one thing more beautiful.

"Did you get anything on Kinsley's employees?"

Rhett shook the thought from his head. He'd run Benji, Lola, and Justin before dropping the key off to Kinsley. "They're clean, but I'm not ruling out Benji."

"Why?" Asher asked. "Because he's slept with Kinsley?"

Rhett knew they'd been intimate only because Boone had shared that info when Kinsley hired him. He'd been against her hiring an ex-boyfriend. She'd ignored Boone, like she ignored most people. She always went with her gut. Rhett liked that about her. "That has nothing to do with anything," he retorted.

"Sure it doesn't." Asher smirked.

Rhett focused back on the road, not allowing Asher to turn this conversation personal. Kinsley had been threatened. Rhett would find out why. "Someone had a way to disable her security system," he said, reminding Asher of that fact. "This could very well have something to do with someone who works there."

Asher didn't look convinced and ignored Rhett's redirect of the conversation. "Speaking of Kinsley, how's things going there?" he asked.

Rhett's jaw clenched and his fingers tightened on the steering wheel. "The only thing I want to talk about is how to keep her safe." He gave Asher a sidelong look. "Got it?"

Asher's brows rose. "In a mood today, huh?"

Damn. Rhett rolled his shoulders and relaxed his jaw, keeping his gaze focused on the road ahead. Both Asher and Boone were his found brothers. They were also the only family he had back in Stoney Creek. "This is…it's…"

"Tense," Asher offered. "I got that."

"That's all it is right now," Rhett said, having nothing more to give. "She's fine. I'm dealing with all this. That's all I got."

Asher inclined his head and didn't push anymore; he simply continued looking out the window.

Most days, Rhett wondered what he did to deserve the friends he had. They were understanding, loyal, and supportive. When Rhett first returned from the Army, he'd been in a dark place, and they had stuck by him. Every single one of them. He kept his focus on the road, getting the subject off Kinsley. Truth was, Rhett had no answers, only pulsing emotions that felt like they were tottering on the edge of control.

They spent the rest of the drive in silence, and by the time Rhett drove along the endless shops and restaurants of The Square in downtown Whitby Falls, he was cemented in his decision to talk with King. He had no clue as to how he could make all this right with Kinsley, but he knew how to protect her.

That was a start.

He drove through the town until they headed back out of the city and into the vast beauty of Maine. Ten minutes later, Rhett pulled into a gated driveway. He rolled down his window, and when the security camera above the gate turned toward him, Rhett announced, his breath clouding, "Detective West and Detective Sullivan to see King."

"Give me a moment, please," a low voice said. After a few seconds, he spoke again. "Drive up until you reach the main house. Security will be waiting for you there."

Rhett rolled up his window and snorted. "Intense setup for a guy who's trying to make others believe he's not a criminal."

The gates opened, and as Rhett drove up the driveway, Asher whistled. "Jesus, look at that house."

Rhett got Asher's awe. The waterfront Georgian Revival red brick mansion sat upon a gorgeous property that likely had impeccable gardens in the summer. Rhett's attention didn't linger long on the property before moving swiftly to the two armed security guards standing at the opening of the circular driveway. Rhett parked a few feet away and cut the ignition. He exited his vehicle and Asher followed him out.

"Detective West," the security guard said right to him like they'd already met.

Obviously they'd done their homework.

"That's right." He gestured to Asher. "Detective Sullivan."

"Identification, please," the man said.

Rhett reached into his back pocket. This show was nothing more than that. A show to make it appear like they didn't have information they shouldn't. Rhett didn't doubt that King knew all about them. Every single detail, right down to their incomes.

The guard examined their badges, then handed them back and said, "I'll need your weapons. You'll get them back when you leave."

Rhett froze.

The guard arched an eyebrow. "Nonnegotiable."

Rhett sighed, then took his gun from his holster. He took out the clip and handed it to the guard, as did Asher. They were both searched for further weapons then the guard led them through the grand foyer of the mansion, passing two more guards before they followed him into a large office. Behind the desk sat Joaquin King.

King's white dress shirt was rolled up at the sleeves, portraying a casual air that Rhett felt certain was manufactured. His blond hair was styled and his dark blue eyes regarded Rhett with every step he took into the room. The only thing about King that didn't scream wealth was his five o'clock shadow, almost as if he needed to rebel against the life that had been handed to him.

"Please," King said, rising from his chair. "Come take a seat."

Rhett settled into the client chair on the left, Asher on the right. Rhett kept his chair angled slightly to keep an eye on those guards behind him.

"Now that you've driven all the way out here just for a talk, what can I do for you?" King asked, returning to his seat behind his desk.

Rhett wanted to see King's expression as he asked his questions. He was sure there was a gentler way of approaching this, but that wasn't Rhett's way. "Did you send your men to trash Kinsley Knight's bar last night?"

Asher exhaled deeply, shifting in his seat. He'd never agreed with Rhett's blunt ways, but Rhett was not wasting time. Not with Kinsley involved.

King lifted an eyebrow. "Kinsley Knight?"

"The sister of Detective Boone Knight," Asher offered.

"Ah," King said, leaning back in his seat and crossing his arms. "Is there a particular reason you think I have involvement here?"

"Because you're a dirty prick," Rhett said.

At that, King grinned.

Asher interjected, using a firm, but polite voice, "We're aware there might be some lingering tension from our recent matter."

"There's no animosity on my end," King said to Asher. To Rhett, he added, "I have never met Kinsley Knight, nor do I plan to."

Rhett stared into King's eyes, seeing something familiar. Rhett had met the worst type of people during his time in the Army. And he'd killed those men. King had that same haunted look in his eye. "I didn't come here today to get an explanation," Rhett said.

King's brows shot up. "Then why did you come?"

"To tell you that if you're behind this, you're a dead man walking."

Asher's head whipped around to Rhett and his frown was deep.

But for King, a man who feared nothing, his grin only darkened. "Do tell me, West, what's your investment here with Ms. Knight?"

Rhett knew he'd shown his cards by coming to King's residence. He also didn't care. "She's pregnant with my child," he told him bluntly. "Last night, her bar was broken into and trashed. That will not happen again."

King's mouth twitched. "Pregnant with your child, hmm? Explains the visit, I suppose." He took in Rhett's measure then exhaled slowly, finally stating, "I assure you that neither my men, nor myself, had anything to do with Ms. Knight's bar being trashed, or have any involvement with anyone in Stoney Creek for that matter. Shall I investigate further to see who may be behind the break-in?"

Rhett snorted and rose, as Asher did the same, ignoring King's remark. He'd come to make a point, and he'd made it. "Do yourself a favor," Rhett warned.

"What's that?" King practically purred.

"Forget her name." And with that, Rhett turned and headed for the door. Just before he left, he glanced over his shoulder, finding King's amused gaze on him. "If you don't, I won't forget yours."

King just smiled.

* * *

Stoney Creek did a few things well. Quaint restaurants and shops. Delicious food and drinks. And Christmas.

In just a few short weeks, Christmas joy would take hold of the town until after New Year's. Even now, as Kinsley entered the small market on Main Street, she spotted old Mrs. Russell, who'd owned the market for as long as Kinsley could remember, sitting behind the counter working on this year's Christmas wreath.

"I really think we need to talk about this," Remy said as she followed Kinsley down the produce aisle.

During the warmer seasons, the market was outside in the parking lot next door, offering fresh local produce. But for now, Kinsley stuck to the organic produce shipped in, thinking the oversized strawberries looked too genetically modified to be healthy for her growing baby. She reached for some romaine lettuce, placing it in the basket, and looked over her shoulder at Remy. "Okay, then talk."

Remy looked like she'd eaten a sour lemon. "I'm really worried about you. I just don't want you getting hurt here, and this entire situation with Rhett is setting itself up for a huge heartbreak."

Any good best friend would be very worried. Rhett was all wrong for her. "Let me guess—you're worried because I'm madly and hopelessly in love with him and you think I'm too emotional for this." They both knew it was true. Loving Rhett had *always* been true.

"Yes, exactly," Remy confirmed, crossing her arms, looking like a fierce, bright warrior. "You're about to go play house with a guy who doesn't play house with anyone. The same guy who has left a trail of women—okay, maybe satisfied women from what I hear—but still heartbroken women in his wake."

Kinsley was definitely one of those satisfied women. She'd always known sex with Rhett would be explosive, but she'd had no idea how explosive. Her mind simply could not have dreamed up how incredible they were together. Even now, if she let herself think of his talented mouth and strong hands…

"Why are you flushing?" Remy gasped then shuddered. "Ew. God. Are you thinking about sex with him?"

"Of course I am." Kinsley laughed, then whirled away to grab some bananas. "Stop worrying about me. I'm going to be smart about this."

"Bullshit." At Remy's hard voice, Kinsley turned around. Blazing eyes met hers. "You've gotta start being honest about all this, or you're going to get hurt, and as your soul sister, I can't stand by and let that happen." Remy barely dragged in a breath before she went on. "You're going to sleep with him again. And you're going to love every second you have with him because it's what you've always wanted. At least be honest about that."

Kinsley lips parted then shut. If given the chance to sleep with him again, she would in a heartbeat. If given the chance to be loved by him, she'd take it in the blink of an eye. "I know that I'm walking a dangerous line with him," she admitted.

Remy sighed heavily, her shoulders lowering. "Good, at least you know that. Just don't forget that line. You need to stay on top of this, and your heart, or he's going to make a mess out of it. So, it's not about being smart: it's about what you want from him."

Kinsley felt that wound in her heart reopen. The same wound that got bigger every time Rhett took a woman home from the bar. Every time she had to hear about him going on a date. Every time she had to watch some woman hang off him…despite not even really knowing him. "Okay, so maybe I don't have this all completely figured out," she said. "But I'm trying to figure it out. I know it's complicated."

"Complicated?" Remy snorted. "Dude, this is so far past

complicated. And I'm really worried that when the dust settles, you're going to be left more heartbroken over him than you already are."

Kinsley stared into Remy's unusually fiery eyes. She smiled and wrapped her arms around her friend's strained frame. "Thank you for loving me so much in the way that you do. I'll never know what I did to deserve a friend like you." Everyone needed that one person who told them things straight. That was Remy, always had been.

Remy squeezed back. "You deserve me because you're as good of a friend back." She leaned away with honest concern in her expression. "Rhett will step up. He'll do what he can. But let's be honest here, it's Rhett. He's not going to love you like you need or deserve."

"I know that." Hell, did she know that well. Kinsley gave herself a couple seconds to rein in her thoughts, knowing she had to get this right. "I don't know how to explain any of this to you. It doesn't even make sense in my head. I know I should keep Rhett at a distance. I shouldn't let him get so close. But everything inside of me is telling me to do the opposite. That if I do, this is all going to be okay and work out."

"But what if that's your heart getting in the way?" Remy asked behind her.

Kinsley continued on, turning down another aisle and grabbing a package of bacon from the fridge. "Maybe it is, maybe it isn't, who knows. But I'm telling you, when he said he wanted me to stay with him, I wasn't thinking that this might mean anything between us, I was only thinking that this was the right thing to do." She walked farther down and reached for a jar of Caesar salad dressing before she faced Remy again. "I know my heart is currently in the danger zone, but I feel like"—she shrugged—"things are going to be okay as long as we're moving forward. Eventually. Maybe not now. But I think, if anything, I need to follow my gut, and my gut tells me that staying with him is the right thing to do."

Remy's eyes lost some heat. "Well, I've already told Asher that I want him to punch Rhett if he makes you cry."

Kinsley laughed. "Did Asher agree?"

"Of course." Remy smiled, then peeked up through her thick lashes. "You're really gonna be okay here?"

"I really am. This is a shock for everyone, not just me. This baby is totally changing my life, and it'll change Rhett's life too. I can't think of what my heart wants right now. Or what it wanted. All I'm thinking is that I have to give him space to accept this news like I did. Then we'll go from there. One step at a time."

"But not to his bedroom, right," Remy said firmly, "because that's a terrible idea."

"Totally terrible," Kinsley stated, though she wasn't sure if she was fooling herself.

A frown tugged on Remy's mouth. "You don't sound convincing."

Kinsley kept quiet and strode forward. She couldn't make that promise about not going back to Rhett's bed, because she knew she couldn't keep it. All she had to do was not expect things he couldn't give. Easy.

"Kinsley," Remy called after her. "Might I remind you that sex with Rhett is what got you pregnant?"

"You're pregnant with Rhett's child?"

Shit. Remy cringed and gave a look full of apology. Kinsley slowly glanced over her shoulder at the other thing Stoney Creek did well. Gossip. And Mary Jane Abbott, who was all purple curls, warmth, and a mother to everyone in town, was a top-notch gossiper. "I am, and yup, Rhett's the daddy," Kinsley said. The news had to get out sooner or later.

"Oh, what fabulous news. I had no idea you were dating," Mary Jane said, eyes twinkling. She had a full basket of food in her hands. "Is there a wedding in the future?"

"No wedding. We aren't dating." Kinsley leaned in and nudged Mary Jane's arm. "Those bad boys are trouble, aren't they?"

Mary Jane's eyes went huge. Big enough that Kinsley laughed.

Remy laughed nervously, glancing between them.

Still smiling, Kinsley moved away, overhearing Remy mutter a goodbye and quickly following behind.

"You do realize what you just did, right?" Remy asked when she caught up to Kinsley.

"I know exactly what I did," Kinsley replied, reaching for the bag of croutons on the shelf. "You're right—I can't do things the way I used to do them. I can't love all over Rhett and hope he sees me standing there wanting him. I can't be blind to just how risky this is with him. I can't keep this all quiet and somehow hope it works out. I've got to handle this all differently. I've got to step up myself and take control of this. Now everyone will know the truth. Now we can all move forward." And with that came a plan. One that put her back in control of her life with her chin held high.

Remy blinked. "I don't even know who you are anymore. Look at you being all sensible and honest with your feelings."

Yeah, Rhett wasn't the only one who was emotionally closed off. That was Mom's going-away present that had stayed with Kinsley ever since she'd left. "I've got seven months and some change to get my life stable for this baby, which includes figuring all this out with Rhett. And I get one shot at being a good mom. I'm not going to mess that up on some guy with major commitment issues."

"Good. There's my girl. Just had to make sure she was in there," Remy said, giving her a beaming smile and sliding her arm through Kinsley's. "Luckily for you, I've got some of the best herbs and salves to make sure that happens."

Kinsley's stomach churned. It was going to be a long seven months.

* * *

At eleven minutes after seven, Rhett finally pulled into his driveway and the large spotlight on the side of the house turned on as he drove by. Large snowflakes danced in the beams of his headlights. He'd dropped Asher off at home, and Remy caught him at their place and sprayed him a couple more times with whatever flowery-scented shit she thought he needed. He stank even worse than this afternoon. Then he made another quick stop before finally calling it a day. When he pulled into his driveway, he spotted Hank's silver Ford truck. He parked next to it then got out, unsurprised when Hank exited his house. Hank had been a second father to Rhett growing up. And after his parents moved away, he'd become the only family Rhett had. Rhett knew this talk had been coming since last night.

Heaviness sank into Rhett's chest when Hank met him halfway, stopping beneath the spotlight. "How did the meeting with King go?" Hank asked, his tone not the commanding chief of police voice he used in the station. This one was warmer, more personal. The one Rhett had heard many times over the years when he, Boone, Asher, and Kinsley got into trouble.

Rhett snorted, crossing his arms and leaning against Hank's truck. "Did Asher tell you we were going?"

"It didn't take much to know you'd go there." Hank's eyebrow winged up. "And?"

"I doubt King's involved. I got very little off him, but a mild amusement that we thought it was him."

"I'd say it's good it's not King, but I'd almost rather it was so at least we'd know who we're dealing with." Hank rubbed the back of his neck, glancing down to his worn black boots. "It's such an odd situation," he finally said, looking up. "To trash her place, and not rob her. It just doesn't add up."

Rhett nodded, feeling the same frustrations burn through his blood. "We'll start with fresh eyes in the morning. We've got calls into Whitby Falls. Hopefully, we'll also have some evidence by then to go on. There's a reason she was targeted. I'll find out what it is and who's behind it."

"I've got no doubt that's very much true," Hank said, then he hesitated, his intense eyes boring deeply into Rhett's. "Listen, it isn't my place to stick my nose into your and Kinsley's business, but for my own peace of mind, do I have anything to worry about here?"

Rhett remained quiet for a long moment. The answer wasn't so easy, and he wouldn't make false promises. He respected Hank, as much as he did his own father. "I'll protect her," he finally said. "I'll keep them both safe." That he knew how to do. "As for the rest…"

Hank chuckled. "I'm sure Kinsley will tell you how she wants the rest to go." His smile faded and he gave Rhett a long regard. "She's been through a lot," he said with heavy regret. "With her mother, as you know." He paused and then gave him a firm nod. "Protecting her, keeping them both safe, that's all I can ask from you." He took a step forward and cupped Rhett's shoulder. "You do that, Rhett, and we'll be just fine. Got it?"

"Yes, sir."

Hank's expression shifted, filling with his usual warmth before he said, "All right, I'll get out of your hair. See you in the morning."

Rhett nodded, then gave Hank a wave before he drove off. He didn't deserve Hank's warmth and affection. He deserved having Hank yell and punch him for knocking up his daughter, but that wasn't Hank's way.

With a sigh, Rhett turned to his house, feeling about a second away from crawling out of his skin. He forced his feet to take him in that direction, and when he entered through the back door of his house, the aroma of spices slammed into him, bringing memories of when his mother cooked. He could almost hear her yell, *"Get those dirty boots off and wash up for dinner."*

It'd been a long time since his parents had come home, busy with their new lives far from Stoney Creek.

Tonight, though, it was Kinsley who stood at the sink with two T-bone steaks already grilled, mixing together a Caesar salad. Rhett was monetarily stunned by the view, and his reaction to it. He never brought women home to *his* space, and yet with Kinsley, he didn't mind her there. Oddly, a slight flicker of warmth eased over his chest. His house was always so empty, cold almost.

But *her*…nothing about Kinsley was cold.

"Wow, you survived the dad-talk," she said with a laugh, giving him a full once-over. "I had this ready for you just in case it went badly." She handed him an already opened beer.

He accepted the bottle. "You thought your dad planned to rip into me, huh?"

"It was a toss-up, but I'm glad to see he actually listened to me and is letting me handle my own life." She leaned closer and sniffed him. Her grin widened. "I see Remy got to you again, didn't she?"

He felt a frown tug on his mouth. "I smell that bad?"

"It's actually a nice smell." Her mouth twitched. "Just not on a man."

"Great," Rhett groaned, still standing by the doorway. He should say something. But the only thing he came up with was, "Can I do something to help you?"

"Nope." She fixed another plate and gestured to the full plate on the counter. "Just eat."

A cold rush rooted him to the spot. He stared at the plate then at her. "I don't know how to do this."

"You don't know how to eat?" she teased. But at his silence, she turned around and stared at him for a long moment then nodded like she had the answer to a question he never asked. She added utensils to both of their plates, then took her food and headed for the living room, not saying another word.

A second later, his television turned on.

Before he followed her, he stopped to get her water with ice, realizing he had no idea what she liked, and whatever it was, he probably didn't have it anyway. *Bad move, West.* He should have thought of that. He cursed and grabbed his plate, keeping hold of his beer and her water, and entered his living room. The space lacked warmth. Like Rhett's soul, it contained only the necessities, not offering much of anything except a cold space to rest awhile. But pure warmth sat on the chair facing the television.

"Have you ever seen *The Office*?" Kinsley asked, cutting into her steak.

He glanced at the television screen, realizing she was on his Netflix. "No."

"No?" she asked. "Oh, good, then I know what we're doing while I'm here. Total *Office* marathon. You'll love it. It's so funny."

His heart raced as he set his plate and beer down on the coffee table. "Here," he said, handing her the water.

She glanced up. "Oh, thanks," she said with a full mouth. She took the glass, set it down, then focused right back on the television.

He couldn't help the amusement that drifted up, bringing a smile to his face. Kinsley had always been this woman who seemed cut from a different cloth than anyone else. She didn't have manners like other women. Her hair wasn't neat, her messy bun obviously just thrown up there without a look in the mirror, and if she had makeup on, he couldn't see it. He assumed that was because she was raised by her father and not her mother. But he liked that about her. Christ, no, he found that sexy. Low maintenance was *hot*.

He clamped that thought down immediately, forcing his gaze to his plate, not blind to how her sweet laughter touched tender places in his chest and how he remembered hearing that laugh when his kisses tickled her sides.

"If you're waiting for your dinner to somehow taste better, you're out of luck. I'm a terrible cook."

He glanced into those bright blue eyes and felt sucked right in. Any other woman and he'd have to find something to say, but not this woman. He smiled softly. "As long as it doesn't kill me, I'll think it's good."

Either he said the right thing or his smile warmed her because her expression went utterly soft. "Well, I haven't quite decided if I'm going to kill you yet, but don't worry, I have no plans to do so tonight." And with a wink, she turned her attention back to the television and all but shoveled her salad into her mouth.

He decided to do the same.

Chapter 7

A loud bang jolted Kinsley awake from a deep sleep. She sat up in Rhett's queen-size bed, with a dark gray duvet over her, and glanced right, finding the clock on the nightstand that read 4:22. Darkness encased her, telling her she should still be sleeping. Another loud grunt sounded again, and she shoved the covers off, hurrying out of bed. Just as she reached the open door, Rhett's yell froze her in place. "Run!"

Her heart leapt up into her throat, the sleepiness gone from her eyes, as she scanned the area quickly for a possible threat.

Rhett's sharp intake of breath jerked her attention to the couch, where he suddenly sat up. Moonlight shone in through the window, detailing the hard lines of his body wound tight, sweat glistening off tense muscles. "Fuck," he said, running his hands through his hair.

Not wanting to make a big deal out of an obvious nightmare, Kinsley slowly backed up until she climbed into the bed again. She lay her head against her pillow, sure he couldn't see her through the darkness, and watched Rhett rise, scrubbing his face. Even from where she lay, he looked visibly shaken. The sound of his voice moments ago had made her blood go cold. She'd never heard that tone from him. There was no fear, no emotion, no nothing, just an order that was meant to save lives.

That was the soldier.

The man she didn't know.

The bed felt cold, the sheets impossibly wrinkly and suddenly uncomfortable, as she heard the shower go on. With bated breath, she waited, and waited, and waited for him to finish his shower, to know he was all right. Ten minutes went by, then twenty, then twenty-five. No thoughts went through her mind as she slid out from under the blankets again and moved to the bathroom. Only worry for him touching every warm bit in her soul. The door was ajar, and she pushed it fully open, finding the small room full of steam. "Rhett," she said softly.

Nothing. No response.

The all-glass shower was completely clouded. "Rhett," she said louder. "Are you okay?"

Still nothing.

She moved closer and opened the shower door, every second feeling like a lifetime. When she peered inside, she nearly broke at the sight in front of her. Rhett sat against the wall, arms resting on his knees, hands threaded in his hair. Desperate to get closer, she went straight in, cotton nightgown and all, and knelt next to him. She placed her hand on his shoulder, sliding her touch over the rough skin of the bullet wound there that had ended his military career. He trembled beneath her touch, even though the water raining down on them was warm. "Rhett," she said softly.

He finally lifted his head, dropping it back against the tiled wall, and his gaze met hers. His expression revealed everything…his pain…his truth…his horror at the things he'd seen, and she threw her arms around his neck and hugged him, regardless of whether he wanted it or not. She didn't count the minutes she held him, but she relished when he dropped his head into her neck and inhaled deeply. He didn't touch her, not until his trembling stopped. Only then did he wrap his arms around her tight.

Tears welled behind her closed eyes. She didn't even want to think about what he saw in those nightmares. She pulled back from his embrace and met his dark eyes. "Bad dream?"

He nodded.

Pulled in by this hidden force between them, she cupped his face. "What can I do to help?"

He stared at her. She stared back. And in those passing seconds, there was suddenly nothing separating them. There was just this heated intensity that was passion and emotion and things she couldn't even explain to herself. He dropped his chin and breathed so deep that it almost seemed like a weight had been lifted off him. "I can't fight this tonight. Fight you. You've got one chance to get up and go back to bed."

She released a shuddering breath, embracing the burn he built inside her. "I'm not leaving you."

His eyes blazed. "Then kiss me."

And she willingly complied, knowing the danger, but doing it anyway. Because there was something addictive about Rhett, something she never could let go of. Being with him went against everything her mind told her. She risked her heart, and yet it felt right to do so.

A harsh shudder ran through him when she climbed onto

his lap, her soaking nightgown a heavy weight against her. His strong callused hands caressed her thighs, sliding her nightgown up and up until he cupped her bottom. She stared into his eyes, lost in them, owned by them. He didn't look like an empty man. He watched her with heat and passion, turning her bones to liquid. Albeit, with a whole world of uncertainty simmering just beneath the surface.

But all that went away when he kissed her, like he knew her body and how to make it awaken. He *took* and *gave* equally, undoing her completely until she was panting for more. Nothing in how he touched her now was like their one night in the tropics. It wasn't playful and fun; it was raw and needy. It didn't feel like he was caressing her; it felt like he was centering himself, reminding himself what was real and what wasn't, and she wanted to be that for him.

She shifted her panties to the side and then ground her hips, rubbing herself against him, feeding pleasure to where she most needed it. He gave a rough growl, his kiss turning urgent, and she didn't wait, needing him just as much. She lifted her hips, finding the tip of him, taking him deep inside her. He broke the kiss, one hand on her nape, the other on her hip helping her move and gain speed. Every slow stroke brought her higher, made her moan louder, echoed by his groans.

She lost herself in the way he watched her. The need there. And with a surge of pleasure, she sank deeper into this thing between them. The thing that made no sense, defied everything she believed in, and yet somehow seemed perfectly right.

His hands were suddenly gone, grabbing her nightgown and yanking the soaking wet fabric over her head. His fingers threaded in her wet hair again, and his lips met hers with a passion that burned. She felt him everywhere. In her body. In her heart. In her soul. But then his hands were on her breasts, his tongue sliding over a taut nipple.

Heat flowed through her, a building pleasure she couldn't control. She moved harder, faster, as he sucked deeper, bringing her nipple to the roof of his mouth. Then his teeth brushed over the sensitive flesh, dragging and pulling, and all the building pressure suddenly broke apart around her. She vaguely heard his answering roar, his fingers digging into her hip, but the pulsing of her pleasure pulled her under.

The moment she remembered she had working parts was the same instant she realized that Rhett was hugging her tight again, his head buried in her neck. She wrapped her arms around him, holding him close, and did the one thing she knew no other woman had done before her.

She didn't let him push her away.

* * *

Darkness enveloped his bedroom as Rhett stood by the foot of his bed, shaking the excess water from his hair. He had slipped into his boxer briefs, knowing he should reach for his pants and shirt and walk away, but he couldn't find the strength to do that tonight. The dream shook him, more so than it had in months. For years, nightmares had drowned him and whiskey had been his answer to silence them. Women helped them too, burning off the adrenaline and quieting his head. Tonight's nightmare left him feeling raw and Kinsley made breathing easier. As she lay in his bed, his deep inhale felt lighter than it had since he'd come home from the military. Her light had encased him, and there wasn't a damn chance in hell he'd walk away from that.

Alone, he knew. Cold, he understood. This warmth, he wanted to keep it for as long as she'd let him have it.

"If you're going to say that was a mistake, prepare for a throat punch," Kinsley said, her firm voice filling his dark room.

"Since I take that threat seriously, I won't say it was a mistake." He slipped into bed and she turned around to face him, snuggling in closer. "You want to be here, Kinsley," he told her, "then be here." Tonight, he couldn't be stronger than his needs. And he needed *her*.

He lay his head back against the pillow and shut his eyes, feeling the welcome quiet wash over him. "We should, though…" He swallowed against the dryness in his throat.

Kinsley placed her hand on his chest, easing the tightness there. "I know what this was. I know what you can give and what you can't. Stay in the moment, Rhett. I'm fine. This is fine. Everything's okay."

The surety in her voice surprised him, especially considering how she'd found him in the shower. He shifted onto his side, resting his head on his arm. She lay facing him, the moonlight from the window giving him a sudden view that had him hardening again. The line from her ankle to her hip was damn near appetizing. Her skin was so smooth, so perfect, and he remembered how he'd stroked every inch and how she'd moved with every touch he gave. His cock twitched, need overwhelming him as he took in the curve of her hip, the slightly rounder breasts than he remembered in the tropics, and her rosy nipples. But as he looked up into her face again, his eyes finally adjusting to the darkness, he saw her eyes under the moon's beam. So bright, and full of life…Christ, this woman unraveled him. And the truth was, he wanted to believe her words, that everything *would* be okay. He brushed the hair off her face and muttered, "You're a fiercely strong woman, Kinsley."

"I know." Her smile was sweet and soft and everything he expected from her.

But then that smile faded. "How often do you have nightmares?" she asked.

Well aware he owed her some answers after the condition she'd found him in, he answered, "There's no rhyme or reason to them."

Most women wouldn't push. Of course, Kinsley did. "What are they about?"

He debated avoiding the question, but she saw him at his worst tonight. He needed to explain. "Afghanistan."

Her pause lasted awhile, telling him she was mulling something over. "Well, I guess that's to be expected," she finally said. "Anyone coming home from war won't just have physical scars, but emotional ones too."

He let his silence be his answer. She was right: War left wounds, and not just physical ones.

"So, is it a recurring real dream?" she asked, breaking the silence again. "Or is it like a fictional thing?"

"Past memories."

Again, she hesitated. "Can you tell me about the dream you had?"

He leaned back against his pillow, staring at the shadows on his ceiling. The sound of helicopter blades cutting through the air took him back to that day where the guy he once was died and someone else took over.

The heat was nothing he'd ever felt before. It not only scorched the body, but hurt with every breath. Rhett held his weapon steady, moving quickly through the cement structure. Once maybe, the place had been used as a house; now it had been long empty. He exited a small room, quite possibly an old bedroom, then came upon a garden where he found a girl, maybe twelve years old. Beside her was her mother, the woman who had been helping Rhett and his team locate her husband. "Target found, one deceased."

"Roger, moving out," Matthews said.

Rhett rushed forward toward the girl, dropping to his knees next to her. "Who did this?" he asked the daughter, who stared and trembled at her deceased mother.

Rhett took the girl by the arm and shook her. "Who did this?" he asked again.

"My brother," she whispered, tears rolling down her cheeks. "You said they wouldn't know. You promised to keep us safe. You lied. She's dead. My mother is dead."

Her mother had traded information in exchange for keeping them safe from a world she wanted to run from. One that would secure the protection of her daughter. But last night, while a unit drove them from the secure location to the airport to fly them to safety, the vehicles had taken on heavy fire, and the mother and daughter had gone missing. Six soldiers were killed. Four hours later, intel had led them to this location.

Over the communicator tucked into Rhett's ear, his fellow Army Ranger, Collins, said, "Movement on the south."

Rhett grabbed the girl by the shoulder. "Stay behind me. Hold on to my shirt. Stay close."

She nodded, fear shining in her eyes.

He covered the girl with his body, a shield to protect her where they'd failed to do so for her mother, and he raised his weapon. He moved swiftly and quietly through the building, when suddenly he caught movement to his right. A boy, no more than eight years old, held an assault rifle aimed at Rhett.

"Dear God, what happened after that?"

Rhett blinked, and he was reminded that he wasn't in that hot, dry place, and that the heat he felt came from Kinsley's body. She curled into him, and his body trembled slightly. Fuck, he had no idea what he told her. He cleared his throat, breathing deep, trying to settle the rapid beat of his heart. "I got shot."

She cupped his face, her voice filled with emotion. "You couldn't shoot the boy, could you?"

"I hesitated, and it got me shot," he answered, his throat tightening until he could barely get air in.

"Jesus Christ," she all but breathed. "He killed his own mother?"

Rhett loosened a breath. "To him, according to the lies his father had hand-fed him, she was a traitor."

A pause. A long, heavy pause. "Just before you woke up, you yelled, 'Run!' Who were you telling to run?"

"His sister."

Kinsley's breath hitched as she lay in his arms, snuggling her face into his chest. "Did he shoot her too?"

Rhett shut his eyes and forced his words through his dry throat. "The only person who came out of the garden alive was me." And those were the haunting realizations. Three innocent lives were lost.

There was a long stretch of silence, as Rhett felt the dampness drip onto his chest where Kinsley lay her head on him. "Rhett," she eventually said. "I'll never understand everything you went through there. The things you had to see or do for your country to ensure I lived a safe life at home, and for people all over the world to be free from cruelty, but I do know one thing."

He pressed his lips down on the top of her head. "What's that?"

"I'm really happy you came home."

He closed his arms around her and shut his eyes, letting this warmth she offered fill the cold places inside him.

Chapter 8

The next morning, Rhett leaned against the steering wheel, looking at Kinsley through the passenger side window of his truck on Main Street. "I'll text you later today when I'm ready to pick you up."

"That works." She wrapped her scarf tighter against the chilly air, while big snowflakes fell from the dark sky. The day was dreary, and she'd rather still be in bed doing things with Rhett to make the windows steam. "Got any idea what time approximately?"

"Give me until five tonight," he said. "Boone texted this morning while you were in the shower that the lab's results are in, so we'll want to press ahead with the investigation."

Her investigation. She really couldn't even believe it and didn't want to think about all the stuff she needed to do to start rebuilding her bar. Last night had been a good night. Hell, a *great* night. She wasn't exactly sure where this left them, but at least Rhett was not shutting her out. She figured that was a good start. "Okay." She smiled and tapped the window. "I'll see ya later then."

She felt every bit of his stare the entire time it took for her to reach Remy's magic shop. Her hand wrapped around the cool brass handle and the sound of Rhett's engine turning on filled the air behind her. His nightmare stayed heavily on her mind all through breakfast this morning. She'd begun to understand what Rhett had endured. In all honesty, she thought his bullet wound had left him broken. She thought he wanted to be back alongside his military brothers, and because he couldn't, he was pissed off at the world. But now she knew just how horrible the things he'd seen and done were and how they haunted him, and he was struggling to readjust.

Not really knowing how to help him, she opened the door to Remy's shop, and was greeted by an overwhelming whiff of something spicy mixed with something sweet. The shop had cream-colored walls and gorgeous worn hardwood floors. Remy stood behind the black-painted counter, worrying her bottom lip. Leaning against that counter was Peyton smiling ear to ear. "Aren't you two a stark contrast to each other," Kinsley remarked. "One, happy as can be. The other, worried as hell."

Remy shrugged and said all too quickly, "How did last night go? I wanted to call but Asher told me to stay out of it."

Kinsley noted the dark circles under Remy's eyes. "You should have just called, so you wouldn't have spent the whole night worrying." She strode toward a small circular table that had a new cream tester on it. "Everything...well, it went okay."

"Oh, no, you *did* sleep with him."

Kinsley whirled around with a dollop of the peppermint-scented cream on the tip of her finger. "Seriously?" She snorted a laugh. "How do you get that I slept with him out of what I just said?"

Remy lifted her brows.

Kinsley rolled her eyes. Remy knew her, sometimes even more than Kinsley knew herself. "Okay, fine, we slept together."

"Does that mean you're together now?" Peyton asked, nearly bouncing on her feet.

"No," Kinsley said, rubbing her hands together. "It means we slept together again. That's it."

Remy crossed her arms and frowned. "I still say this is a really bad idea. Someone is going to get hurt here, and I'm guessing that someone isn't gonna be Rhett."

"Your concern is duly noted," Kinsley said as she approached them, feeling a slight tingle as she rubbed the cream into her hands. She stopped in front of Remy and kissed her cheek. If Remy didn't worry, she wouldn't be Remy. But it wasn't Kinsley's place to tell them that she'd found Rhett in the shower. Or that when she saw him like that, her heart broke for him. Or that being close to him felt as natural as it did to breathe and there wasn't a chance in hell that she wouldn't be there for him. It wasn't her truth to tell. And she couldn't explain why she was so all in with a guy who could break her heart. She knew better. But she also couldn't walk away. "Now, are we ready to go start tossing everything in the trash?"

Yesterday Kinsley had arranged for a crew to come this morning and clear out all her beloved furniture that was smashed to pieces. She assumed today would be equivalent to getting her nose hairs plucked out one by one, but in order to move forward, she needed to start fresh. Once the insurance money came in, she wanted to get things rolling. The less time the bar was closed, the better.

Peyton hooked her arm through Kinsley's. "Yup. Totally ready."

Kinsley regarded her sister-in-law, who looked a little too perky this morning. "What's up with you?"

"With me?" Peyton asked with wide eyes, pointing to herself. "Nothing."

Liar. "Okay…sure," Kinsley said, not believing that for a moment.

"Let me just grab a few things," Remy interjected, making her way around the counter. She quickly moved through the magic shop, picking up jars and incense and putting them all in a bag with the store's logo on the front. "Ready." She smiled more genuinely now. That was the good thing about Remy's worrying; it was always short lived.

Peyton kept hold of Kinsley's arm as she led her out the door, past Uptown Girl. A gorgeous red lace nighty caught her eye. "Ooh, I might have to come shopping soon," Kinsley said to Peyton.

Peyton glanced at the nighty in the storefront and smirked. "Sure, just don't tell Boone you're coming here. He'll probably have Rhett killed if he knows that you're buying lingerie for him."

Kinsley laughed too, but Boone loved Rhett too much to do that. They all did. Except maybe Remy. Right now, she didn't trust Rhett. At all. Not that Kinsley could blame her. Rhett slept with women and left them. That was his MO. Kinsley was well aware this could happen to her too. Even if she was pregnant with his baby, she knew that she still walked a thin line.

When they drew closer to the bar, she noticed that the parking spaces in front were empty, except for the cruiser with the rookie inside keeping an eye on the bar—and her. She waved then sighed, reaching for the keys in her purse. "I thought the junk guys would be here by now."

"Weird," Peyton said, her mouth twitching.

Kinsley studied her. "*You* are acting weird."

"That's insulting," Peyton said, looking straight ahead with beaming eyes.

Kinsley gave a sidelong glance at Remy, who shrugged and said, "I have no idea."

Peyton just smiled.

Kinsley shook her head then used her keys to open the door. When she walked in, she was sure her eyes were betraying her. Yesterday, she'd left the bar in shambles. Today…

"What…who…" She walked to the middle of the room, which had been cleaned from top to bottom, with new circular tables and wooden chairs. The glass on the floor was gone as was the broken mirror behind the brand-new bottles of wine and liquor, and the part of the bar where the warning had been etched into now had a thin piece of wood stained the same color as her bar nailed onto it. "I don't understand what is happening." She blinked, whirling around. "Did you do this?" she asked Peyton, now understanding the smirk.

Peyton bounced on her toes; her hands clamped tight. "Rhett did this. Oh my God, it feels so good to say that aloud. I've been holding it in all morning, because Boone made me promise not to stay anything."

Kinsley blinked. Again. "Rhett did this?"

"He sure did." Peyton grinned. "Sweet, right? Even Boone was shocked when Rhett called to tell him the plan last night."

This didn't make sense. Kinsley slowly shook her head, trying to knock some sense into it. She failed miserably. "But Rhett was with me last night." She couldn't exactly forget his incredible hard body against hers.

Peyton stepped closer to one of the tables and rubbed her hand along it. "Boone said that he called in a couple of old military buddies to get the job done. I guess one of them is a member of the legion or something, and they borrowed the tables and chairs from there." She tapped the table with her knuckles. "It's not like what it was, but it'll work until you get your insurance money."

"I can't believe he did this," Kinsley admitted then looked at Remy. "Did you know?"

Remy shook her head, looking shell-shocked. "No...No, I didn't know. Okay, so this is incredibly unlike him." She clamped her mouth shut, her eyes suddenly widening, and she exclaimed, "See, I told you that all the juju I sprayed Rhett with was going to bring positivity. Rhett would never have done this before. It's remarkable."

Peyton rolled her eyes.

Kinsley laughed softly. Letting Remy believe her magic had caused Rhett's kindness wouldn't hurt anyone or anything. "This is just..." Kinsley circled around, taking it all in. She wouldn't need to close. The bar could stay open. She wouldn't lose any money. Her throat tightened and her chin quivered..."Oh, no." She burst into tears.

Remy was there in a second, as was Peyton.

"Probably not the reaction anyone expected," Peyton said, rubbing Kinsley's back in big circles. "Are you okay?"

"Yes, I'm just happy. This is"—Kinsley wiped her tears—"so sweet of him. I can't believe he arranged all this."

"I, for one, think all this is good for him," Peyton said. "Rhett needs structure, and he needs someone to care about more than himself. He's doing the right thing. Boone was all smiles when he told me. I guess the guys had been working all night, and just left an hour or so ago."

"Unbelievable," Kinsley said. She turned to Remy. "Maybe your love potion is finally working." Not that Kinsley believed in that, but if she could make Remy feel good, she would.

Remy hesitated, considering. "Maybe, but I always assumed it didn't work because Rhett was closed off."

"You did a love potion on Rhett?" Peyton asked with a burst of laughter.

"In high school," Kinsley explained. "We tried three times to no avail." And just to make Remy feel like her magic had all the strength in the world, she added, "Maybe now it's working."

"Maybe." Remy smiled sweetly, linking her arms with Kinsley.

Kinsley swiped at the dampness on her face and drew in a deep breath. "Well, now we need a new plan since we're not spending any time cleaning up this place. What do you want to do?"

Remy raised her hand. "I vote we celebrate with chocolate cake."

"It's nine o'clock in the morning," Peyton said.

"Chocolate. Cake. Peyton," Remy said slowly.

Kinsley smiled. "She's right. I can't drink wine. Chocolate cake it is."

* * *

I can't believe you fixed the bar for me. Thank you doesn't seem hardly enough but thank you.

Rhett embraced the warmth in his chest as he stared down at

his phone and read the text from Kinsley. Good. He'd made her happy, which was a step in the right direction. Determined to get his day started, he shoved his phone into the pocket of his jeans and set to making himself a coffee in the break room. Lee Matthews, his old military buddy, now owned a construction company, and Rhett paid for the labor of Matthews's guys for the work done last night to get Kinsley's bar back up and running until the insurance money came in. The less time she was closed, the better.

"Dalton's here."

Rhett glanced over his shoulder to find Asher standing in the doorway. The heady amusement in his friend's eyes interested him. "Did the boys have any trouble getting him to come in?" They'd sent a couple of squad cars up to Whitby Falls, and along with their police department, they'd gone to *ask* Dalton to come in for a chat.

"Cameron took a good hit from one of the bikers," said Asher with a grin, "but from what I hear, Cameron responded quick enough that I have no doubt that guy regrets the punch."

"Damn. Would've liked to see that." Cameron was a rookie, but he also had a black belt in jiu-jitsu.

Rhett poured himself a cup of steaming hot coffee, getting his thoughts together. He was determined to get some answers from Dalton. The timing of the bikers coming to Kinsley's bar and then the break-in was a little too coincidental for Rhett's liking. "All right, let's see what this prick has to say." Mug in hand, he followed Asher out of the break room. He stopped by his office and grabbed the file folder off his desk before continuing on to the interrogation room down the hall.

Just before Rhett entered the room, the chief called his name. Both men turned and waited for Hank to reach them.

"Meet me in there," Asher said before he strode into the interrogation room.

Rhett nodded, watching the door shut before facing Hank.

There was a softness in Hank's eyes. He placed a hand on Rhett's shoulder and held his gaze. "Good man." Without another word, he walked away.

Rhett released the breath he hadn't known he'd been holding, pleased he'd gotten something right when it came to Kinsley.

He entered the interrogation room, finding Dalton sitting at the metal table, arms crossed, looking bored. In the corner of the room, a video camera would tape this interview, and Boone sat behind the two-way mirror watching the conversation from another angle. Rhett wouldn't take chances. He wanted all eyes on Dalton now. He took a seat across from Dalton and set his coffee down, regarding the arrogant tilt to Dalton's head, the half smile.

Rhett could have been Dalton. When he returned from the Army, a shell of what he had once been, he had Boone and Asher. A soldier always needed camaraderie, and Rhett found that in his childhood friends. Dalton found that in a motorcycle gang. Rhett owed much to Boone and Asher, who'd pulled him away from the darkness that shadowed his life in that first year after he came home. They had forced him to come out, even when he didn't want to. They made him attend family dinners when all he'd wanted to do was hide in a bar and drink into the pain.

Rhett finally cleared his throat and opened the file. "I don't want you here, and you don't want to be here," he said to Dalton. "Answer my questions truthfully and we can both be spared wasting our time."

Dalton's mouth twitched. "Ah, and here I thought you liked me, West."

Rhett flipped through the file, pulling out the photograph of Kinsley's bar in shambles. "The night you showed up at Whiskey Blues, the bar was ransacked and destroyed." He flipped the photograph around and slid it across the table to Dalton. "Are your guys responsible for this?"

Dalton examined the photograph and snorted. "Not our style," he said.

Truth. When the Red Dragons committed crimes, they didn't hide their faces. They were smart, lethal, and did not fear the law, and usually the younger generation took on the guilt for any crimes as an initiation into the gang. But that was not why Rhett had brought Dalton into the station today. He doubted the Red Dragons were behind the break-in, but after years of honing his skills to read people to keep his brothers safe in the war, he was using Dalton as a stepping-stone to find out evidence he wouldn't otherwise discover. "Have you heard of any new gangs coming into the area?"

"You'd know that better than I would," Dalton said.

Asher asked, "You're dodging the question, which leads us to believe that there is another group in town."

Dalton's gaze cut to Asher. "Didn't say that, did I?"

Rhett clenched his jaw in frustration and turned back to his file to pull out the photograph of the perpetrators. He slid that to Dalton. "Recognize anyone?"

Dalton's eyes breezily scanned the photograph. Until suddenly his gaze stopped, narrowing slightly, his mouth twitching. "Nah, I've never met any of them." He leaned away, shoving the photograph back toward Rhett.

"Bullshit," Rhett said, pointing to the man whom Dalton seemed to recognize. "You know him, tell me who he is."

Dalton's gaze flicked back to photo before lifting to Rhett again. "I already told you, West, I don't know who that is." He rose in one fluid movement, an arrogant prick as always. "And since you've got no reason to hold me here, I'm leaving. Unless I need to call my lawyer."

Rhett bit back a curse. They couldn't force Dalton to talk, no matter that Rhett wanted to do just that, by any means necessary. For now, he'd tread lightly. Besides, he had enough to go on to get the ball rolling. He took the photograph and slid it back into the file. "Cut him loose," he said to Asher.

Dalton's brows shot up. "That was very anticlimactic, West. After our last time together, I thought you'd come at me a little harder." A quick, dark grin crossed his face. "It must be that sexy little brunette that gets you up all fired up."

"She does get me worked up," Rhett said calmly, even as tension roared through him. He pressed his knuckles against the metal table and leaned in. "She's pregnant with my child."

Dalton's smile widened. "Is she now?"

Bored of this game, Rhett said, "If you've got a hand in this, I'll find out, but let me make this clear to you. No one comes near her, and if you know who's responsible for this"—he allowed every ounce of darkness that had once lived in his soul to show on his face—"tell them to run."

Dalton's entire demeanor changed. What once was playful was now serious, and he looked Rhett directly in the eyes. "The Red Dragons have no interest in your woman or her bar."

Rhett hesitated, scooping up the file, playing those words over. Dalton's answer had been specific. A bit too specific. "Keep it that way," Rhett said, turning away.

His hand reached the door handle as Asher said, "All right, Dalton, we're done here."

Rhett whisked the door open, and Dalton replied, "Next time you pick me up for no reason, I won't be so nice."

Rhett snorted, not indulging Dalton in further conversation. He headed straight for his office and took a seat behind his desk. He opened the file, taking out the photograph of the men in Kinsley's bar, as the loud roars of motorcycles thundered outside the station, heading out of town.

Asher entered his office a minute later, followed by Boone. They sat in the client chairs across from him. "What did you make of that?" Rhett asked Boone.

"Dalton knows something," Boone said, crossing his ankle over his knee.

Asher nodded. "But I still doubt it's the Red Dragons."

"He basically hand-fed us that it's not his bikers," Rhett said. "His choice of words, 'The Red Dragons have no interest in your woman or her bar,' was very specific. The second he heard she was carrying my child, his demeanor changed. Was it a warning that while he and his men aren't interested in Kinsley, someone else is?"

Boone scrubbed his unshaven face. "You're certain King has nothing to do with this?"

Rhett nodded. "Got no doubt in my mind."

Asher added, "As much as I'd love to jump on King and get him for this, I agree, this doesn't have his flavor on it."

"We need to put this to bed," Rhett said, running his hands over his face.

Asher broke the silence. "You saw something from Dalton."

Rhett hit the spacebar on his keyboard to awaken his computer and reached for the mouse. "Dalton recognized that guy. I saw it in his face." Rhett pulled up the photograph of the men and zoomed in on the picture until he had what he needed.

Rhett turned his monitor toward the guys and tapped the man's tattoo on his wrist. "He recognized that."

Asher studied the tattoo then his brow arched. "How sure are you?"

The military taught Rhett not to miss subtle physical clues. To do so meant lives were lost. "I'd wager that he not only knows of the guy, but he's met him personally. We want to find out who's behind this," Rhett said, stabbing his finger against his monitor. "We need to find out who this tattoo belongs to."

Asher sighed. "That's not hard at all."

Rhett nodded, knowing their lead was a terrible one. "If there's another biker gang in town, there will be unrest in Whitby Falls. I'll call Anderson"—a homicide detective Rhett knew well—"and see if I can go up tomorrow to revisit some recent cases. There might be a connection there that will give us one of these guys."

Boone nodded and rose. "Want me to come with you?"

Rhett shook his head. "Stay here. Close." *To Kinsley. Keep her safe.*

Boone gave him a look of understanding and tapped the door frame. "Call if you need me. Asher, you're with me. Let's dig into seeing if there've been similar break-ins close by."

"Keep us in the loop of anything you find," Asher said, then followed Boone out of Rhett's office.

Rhett turned back to his monitor and the man with the tattoo. The gesture that man had made of cutting his neck with his knife had never left Rhett's mind. The warning there was clear. Rhett reciprocated with his own warning now to Dalton, and no doubt that warning would spread throughout Maine. Touch Kinsley and his child, and there was nowhere they could hide that Rhett wouldn't find them.

Chapter 9

"What was up with Detective Hard Ass yesterday?" Benji asked by way of greeting as he strode out from the back room. "I thought his glare was gonna burn me alive."

Kinsley finished cutting up the limes for the busy night ahead. The last customer had left five minutes ago, but soon, the bar would be full again, all to watch the folk singer who hailed from New York City. "Oh, I'm just pregnant with his baby, so he's getting...moody."

Benji froze mid-step. He blinked and then slowly lowered his foot to the ground, his mouth wide open.

Kinsley burst out laughing. "I'm surprised you hadn't heard already. Mary Jane overheard me talking to Remy about it yesterday at the market. I thought for sure *everyone* would know by now."

"No, man, I hadn't heard." Benji glanced at her belly before his gaze lifted again. "Pregnant, whoa." He blinked again. "So, are you two a thing now?"

"Lord, no," she replied with a dry laugh. "He only found out the other day."

Benji shook his head, obviously clearing the shock away, then approached her. "Well, he's certainly handling the news well, and stepping up, considering he fixed your bar last night."

"He's an incredible guy. I'm just glad everyone's finally seeing it," was her carefully worded reply.

Benji chuckled softly. "*An incredible guy* is not exactly how I think anyone in town would describe Rhett."

Playboy. Tough. Those probably sounded right to everyone in town. "Yeah, but you don't know him like I do," she replied.

Benji kept quiet after that, and she grabbed the rag from the sink to wipe up the condensation left from the last customer's beer. The bar wasn't hers anymore, or at least it didn't feel like hers, but soon, once her insurance claim was processed, she could get decorating. "I'm sorry I didn't tell you sooner about the baby," she said to Benji, suddenly feeling terrible about that. "It's just been a whirlwind."

"Hey, no worries, Kins, this had to be a mega shock." Benji dropped his backpack under the bar then enveloped her in one of his warm hugs. "Are you happy?"

"Happy and scared," she admitted, leaning into his comforting embrace. "And everything in between that."

His hug barely lasted three seconds. It didn't take much to realize he feared Rhett walking through the door and seeing them again. Oh, the power Rhett had. Kinsey was sure he'd find Benji's reaction amusing.

Benji organized the liquor bottles in the way he preferred them, switching out an empty bottle of vodka for a new one. "I guess that explains why you haven't been working as many late shifts."

She nodded then took her purse out of the drawer. She'd already grabbed her winter coat from the back, and quickly slid into it. Outside, the sun was already setting, the long dark nights of winter ahead. She wrapped her scarf around her neck. "I just can't do it anymore. I'm so tired all the time."

"Well, that's what you've got me and Lola for," Benji said, giving her a nudge toward the door. "Go rest. I've got everything here for the night."

She let him lead her around the bar but paused before leaving. "If anyone comes in tonight who feels off to you or anything, call Boone. He wants us to keep an eye on the customers."

"Sure, no problem." Benji pointed at the door. "Goodbye, Kinsley."

She blew him a kiss then left through the front door. Many nights, she'd seen people come into the bar and take for granted the good people in their lives. Once, she'd overheard one man boast about his wife at home with their kids, when he came in every night to the bar after work. That mistake wouldn't be one she made. She knew how good she had it, and that's why she didn't have lingering trauma where her mother was concerned. She'd spent ten years in therapy after her mom left. The *good* was all she wanted in her life, and everyone in her life brought something wonderful to it.

When she stepped out, the cold night and a dark sky of sparkling stars greeted her. She drew in the brisk air. With all the cloudy days lately, she hadn't seen the stars in a while. Those little twinkling lights often reminded her of how small she was, and how life could sometimes be full of magic. She reached into her purse for her cell phone, discovering that Rhett was twenty minutes late in picking her up.

The rookie, Cameron, sat in his cruiser. He was the youngest rookie on the force, only twenty-one. Cute, too, with his all-American blond hair and blue-eyed good looks. Kinsley approached him, and after he rolled down the passenger side window, she said, "I'm going to go meet Rhett at the station."

Cameron nodded. "I'll keep an eye on you while you do."

"Thanks." She smiled. "Have a good night."

"You, too."

She turned away from him, tucking her cell phone back into her purse. "Once a cop, always a cop," she muttered, heading down Main Street. Being late, sadly, came with the job description.

A few minutes later, she entered the station and was greeted with smiles and waves. Every set of eyes went straight to her belly, telling her they'd all heard the news. But only Doreen, the receptionist, made a move toward her.

Doreen had worked at the station for as long as Kinsley could remember. "Oh, my dear, Kinsley, I heard about yours and Rhett's exciting news. A baby!" She threw her arms around her tight. "Your father was just beside himself when he told me. How are you feeling?" she asked, leaning away, bright eyed.

"Better every day," Kinsley answered. It was partly the truth. She'd lost her breakfast immediately after she ate it this morning but then she ate another meal an hour later and was totally fine. Progress.

"Wonderful news," Doreen said. "You'll let me know if you need anything at all?"

"Thanks, I will," Kinsley said with a smile. "I'm actually here to see Rhett. Is it okay if I go back?"

"Not a problem, dear," Doreen said. Kinsley cupped her hands, looking properly pleased, then gave a quick wave and headed off.

She felt more weight vanish off her shoulders that she didn't know was there. Everyone who needed to know she was pregnant knew, and everyone seemed happy. Well, Rhett still seemed tense, but things were moving in the right direction. She walked past her father's empty office and found Rhett sitting behind his desk, his head down as he studied the papers scattered around him.

"You're late," she said.

Rhett jerked his head up and glanced at his monitor. "Shit." He jumped to his feet, guilt raging in his gaze.

"It's okay," she reassured him, pointing at herself. "Kid that grew up surrounded by cops, remember?" Rhett looked torn between leaving and finishing whatever he was working on, so she sat in the client chair. "I take it this is my case." She waved her hand at the papers on his desk.

Rhett nodded, returning to his seat and rubbing his hands over his face. "I got sucked in. Did you walk here alone?"

She nodded, and at his deep frown, she added, "The street is really busy tonight. Perfectly safe. And Cameron's sitting at the bar in his cruiser. He kept a good eye on me. What have you found out?"

He angled his head, watching her. She knew he couldn't tell her everything about her case, even if her father was the chief of police. He finally said, "We're drawing closer to identifying one of the suspects."

"That's good," she said.

He nodded, his gaze sweeping over the documents like he could find all the answers there. "I'll feel much better once we know the reason why your bar was trashed. The unknown..." Those dark intense eyes met hers again. "It's an unfavorable position."

"You'll figure it out," she said with a confident smile. "You guys always do."

He inclined his head then searched through his papers. "Do me a favor, though," he said, finally handing her a photograph. "If you ever see a guy with this tattoo on his wrist, don't approach him. Just get somewhere safe, all right?"

Her heart skipped a beat, her hand falling to her belly. His oath to the badge made it impossible for Rhett to disclose direct information about the case, but that sure sounded like a warning. "Is he someone I should be afraid of?"

Rhett's mouth tightened before he said, "He trashed your bar. Which means he is a threat to you. Promise me you'll stay away."

She held his intense stare, which was also oddly filled with a new warmth she saw in him. "Okay, I'll stay away."

"Good." He tidied up his papers and put them in the file, which he then shoved into his desk drawer before locking it. "Want to grab some grub on the way home?"

She'd been thinking about this all day. "Actually, I thought we could grab some fast food and then you can show me what you do for fun."

He frowned. "Why?"

She rolled her eyes. "Is it really so awful to show me something I don't know about you?"

"No, it's not awful at all," he said, reaching for his winter coat on the back of his chair. "But you're not going to like what I do for fun."

"Oh, yeah, try me."

* * *

A half an hour later, Rhett dodged the first fist coming at his face, but the second landed squarely on his jaw, sending him flying back against the boxing ring padding.

"You're right, I don't like this."

Rhett turned his head and gave Kinsley a bloody-mouthed grin, while she sat on the bench, arms crossed, one leg bouncing over the other. He turned back to his target, and longtime friend, Theo, and hopped to his feet. He charged forward and took his opponent down with his forearm pinned to Theo's neck.

Theo had retired from the Navy a few years ago and opened Sailor's on the outskirts of Stoney Creek, but Rhett had known him in high school. Theo filled the void that many military guys needed filled. Most people thought that adjusting to civilian life was a challenge because of the painful memories they took home with them, and while Rhett had his own nightmares and knew that his time in the military fundamentally changed him, one of the hardest parts of returning to civilian life had been the adrenaline. He'd spent his days and nights being on alert, looking for that threat that would kill him or his men. Letting go of that adrenaline had been impossible, which only fueled the nightmares. He knew the pregnancy was why his dream had come back the other night. Any change brought the nightmares back. But that's why he came to Sailor's, to get control of himself, and the adrenaline coursing through his veins.

Once a warehouse, now the boxing ring was in the center, with a weight area off to the right, and on the other side were a few punching bags. Theo gave members a keycard to gain access to come and go as they pleased. Only a soldier understood a soldier, and nearly all the gym members came from a military background.

When Theo couldn't break the hold, he tapped Rhett's

shoulder, and Rhett lurched to his feet. Theo followed. "Leave her at home next time," Theo said with a grin, his dark blue eyes laughing. "You fight better with her here."

Rhett wiped his mouth with his forearm then caught the blood there. "I'm not the only one showing off here."

Theo grinned. "Bring me a pretty lady and a guy's gotta do what a guy's gotta do."

Rhett shot forward with a front kick, but Theo blocked the hit and reciprocated with a body grab. Rhett shifted, latched on to Theo's wrist, and escaped the hold, sending Theo slamming down hard on the mat on his back.

His laughter boomed in the open space all the way up to the exposed rafters. "Prick."

Rhett grinned and offered a hand. Theo accepted it and was on his feet a second later. Rhett's chest felt lighter, his tense muscles slowly relaxing. Only one other thing made him feel so quiet, so calm, and he felt that same tug to get close to Kinsley again. Her soft moans brushing over his body. The scent of her, a pleasing scent he could still smell now. It had been on his mind all day. He'd had sex. A lot. He loved sex, but with Kinsley, sex was…*different*. Addictive.

Theo bent at the hip, catching his breath, sweat coating his flesh. "And now that my pride has been beaten into the ground, I better get home to the wife." He cupped Rhett's shoulder, his hand wrap rough against Rhett's sweaty skin. "You better go fix up that lip." He grinned. "Looks like I got a good one in."

"Please. It's barely a scratch."

Theo laughed. "Sure, let's go with that." He strode off toward the change room.

Fighting, using muscles and skill for combat, Rhett had trained for years to hone this abilities. The soldier in him needed to be fed, kept in control, and sharp, and he felt perfectly aligned when he turned back to Kinsley. She still sat on the bench with her arms crossed. The old factory lighting flickered, but there was enough on her to let him see her. A brunette beauty in a grungy place, and yet she seemed to suit the place too.

He stepped through the ropes then moved down the stairs, beginning to unwind his hand wraps. When he met her at the bench, she asked, "Seriously, you honestly think that getting the snot kicked out of you is fun?"

"Yes, it's fun, and I also don't recall losing the fight, so I'd say I did the snot kicking."

She slowly shook her head, frown in place. "Honestly, how that is fun is beyond my comprehension."

Rhett grinned, knowing there was blood in his mouth. "Getting physical and sweaty doesn't seem like a good idea to you?"

She cringed. "Ew." His face was in her hands a second later. "Do you need to see a doctor?"

"Yes," Theo yelled from the other side of the gym as he walked out of the change room. "Maybe get him his blankie too."

Rhett gave him a rude gesture and Theo barked out a laugh. He headed out the front door with a wave, and it slammed shut behind him. Rhett faced Kinsley. "I'm fine. Give it a few minutes and the bleeding will stop."

"What about *that* is seriously fun to you?" she asked, pointing to the ring.

He shrugged. "Just burns off adrenaline, and I'm good at fighting. Would you ask a tennis player why they like playing tennis?"

She hesitated. "Okay, I see your point…sort of." She scanned the area and asked him, "Does Theo own this place?"

Rhett got a good look at the cleavage in the vee of her shirt before he nodded, and once he'd finished unwrapping his left hand, he moved on to his right. "He doesn't make money off the gym. He holds a fund-raiser every year to buy new equipment and pay for the space."

"Really?" she asked, glancing around again, reassessing. "Why?"

Rhett shrugged. "He gets that military guys need this when they come home."

Her brows shot up. "To fight each other?"

"To readjust to civilian life," he countered. "You train for years in the military to be a fighter, to respond on instinct, to always be on the alert. It's difficult to turn that off when you come home. This helps."

"Oh," she said. Then soft understanding crossed her face. "Okay, I guess that actually makes a lot of sense." He liked how she seemed to get him. More than anyone else. "It's good you all have this," she added softly. "To come to a place to be together."

Rhett gave a firm nod then tossed his hand wrappings into the trash can. He turned back to her and took a step closer. He saw the hitch of her breath, and fuck, he got that. Whenever he got close to her, his body responded. Being around her spoke to a very primal part of him. "Other than this, I'm either at work or with your brother and Asher or at a bar." He took that last step, closing the distance between them, then glanced down into her pink-cheeked face as she looked up at him with those blue beauties. He tucked her hair behind her ear, and the way she leaned into his touch slowly unraveled him. "But there is one other thing I also do for fun." He lowered his voice. "One other thing I'm very good at."

Her lips parted, inviting him in for a kiss. But then she blinked, and the heat faded a little from her gaze. A sudden softness crossed her face that had him wondering what was on her mind. "Not interested tonight?" he asked.

"I never said that, but later." She gave him a little push. "Go shower."

He held his ground, not moving an inch. "Why?"

"Because you're gross, sweaty, and stinky, and your mouth is still bleeding." She tried to push him again. "I want to take you somewhere before I forget I want to take you there."

He didn't budge. "Is it going to involve that show you and Remy watch...*Housewives of...*something?"

"*The Real Housewives of Orange County*?" She stopped pushing and laughed softly. "No. Why would you even think that?"

"Because you and Remy talked about that show for two years straight." It had been a punishment to everyone who had to endure it.

She rolled her eyes. "Okay, fine, we do love that show, but no, I'm not going to make you watch it."

He grabbed her shirt and yanked her closer, loving the hitch of surprise in her breath. "Does it involve bubble baths?"

"No," she rasped, wide-eyed.

He dropped his head and dragged his nose along her neck, drawing in her scent, which called to him on every level as a man. When he leaned away, he grinned at the heat burning in the depths of her eyes. He lifted an eyebrow. "Long talks about girly things?"

"Oh, my God, Rhett, you'll see," she said, giving him a final hard shove. "I promise it won't be painful. Go."

"All right." He began to turn but then stopped to scoop her up in his arms.

"Hey!" she exclaimed.

"I'll go shower," he said with all the heat he felt burning between them. "But you're coming with me." And then his lips found her neck, permanently ending the conversation.

* * *

With a steaming hot chocolate take-out cup in her mitten-covered hands, Kinsley sat on a blanket next to Rhett on the tailgate of his truck an hour later, with another cozy blanket over her lap. Her body still hummed from their shower together, and luckily, no one had come in and disturbed them. Rhett wore his black winter hat and leather gloves. She, her cute slouchy winter hat. Acadia National Park was south of their location, but she'd taken him up the summit to a parking lot that led to one of the hiking trails.

"I gotta admit, I wasn't expecting you to find this place fun," he finally said after many long minutes of silence.

"Well, there's probably a lot you don't know about me."

Unusual softness reached his eyes. "I've got no doubt that's very much true." He watched her a moment longer then asked, "Maybe we should change that, so why don't you tell me what you love about this place so much?"

She tore her eyes off the stars shining down on the Atlantic Ocean. "It's just…quiet. The type of silence I can't find anywhere else." She had started coming here when she was old enough to drive. When she really started dealing with her mom's absence. The tourists didn't know about this place, and for the most part, no one else came to this parking lot atop the mountain, unless they were hiking the trails throughout the day.

Rhett drew in a deep breath and exhaled a cloud, leaning against his leather-covered hands. "It is quiet. Peaceful."

She nodded at him, figuring he would like this too. Rhett's world seemed so small. Work, fight, go out with friends when they asked. Her heart couldn't help hurting a little at that. Soldiers were brave and strong, and the world owed them a great service, but there was a price to be paid, and Rhett had paid that price. Hell, he was still paying it. "Whenever things get heavy, this just lessens that load."

He tipped his head back and his gaze went somewhere else when he looked up at the sky. "If you like this view, you would love the stars in Afghanistan. I'd never seen so many stars like I did in the sky there."

"God, over the desert, the sky must have looked so black."

"Yeah," he agreed with a soft nod. "The blackest black I've ever seen. The stars were so bright. The whole world looked different there." His Adam's apple bobbed. "Nothing like here."

She sipped her hot chocolate, wondering over all the things he'd seen, all the missions he'd taken. "Do you miss the military?"

He tipped his head to the side, his curious eyes on her. "Why do you ask?"

She shrugged. "You were in the Army for a long time. You must miss it."

He loosened a breath and stared up at the stars again, his jaw bunching. "Yes, I miss it."

"But are you happy being a detective too?"

"It's satisfying."

She swallowed another sip of hot chocolate then laughed softly, shaking her head. "That was a piss-poor attempt at dodging the answer—you realize that, right?"

His mouth twitched before he looked at her again. Their gazes held for a beat. Then a haunting darkness fell over his expression. "I might miss military life, but I also can't trust myself anymore."

Her gut twisted at the raw pain in his expression. "What do you mean?"

He glanced back up to the sky, his brows drawn together, and his eyes grew distant, going back to a different time. "I couldn't trust my shot after I got wounded," he explained. "I'd go back to Afghanistan in a second if I could repair my shoulder enough to know that if I fired off a shot, I wouldn't miss. Being a soldier was my calling."

Her heart squeezed tight. "Even with the nightmares you suffer, you'd still go back?"

"In a heartbeat," he said in an instant. "I've never felt purpose like I did when I was a soldier. To protect, to defend, to lead, I lived and breathed that life, and I was very, *very* good at my job. But the injury has made my reflexes slower. That could kill the men I'm trying to protect."

"So, you're saying that being a detective is second best."

His head fell to the side again, those intense eyes landing on her. "It's not second best. It's just another life, not the one I thought I'd have."

The pain in his eyes was palpable. It hadn't been there before he went off to the military. She wished she could remove it. "Well, I think you did your job. You saved lives, and they got a good eight years of your service. But considering how you came home, I'm not so sure that it was a bad thing you got shot."

His brows rose up. "You wanted me to get shot?"

"No," she said, nudging her shoulder into him. "Of course not. All I'm saying is that you were different when you came home, and if you'd stayed longer, I'm not sure how that would have been for you, you know?"

"I never thought I'd come home." His lips clamped shut, like he hadn't meant to say that.

She pushed, feeling her blood heat a little. And not in good way. "Ever?"

He gave a firm shake of his head. "I thought I'd die in those deserts," he said, so cold and distant. "I almost did."

She reached for him, placing her hand on his arm, and she was so damn glad when he didn't pull away. "Did you want to come home?"

There was a long pause. He didn't even look like himself when he glanced at her. "No."

"Oh," she whispered, suddenly feeling like the air had been knocked out of her.

He took in her expression then slowly shook his head as if he hated himself for making her look like that. "You have to understand, Kinsley, that when I left for the Army, that had been the life I wanted. It suited me. The brotherhood, the cause to make this world a little bit safer, and to fight for those who can't fight a bigger evil, it was all I wanted to do, but there was a cost, and that cost was that you turn off a part of yourself to get the job done. You don't see faces or genders or ages. You see killers wanting to kill the brothers beside you." His voice changed then, growing harder. "I trained. Hard. I did my job. And I was good at that job. This civilian life…I never thought I'd ever come back to it. My life in Stoney Creek ended when I entered the military."

She swallowed the emotion that clogged up her throat. He didn't need to fill in the missing pieces. The short affairs with women while he waited for a new mission. The danger. The risky adrenaline rush. That *was* Rhett, through and through. And when he returned home for good, he'd been forced to be something he never wanted to be. She nearly kept quiet, but something in her gut told her to push. "So that's why it was hard for you when you got back?"

"Just changed the direction of what I thought my life would be." He paused and gave her a quizzical look. "Out of curiosity, what did you notice that seemed hard for me?"

"Smiling," she said.

He gave her a look that revealed a whole lot of his raw emotions without saying much at all. "Smiling?"

She nodded. "It's just...different now." Haunted. When he silently watched her, she added, "Do you remember when you saved my ass at a bush party one night?"

He shook his head.

Her throat tightened. She wondered how many happy memories had gone away. "I'll never forget that night. You came to the bush party and picked Harry Sanders up by the back of his pants, hooked his belt hook onto a tree branch, and left him hanging there."

Rhett's brows drew together. "I don't remember that."

"No?" She chuckled at the memory. "We were in the forest down by Old Man Butler's. Harry had been feeding me shots all night. I guess you and Boone got wind of my being there and being drunk, and suddenly you came over and had Harry hanging like he was a two-year-old." Warmth touched her at the lightness in Rhett's eyes that night. It'd been a long time since she'd seen that. But that had been the first night she'd suddenly looked at Rhett differently. Hell, she thought at that time he looked at her differently too, protecting her when he really didn't have to, considering her brother was also there. But the moment Boone marched up and glared at a very drunk Kinsley, Rhett shut off all emotion on his face.

A cloud of air escaped from Rhett's mouth. "Shit. Right. Yeah, I remember that now." He chuckled, shaking his head. "I'd never seen you like that. Or Boone so pissed." His gaze fell to hers and he broke into a smile. "I gave you a piggyback ride, and you laughed the entire way home."

Her breath caught in her throat. "See," she said, pointing to his face. "That's it. Right there."

The smile stayed in place. "What's it?"

She nudged his shoulder with hers again. "That's the easy smile you used to have. I think that's the first time I've seen it in a really long time."

He stared at her for a long moment then turned his head and looked up at the stars again. She did the same, thinking that this was the first time in a very long time that Rhett looked comfortable.

Long minutes went by, and she thought that would be the end to the conversation, but Rhett surprised her. He took her hand in his then lifted it up to his lips. Eyes on hers, he pressed his mouth to her hand. "Thank you, Kinsley. For that story. For sharing this place with me."

Warmth touched everything cold. "You're welcome."

Chapter 10

The next afternoon, on the way home from Whitby Falls, Rhett was ready to crawl out of his skin. He'd spent all day with Detective Anderson in the Whitby Falls PD, doing the hard and long detective work that, in the end, usually solved cases. Sadly, nothing had jumped out at Rhett as trouble within the biker gangs in the area. Dalton had recognized the guy in the photograph, and Rhett's instincts told him to stay there. Bikers knew bikers. While Rhett doubted this was the Red Dragons, he felt that tug in his gut that there was a connection to Dalton. But that connection didn't lie in Whitby Falls. He found no restlessness within the streets of the city that spoke of trouble. The past month had been full of petty crimes, domestic disputes, and a few minor crimes within the Red Dragons, but nothing that stood out as dangerous or serious.

Frustration cut through him as he drove down the snow-covered two-lane country road heading back toward Stoney Creek. He took the roads slow and easy but wanted to do the exact opposite. He wanted to get to Kinsley. Last night she'd touched on something inside him that still shook him this morning.

Rhett didn't do shaken.

And with his frustration building over the case, as well as this edginess she brought out, he couldn't stand it any longer.

Only ten minutes away from town now, he hit the phone button on his steering wheel. His Bluetooth kicked in. "Call Boone," he said.

The phone rang twice. "Knight," Boone answered.

"Any updates?" Rhett asked.

"Tattoo recognition is still running," Boone reported through the car's speakers. While tattoo recognition software was in the works, it was still in its infancy, and Rhett doubted they'd find anything there. He kept the thought quiet as Boone added, "Asher's making some calls within two hundred call radiuses to see if any arrests have been made with a similar tattoo, but nothing yet on that front."

"Nothing else?"

"Nope," Boone said, sounding as frustrated as Rhett felt. "Nothing on your end?"

"Negative," Rhett said. "I'll be back at the station in forty-five."

"I'll be here." The phone line went dead.

When Rhett finally rolled into town and stopped at the stop-light, his gut twisted, his chest impossibly tight. He bounced a knee, tapping his thumb against the steering wheel to the beat of the music playing on the radio, but nothing helped. What he needed to do was shed the restlessness burning through him to center himself again. He considered calling Theo, who Rhett knew would come no matter what he had going on, because that's what they did for each other. When the adrenaline rose, once Rhett gave up counting on Jack Daniel's to calm himself, they got into the ring to discharge the excess energy. Though today, Rhett's agitation wasn't only about the job or about settling back into civilian life. It had to do with why he could barely sleep last night. Kinsley, and the shit she was making him feel. And instead of driving himself crazy, he decided to do something about it.

He pulled over to park in the first spot he found and got out, locking the doors behind him with a loud *beep*. The bright sun warmed him as he walked along Main Street, a stark contrast to the brisk air. He shoved his hands into his pockets and kept his head down, not wanting to see or speak to anyone. Only one person was on his mind now.

A handful of minutes later, he found that woman sitting at her desk in her small office. She wore a big cozy-looking cream sweater and dark gray leggings, and just the sight of her hardened his cock to steel. The bar had been busy when he walked in, but the people out there were none of his concern.

Kinsley slowly turned, surprise in her eyes. "Oh, hey. I wasn't expecting—"

He turned back to the door and locked it. "You have to understand something," he said, facing her again. Uncontrollable heat slammed into him in her presence. He did well to stay away from anything that made him feel too much, but she'd crossed that line last night, and he couldn't uncross it. "I get edgy."

Her chest rose and fell quickly with heavy breaths as she stood from her chair. "Okay," she said slowly.

He took a step toward her. "I usually manage that restlessness by sparring with Theo." Then another step, needing to get closer, to breathe the same air she did. "That's not how I want to manage it anymore. At least, not all the time, and certainly not today."

She visibly swallowed, her cheeks flushing. "Okay," she repeated.

He stopped, his boots right in line with her feet. The heat poured off her, and he wanted to absorb it. Every little bit until he only made them burn hotter. He slowly raised his hand and stroked her cheek, finally threading his fingers into her hair. "Because I've realized there is something more potent than my restlessness."

"What's that?" she whispered, her lips parting, ready for his kiss.

He dropped his mouth close to hers. "How fucking much I want you." He slid a hand across her lower back and yanked her closer. "The way you feel." He dropped his head into her neck and slid his nose up her warm skin, feeling a hard shudder run through her. "How it draws me in." He nipped at her flesh and she pressed herself closer, running her hands up his biceps. He leaned away, tucking his thumbs to angle her chin up. "And the way you taste…it's so fucking good. All day you've been in my head. I want you. Right now."

"Too much talking. Not enough kissing," she said huskily.

He didn't need to hear more. He sealed his mouth across hers, maneuvering her until her back bumped against the wall. Rough, hot, quick, he needed her now. She held on to his shoulders as he opened his jeans, exposing his hardened length. Her leggings were soon down, one still halfway up her leg, the other all the way off. He didn't hesitate, and by the looks of her hooded eyes, he knew she didn't want him to. He grabbed her ass cheek with one hand, his cock with the other, and entered her. Slowly, relishing how she squeezed him, he pushed inside her, feeling the drag of her hot flesh against him, until he was seated in deep.

She moaned his name, and he pulled back once, letting her adjust to him. Christ, she was ready. Wet and silky and warm, and everything he needed. He worked her in slow strokes, feeling her completely, as her body tightened around him like she didn't want to let him go.

His heart thundered in his ears, the adrenaline pumping through his veins, calling for him to unleash himself, the edginess controlling him. He needed that gone. Urgency took over, shifting him from a pursuit of her pleasure, to only a raw need taking over. He hooked her leg onto his arm. Pinning her between his body and the wall, he stared right into her gorgeous sparkling eyes as he pumped his hips. Hard. And fast, careful not to go too deep. Over and over again, until he breathed harshly, sweat trailing down the side of his face. Her eyes went wide with the pleasure until they clamped shut. Her chin angled up and her breath cut off, the moan she nearly gave only coming out in a puff of air. He nearly went cross-eyed with the pleasure, and he grew harder with every thrust as skin slapped against skin. His breathing was rough, and there was nothing sweet about how he touched her. This was something primal, something that came from deep in his chest, a part that needed her to be the reason he felt better. And as her mouth fell open in a perfect *O*, and her moan finally spilled from her mouth, she began clenching him like a vise. He growled, thrusting harder, his muscles burning in delight at being fueled.

And two thrusts later, she broke apart around him, and he followed her in a hot rush and a hard shudder, releasing something deeply haunted in his soul.

* * *

The day had come and gone, and still Kinsley rode the high that Rhett had sent her on earlier. She'd always wondered what it would be like to be on the receiving end of Rhett's affection. Now she had that answer and she liked it. Scratch that, she wanted all of it…all the time. Sure, Rhett wasn't one for long romantic walks by the beach. She doubted he'd ever say, "I love you," but he brought passion and intensity, and those were certainly things she'd never had in her life before.

What she didn't like was her current situation. "This is depressing as shit," she said to their inner circle, minus Rhett, while she sat at one of the tall tables at Merlots. The classy nightclub was on the other side of Main Street, the only other bar in town. Luckily, they had different crowds, so the competition between the two had never been a big deal. Which was good, since Kinsley really liked the owner, Bernie.

Boone snorted, sitting across from her, a beer set in front of him. "You only hate this because you're our designated driver tonight."

"No, I hate this because the *only* time I should be at a bar sober is when I'm working," she countered, then glared at her glass of water before taking a sip. "You all never wanted to come here whenever I've asked you before, and now you do it when I'm pregnant so I can't drink my face off and dance like an idiot." Eighties music filled the space, and Kinsley craved to be right there with the gyrating crowd, only she needed a couple of glasses of wines to bring out her spectacular moves.

Boone arched a brow. "You can still dance like an idiot. I've seen you. You're good at it."

She gave him a rude gesture, which had him laughing.

Peyton nudged his shoulder with hers. "Stop bugging her."

She gave Kinsley a sweet smile. "We thought you could use a night out, away from the bar. And sadly, this town lacks anywhere else to go. Unless you're up for some midnight bingo?"

Kinsley barked out a laugh. "Please, God, never let me go there." She returned a soft smile back at her ever-so-sweet sister-in-law. "And you're right. I could use a night out. Thank you." Even though she could tell that what Peyton had said was only a half truth. They all wanted to drink and dance, but they were trying not to make Kinsley feel bad about it.

From her spot next to Kinsley, Remy asked Boone, "How's the case going anyway? You guys getting anywhere?"

Boone's mouth flattened into a thin line. "It's slow going."

"You'll find them," Peyton encouraged him, sliding her arm through his. "You guys always do."

Boone's eyes darkened when he looked at Kinsley. She'd seen it before, and she knew why Rhett had been so wound up earlier. The case was stalling. Even Dad looked frustrated when he stopped by the bar a couple of hours after Rhett had arrived and made her day immensely better.

A thought that had lingered on her mind all day suddenly sprang up again. "What if it's nothing," she said, swirling the straw in her glass.

On the other side of Boone, Asher's brows shot up. "Care to explain how it could be nothing when they demolished your place?"

Kinsley considered the same thought that kept repeating in her mind then she shrugged. "Nothing has happened since that night. Maybe it really was the Red Dragons, and they were pissed that Rhett got all hard ass with them. They made their point of payback, and now they're done."

Neither Boone nor Asher looked convinced.

Boone finally said, "It's something to consider, but I'd bet my money that something more is going on there."

Asher nodded in agreement.

Remy said, "Well, I, for one, am crossing my fingers that it was a one-time thing and you can put this behind you." Something caught her gaze over Kinsley's shoulder and all the warmth vanished from her expression.

Before Kinsley could turn around, strong arms wrapped around her and Rhett leaned down to kiss her cheek. "Hey," he said just to her. Then he gave everyone around the table a quick look before he added, "Be right back. Let me grab a beer."

He strode off to the bar, and Peyton said, "Okay, that happened, didn't it? Rhett just kissed you on the cheek, right?" When no one answered her, Peyton went on. "Did I imagine that?"

Even Kinsley wondered if she'd imagined that. She finally blinked, following Rhett with her gaze as he made his way toward the bar.

"You're not imagining anything," Boone said. Was that a bit of pride in his eyes? "That happened."

Remy looked the exact opposite. She crossed her arms and scowled. "Are you guys together now?"

"Remy." Asher elbowed her gently.

Her frown only deepened.

Every other face but hers was lit up. Kinsley rolled her eyes. "Do we need to talk about it?"

"Nope," Boone said.

"He's such a liar," Peyton said, reaching for her chocolate martini. "He totally wants to talk about it."

"It's not our business," Asher said sternly to Remy, who still hadn't taken her eyes off Kinsley.

"What's not your business?" Rhett asked, sidling up to the table with a beer in his hand and a fresh glass of water with lemon.

"Thanks," Kinsley said, smiling at him as she took the beverage. She studied him, looking for any of the intensity she'd seen earlier, but it just wasn't there. He seemed…calm…settled.

Remy's voice snapped like the end of a whip, answering his earlier question. "If you and Kinsley are dating now."

"Ah, I see," said Rhett, grabbing the stool next to Kinsley and then pulling her in between his legs. He rested one foot on the bottom of her stool.

If Remy really did have magical abilities, Rhett would be set on fire by now. Kinsley reached for the straw in her glass and sucked back the biggest sip of water of her life, wishing the ground would open up and swallow her.

"Well," Remy growled. "Are you going to answer me?"

Rhett gulped his beer then set the bottle down on the table. "Asher's right, it's none of your business."

The air felt charged with electricity, like right before a thunderstorm. A thunderstorm that was going to suddenly produce lightning that could kill you. And that lightning was aimed right at Rhett.

Boone finally broke the silence. "Did you catch that fight last night?"

"That finishing blow was spectacular," Rhett commented.

And just like that, the personal conversation was over, thanks to her big brother. She glanced up at Boone and he gave her a quick wink before continuing his conversation with Rhett and Asher over the upcoming Mixed Martial Arts fight next weekend.

Kinsley exhaled the breath she'd been holding. She leaned

back against Rhett, and he snagged an arm around her waist and pulled her closer against him. Everything felt good and right, and yet, there was a tingle in the back of her mind telling her this was too easy. She pushed that thought aside.

Rhett was making a statement here tonight. What that statement actually meant, only time would tell. But Kinsley wanted to let things unfold how they were meant to. Rhett was there, present, and that, for right now, was more than she had expected.

Remy's tension wafted off her. To ease her best friend's worries, Kinsley reached for her hand under the table and Remy squeezed back. They had been friends since they were ankle biters, and she knew Remy was worried. Very worried. "I know it's hard to understand," Kinsley said softly, keeping the conversation private. "But I'm okay with how things are."

"Yeah, you keep saying that," Remy grumbled.

Yet Remy still didn't believe her. Not that Kinsley could blame her. For as long as Kinsley could remember, she'd wanted the engagement ring, the wedding, the happily-ever-after. Being with Rhett meant she'd get none of those things. But life wasn't all sunshine and roses, and she wanted Rhett. Always had.

Before she could think more on it, an ice cream sundae was suddenly placed in front of her. "Oh, dear God, I am in love with whoever got me this!"

Rhett's soft chuckle brushed across her cheek. "It's not fair that we get to drink, and you don't. I figured this was second best."

"Oh, my, my," Kinsley purred, her mouth watering. She turned to him slightly and grinned. First, a mind-blowing orgasm earlier, then a thoughtful glass of water, and now ice cream. Who was this guy? "Thank you."

He gave her a firm nod and a genuine smile.

The ice cream only made Remy's frown deepen. And she *never* frowned at ice cream.

"I gave ya the works, Kinsley," Bernie said, his brown eyes creasing, creating more wrinkles. Bernie was an average-looking guy. Average height. Average weight. But his personality was anything but average. Warm and charismatic, when he spoke, people listened. Bernie had owned Merlots for as long as Kinsley could remember, even though his son, Joshua, now ran the show. "Thought it was a good way to congratulate you and Rhett on the baby."

Mary Jane's gossip had obviously gotten around town. "Thanks, Bernie," she said. "How's Eleanor doing?" His wife had gone through chemotherapy for breast cancer last year.

"She's in remission," he replied with a glowing smile. "She's happy to be back working at the library."

"So glad to hear that, Bernie," Boone interjected. "Please tell her we all say hello and that we're so thrilled to hear she's feeling well."

"Will do." Bernie handed Kinsley napkins before offering spoons to Remy and Peyton. "Knew better than to come with ice cream and not make it big enough for all of you."

"Yum," Peyton said, taking her spoon. "Thank you."

As Remy took the spoon from Bernie, Rhett asked, "The bar's looking really good. Did you do some renovations?"

Bernie nodded. "Josh wanted to modernize the place a bit last month, so we had some work done." He scanned his club, then glanced back at Rhett and gave a shrug. "Not quite what I would want, but the customers like it."

Kinsley heard every word Bernie said, but she was stuck on what Rhett had said. He knew this place intimately, which told her that he came here a lot...to find women to warm his bed. She glanced up at Remy, and her friend's earlier irritation turned into hot anger, burning there in her eyes.

The guys continued to talk to Bernie, but Kinsley put her focus on the ice cream and dug in. Rhett had a past; one she could live with. His present and future were all that mattered now.

* * *

An hour later, Rhett's stomach was heavy from his beer as he headed up to the bar to pay his tab. Kinsley looked tired, and he felt exhaustion roll through him too. Next to him was a pretty brunette that kept making eyes at him. She was exactly the type of woman he'd have taken home before. She wanted one night with the bad boy, and Rhett was that guy. Or he had been. Now he wasn't exactly sure what he was, other than the guy trying not to fuck up.

He settled his tab with the bartender quickly, thinking to himself that tonight had gone better than expected. He knew he'd rock the boat and make a statement when he kissed Kinsley in public, but he figured why prolong the secrecy? They were having a child together, and things were heating up between them, more than cooling down. Why hide that fact? Whether that would blow up in his face, only time would tell.

When he placed his debit card back into his wallet, from behind him, Remy snapped, "What in the hell are you doing?"

He glanced over his shoulder. Typically, she was sunny and bright, but now she glared daggers at him. "Paying my tab. Is that all right?"

Her eyes slowly narrowed into slits. She took his arm and he allowed her to pull him around the bar to the hallway where the bathrooms were located.

She placed her hands on her hips. "No, nothing you're doing is all right. Asher told me to stay out of this, but I never thought you'd do *this*."

Rhett arched an eyebrow. "What exactly am I doing?"

"Pretending that you're actually going to make this work with Kinsley."

All through the last hour, he'd caught Remy giving him a glare promising death. He couldn't fault her for it. Kinsley and Remy were as close as sisters. They had each other's backs through thick and thin, and Rhett knew if the roles were reversed, Kinsley would be up in Asher's face. Rhett had a past, and he was well aware that he walked on shaky ground now. "Who says I'm pretending?"

Her brows shot up and she gave a dry laugh. "Seriously, you're actually going to fucking go there. You knew since high school that Kinsley had a thing for you. You knew when you came back that what she felt for you was even stronger. And you did *nothing*. You didn't even give her the time of day or notice her."

Remy had it all wrong. He had fought not to notice Kinsley. He had stayed away to protect her. But he simply didn't feel it necessary to explain that to Remy. "If there's something you're trying to say, Remy, then get to it."

She pointed a polished black fingernail at him. "I keep hearing that this is none of my business. Maybe it isn't, but Kinsley isn't just my best friend, she's like the other half of my soul. She's good and deserves every good thing in life."

"I never said she didn't," he countered, frowning now.

Remy held his stare in a way he'd never seen before from her.

Firm. Unyielding. She continued like he hadn't even spoken. "She deserves a man who wants her with everything that's inside him. She deserves for someone to love all the parts of her that make her so amazing." Remy drew in a long deep breath, her nostrils flaring. "If you cannot be that man, then don't make promises."

Rhett paused. He looked around, seeing two women laughing as they walked by, obviously thinking he and Remy were in a lovers' spat. He turned back to Remy and softened his voice, hoping that would calm her down. "I haven't promised Kinsley anything."

Remy snorted and poked his chest. "Which is exactly the fucking problem, you idiot."

At that, Rhett raised his eyebrows. He couldn't recall ever hearing Remy curse like that before. Or calling anyone a bad name. Damn. He'd *really* pissed her off.

Her voice only tightened as she went on, snarling at him, ignoring everyone walking around them. "Kinsley deserves a guy to promise her everything and to give her the whole goddamn world. She'll want you, even if you cannot give her that. She'll take any little piece of you that you give her, because for some unknown reason she loves you."

She loves you… Rhett's chest tightened, and the room spun a little. "Am I really that terrible of a person, Remy?" he asked in his own defense.

"As a friend, no," she said, and some of the heat left her eyes. "You're wonderful. We all love you. I love you. But you're not the guy who wants marriage, who wants to wake up Sunday mornings in the arms of his *wife*."

She wasn't wrong—Rhett couldn't imagine that. Walking down the aisle, promising anyone forever. He'd never lived with a woman. He wasn't even sure how that would work. Where would they live? Her house? His? It seemed easier to keep separate houses...separate lives. He liked his space. Needed it. "I understand that you're worried about her, Remy," he said again, softly but not weakly, "but Kinsley seems perfectly fine and happy with how things are going right now."

"Of course she is," Remy countered. "She wants you so bad that anything is better than nothing at all."

Rhett's chest took a direct hit at that. He knew what sacrifice meant. He hadn't wanted that for Kinsley, and yet now, he couldn't seem to stay away.

Something must've crossed his face because Remy stepped forward and placed a hand on his shoulder. "No one will say it to you because they're all secretly hoping that this thing between you and Kinsley works out. Hell, if I thought it could, I wouldn't say a damn thing either."

He'd been running from this truth, but it was there, always on his mind too. "You think we're doomed to fail?"

"I think you could have it all. Have the life that she, and you, deserve, but not like this." She snapped her fingers. "You want this, Rhett? Truly want this? Then do the one thing you never do."

He arched an eyebrow. "Which is?"

"Work at it. Truly. Work out your shit and figure out what's going on in here." She tapped his chest. Hard. "Then, after that, marry her."

The thought was so absurd, he burst out laughing. "Remy," he finally said. "We've only been seeing each other for a week."

"So what?" Remy countered. "You've known her your entire life, and she's wanted you pretty much for that entire time." Remy took a step and closed the distance between them. Under her scrutiny, his heart began to race, sweat building on his flesh. "She deserves your commitment. Totally in. One hundred percent."

Rhett gave her an incredulous look. "She wouldn't say yes, even if I asked."

"Maybe not," Remy said with a shrug. "But at least you'll have shown her that you're serious. That this isn't just you going with the flow, taking what you want, and having fun. Because soon this is going to get serious. Very serious. You're having a baby together."

His back went ramrod straight. "I'm quite aware of the serious nature of things, Remy."

Her brows shot up. "Are you? Really? Because one day, that little baby is going to grow up and be a kid and ask you, 'Daddy, why aren't you and Mommy married?' And what answer will you give?"

He glanced away, taking in what she'd said. He'd expected Boone to have this conversation with him, but he was actually more supportive than Remy. He waited for a couple of women to enter the bathroom before he said, "You're talking years ahead. Things are good right now. We're taking this day by day, slowly." He placed a hand on her shoulder and dipped his chin, looking into her eyes. "I know you're worried about Kinsley. I know that my track record doesn't bode well to ease those worries, but this is Kinsley's show. The moment she's not happy, things will change, and I'll do what I can to ensure that I don't hurt her." He gave her an honest smile. "You're a good friend to corner me and give it to me straight, but hurting her is the very last thing I want to do."

Remy considered him for a good long moment then sighed and stepped back. "All right, I can live with that." She began to turn away but then stopped and looked back at him. "Just so we're clear, if you do hurt her, I'll hex you."

He laughed, shaking his head at her. "You know I don't believe in that magic shit."

"Yeah, well, hurt her, and kiss your erections goodbye, buddy." She spun on her heels and marched away as if she meant every single word.

Rhett frowned after her. She couldn't…she wouldn't…

Her grin back at him declared she most certainly would.

Chapter 11

"Wild night last night?" Benji asked by way of greeting as he entered the bar from the back room the next afternoon.

"Wild night for everyone else in town but me," Kinsley said with a smile, adding more beer bottles from the box to the fridge. Truth was, as much as she loved a good party, she had to admit that not being hung over this morning wasn't horrible either. She'd done her laundry, and Rhett's too. Her to-do list was basically down to zero, and her accounting had never been this up to date. Though all day her mind had been stuck on when she saw Remy pull Rhett away for an obvious talk last night. When Kinsley had asked Rhett about it later, he muttered something about Remy loving her and something about his erections. The conversation was confusing, and Rhett looked a little pale about the erection part, so Kinsley left it alone, figuring Remy had threatened him somehow. "We went to Merlots," she explained to Benji, folding up the box. "They all drank. I ate ice cream."

Benji laughed. "Not as good as the chocolate martinis you love so much, but a close second, right?"

"It made me happy," Kinsley agreed. She shoved the box in the recycling bin before addressing him again. "Last night looked busy." When she'd come in this morning and took a look at the sales report Benji had left for her on her desk, she'd nearly jumped up and down. Whiskey Blues was having its best year yet. "You should have called me in."

"Yeah, it was nonstop," Benji said with a shrug. "I called Lola in. She didn't mind, and really, we got this place handled."

Benji was a godsend employee. "I hope the tips made up for the rush."

A bright grin filled his face. "Lola said she made enough to buy a purse she'd been looking at. She left a happy girl. And I basically made my car payment. We're good, so stop worrying."

"Okay, fine, I won't worry then." Kinsley had worked so hard after college getting the bar up and running. To step back felt completely unnatural.

"Anything from the insurance adjuster?" Benji asked.

"Nope. I called him this morning for an update, but he said these things take time, and it'll be another few days or so before anything happens."

Benji leaned his hip against the ice bin, crossing his arms. "How long do you think we'll have to close to get in all the new stuff?"

"I'm hoping just a couple days," she answered. "We'll shut down on a Monday and Tuesday when things are dead."

"Cool," Benji said. "My parents have been nagging at me to come see them. Maybe I'll go head out there." Benji's mom and dad were snowbirds and spent the winter in Florida.

"The beach sounds very nice right about now," Kinsley said, glancing out the window. The current storm was dumping heavy snow on the town. Usually that meant fewer customers.

Benji followed her gaze and snorted. "Yeah, no kidding. They've got a killer condo down there right on the water. You'll have to come sometime."

The thought of bright sun and warm days nearly had her saying *yes*, but...she placed her hand on her belly. "I doubt I'll be going anywhere for a while. I kinda got my hands full."

"Right," Benji said with a wink. "I guess the baby will make traveling a bit hard now."

Everything was changing now. Good changes. And scary changes, too. The unknown never made her feel great. Ready to end her workday and curl up on the couch with a bag of chips and Netflix, she reached for the garbage bag, determined to help Benji before she headed out for the night.

As soon as her fingers brushed against the bag, Benji nudged her hand away. "I'll take it," he said.

"Touch that garbage bag and die," Kinsley stated very slowly.

Benji barked out a laugh and held his hands up in surrender. "Damn. I almost forgot the bite you have."

"I'm pregnant, not fragile," she reminded him. "Please don't baby me. You know I'll hate every second of that."

"I do know that." His smile beamed as he shook his head. "I'll never understand you. Most women want a gentleman."

"Yeah, but those women probably didn't grow up surrounded by a bunch of big tough guys." She'd always liked standing on her own two feet. "Trust me, if I need help, I'll ask, okay?"

"Deal," Benji said, turning away to do more bar prep.

Kinsley finished tying up the garbage bag then carried it into the back. Justin stood with his back to her, his headphones stuck in his ears. He was bobbing his head to the beat of his music while he organized his kitchen for the night ahead.

"Hey," she called.

Nothing. No response.

She laughed, honestly wondering how Justin didn't have hearing problems. Until the night got busy, he shut out the world with whatever music he was listening to. She lifted the garbage bag a little higher, noticing there was a hole in the bottom dripping whatever grossness onto the floor. As if on cue, her stomach roiled at the retched stench coming from the dark liquid. She hurried to get outside and breathed deep past the somersaulting of her stomach, keeping her lips shut tight. The snow fell from the sky in huge flakes. Kinsley loved nights like this. As a kid, she used to stand out in the snow and eat the snowflakes as they came down. She shivered now, thinking kids had to have inner furnaces or something. She used to spend hours outside. Now she'd much rather sit by a cozy fire, curled up with Rhett, if she was being honest with herself.

By the time she'd tossed the garbage bag into the larger bin outside, and took in two deep gulps of cold, fresh air, the nausea settled. That was a step forward in the right direction. Maybe this morning sickness was finally over. She hoped so.

She relatched the metal clamps on the side of the garbage bin to keep the raccoons and bears out. Not that there were a lot of bears that came into town, but there had been at least two since she'd owned the bar. Both were shot with darts and relocated before anyone got hurt. With a final wipe of her hands on her leggings, she turned around, walking right into a wall of hard chest.

"Shit," she exclaimed, taking a step back.

One look at the ski mask covering the man's face, and cold fear bit into her. Everything happened so fast after that. She glimpsed dangerous blue eyes narrowed on her. But then those eyes were gone as fingers caught her by her throat and she was spun around and pressed against the wall. His fingers squeezed and squeezed, her cheek burning against the brick cutting into her flesh.

"You do not take warnings well," he said, his voice deep…dark. But that's not the only thing she noticed. His free hand pressed against the wall in front of her face, and there peeking out from the arm of his jacket was the tattoo on his wrist. The man currently immobilizing her was the same man that Rhett had told her to run from.

But she couldn't run.

He squeezed her neck tighter. "Apparently, you can't fucking listen," he growled in her ear. "This is the last warning you'll get. Close down and stay the fuck closed." He leaned in and his hot breath, smelling of cigarettes and alcohol, brushed across the side of her face. "It's not in your baby's best interest to ignore what I've told you. Do you understand fully this time?"

He released her neck enough to let her wheeze, "Yes."

Then she learned the he'd come there to make a point. One that he made clearly as he sent her flying to the left. Her head smashed into the brick wall next to her, blinding pain slamming into her. Darkness crept into her vision, and tiredness sank in deep as the icy wetness beneath her suddenly began to feel cold. A fear she'd never known froze her. She fought to keep her eyes open, narrowing her focus on his black boots right in front of her. *The baby…the baby…the baby…* She blinked, her eyelids heavy and slow, and then the boots moved away

from her, leaving footprints in the snow as he left her on
the ground.

Get up.

Move.

She tried to push up, but her limbs felt impossibly heavy.
Rhett…

* * *

The hard thumping of Rhett's heartbeat thundered in his ears.
He breathed in and out, relying on his training to control
his emotions, and yet nothing eased the tightness in his chest.
Fear, he realized when he pulled up to the hospital. But he
didn't know this emotion. Fear usually made him sharper,
quicker, and enabled him to act until that fear drifted away.
Now desperation cut through him like a sharp blade, leaving
him more wounded than the bullet that had ended his military career.

At the emergency entrance, he slammed on the brakes of his
truck. He darted out a second later, leaving the door open and
the keys in the ignition, thinking only of Kinsley and the baby,
the worst thoughts filling his mind. He charged through the
hospital doors, running down the hallway. He'd been in Whitby
Falls when Boone told him that Kinsley had been found outside
her bar knocked out cold. *A clear attack*, Boone had said, and
Rhett had never known the type of fury that came over him.
Her body temperature had dropped to a dangerous degree, and
that's what the doctors were most concerned about. The last
update Rhett got was that Kinsley was under heating blankets
and was awake and alert.

The sweat felt cold on his flesh, his T-shirt slicked to him beneath his leather jacket. He skidded to a halt at the nurses' station and slapped a hand on the desk. "Kinsley Knight."

The nurse on duty slowly rose, giving Rhett a hard stare. "Are you family?"

"I'm her boyfriend." The words left his mouth in such a rush that his brain didn't get a chance to catch up to what he'd said.

The nurse frowned. "Identification, please."

On any other day, Rhett would applaud this nurse's firmness. Not today. "It's Rhett West." He slapped his badge on the counter. "The room number. Now."

Another nurse poked her head out from the doorway to the right. "It's fine, Joy, he's the father of her baby," the brunette said. "She's in room one hundred and seventy."

"Thank you," Rhett breathed to his one-time lover from after his first tour in Afghanistan. He didn't wait for Shannon's response, just took off running down the hallway, passing doctors and a couple of cops on his way. *140...154...* He turned right and slowed when he saw the rookie, Cameron, stationed outside a door.

"She's in there," Cameron said, gesturing to the door on his left.

Rhett bolted through the door, stopping short when he spotted Kinsley lying in the bed. "Jesus fucking Christ," spilled from his mouth. He was well aware their inner circle was in the room, as was Hank, but Rhett's attention stayed fixated on the deep scratches on her cheek. A dark purple color shadowed her cheekbone, the early signs of a bruise. Monitors surrounded the hospital bed, and the lumps on her belly beneath her hospital gown indicated some of those monitors were keeping an eye on their baby.

He slowly looked up at her face, staring into those gorgeous eyes. He'd known anger and rage and everything in between. *This*, he'd never known. He wanted to peel back the skin off whoever had touched her in a way that went against everything he believed in.

Whatever she saw on his face only made hers tighten. "I'm okay."

His nostrils flared, the rage burning white-hot in the blood in his veins. He stood there, feeling the tremble of his body, the clench of his fists.

"Rhett," she said softly, but not weakly, as she reached out a hand to him. "I'm okay. We're okay."

Unaware of anything but *her*, he moved to her, tangling his fingers with hers. He sat next to her and raised her hand to his mouth. Jesus Christ. He had never felt this kind of fear, one that crippled him. Didn't understand it. When he finally felt a smidgen of control, he looked at her again, and she had tears in her eyes. "How hurt are you?" he asked.

"My cheek, but it's not that bad." She touched her neck and winced. "Here's a bit tender."

Rhett stared at that spot on her neck. A spot he'd kissed. A spot that another man had no right touching, especially to hurt her. He released a breath, gaining back more of the control that had been slipping away. Slowly, so he didn't scare her, he cupped her face. Something broke and warmed simultaneously as she leaned into his touch. "What did he do to you?" he asked her. "Every word. Every hurt caused. Tell me all of it." And then he'd make the person pay.

"I went outside to put the garbage out," she said. Her chin quivered, tears filling her eyes. "He was just *there*. Out of nowhere. He grabbed my neck and had me up against the wall."

Rhett stared at those marks on her cheek. "He pressed your cheek to the wall?"

She nodded, another tear sliding down that injured cheek. "That's when I saw the tattoo."

Rhett wiped the tear away, careful not to touch her scrapes, and she drew in a shuddering breath. "The same tattoo I showed you?"

"Yeah," she said with a nod, her dark hair blanketing the pillow. "He said I was stupid to ignore that first warning and keep the bar open. That the next warning wasn't in the best interests of my baby."

Rhett's chest hollowed. He placed his hand on her belly, just beneath the strap and monitors there. "He threatened our child's life?"

Her voice broke. "Considering he said it with his hand cutting off all my air supply, I got the feeling he meant me too."

Rhett shut his eyes and breathed deep, struggling not to explode. He called in every ounce of training the military had instilled in him.

He let a beat pass.

Then Hank said behind him, "I've got every unit on the streets looking for someone who matches this sonovabitch's description. But I've got no doubt he knew how to get in and out of town quickly."

"He most definitely had a plan," Boone added. "The move was ballsy. He attacked in broad daylight."

Rhett slowly opened his eyes, feeling near breathless at the tightness in his chest. They would catch this fucker; Rhett wouldn't stop until he did. Right now, he thought of Kinsley and their child. "Are you warm now?" he asked her, stroking her cheek again with his thumb.

"Yeah."

He examined the monitor, not knowing what he was looking at. "The baby?"

"Strong," she said.

He glanced back at Kinsley, squeezing her hand tight. "You must have been very scared."

Her breath hitched, voice wavered. "Really scared."

Not caring about anything or anyone but her, he gathered her in his arms. She held him tight, and he felt the tension rolling through her. Until suddenly she went limp and her soft sobs filled the room. Rhett didn't move. Not a goddamn inch.

He vaguely heard Hank kick everyone out of the room and shut the door behind them. And still, Rhett didn't let go. He held her through every single one of her tears, feeling her pain rip into him the same. He'd fought wars. He'd protected lives. But these two lives in his arms right now, Kinsley's and his unborn child's, were beginning to mean more to him than anything he thought once mattered. Including himself.

When she drew quiet and the tears were gone, she leaned back, and he cupped her face again. She didn't need him to say a word; he saw everything on her face. He gave her what she needed, and for once in his life, he felt like he was getting things right. *Finally.* He dropped his mouth to hers and kissed her with all the warmth she brought to his life.

"Thank you," she said when he broke the kiss. She released a deep sigh, her eyes red-rimmed. "I think I needed a good cry."

"Of course you did," he said, taking her hand again, stroking her uninjured cheek with his knuckles. "What else do you need from me?"

The pain and the fear no longer lived in her gaze; something else burned there. "Find that fucker and get him behind bars."

Rhett let the raw intensity fill him. He slowly grinned, a smile he knew looked deadly. "Now that, Kinsley, is my absolute pleasure."

Chapter 12

It took longer than anyone had expected for the doctor to discharge Kinsley, but some of that was also because Asher took her statement there at the hospital. *The attack is fresh on your mind*, he had said. Yeah, it was fresh, and so was the fear. There, lingering right in her chest, just above her baby. She was curled up on Boone and Peyton's couch by the crackling fire when she slid her hand under the warm blanket to rest on her belly. She'd never been that scared before. A fear that felt all consuming. From the attack, yes, but also from not knowing who wanted her to close the bar or why. She lived in Stoney Creek, a small town of quiet people. She had no enemies that came to mind. No matter how she looked at this, nothing made any sense.

It had started snowing again the moment they left the hospital, and Kinsley watched the snowflakes flutter down from the living room window of the lake house that had ivy climbing along its left side. Peyton had bought the place when she moved to Stoney Creek, furnishing it with antiques, and what once was in desperate need of repairs now looked brand new again with a fresh coat of cream-colored paint on the walls. The entire house screamed French country cottage. Kinsley had to squint to see the snow-covered frozen river past the big shade trees, with their branches dipping under the weight of the fallen snow.

"Hot chocolate makes everything better," Remy said.

Kinsley glanced away from the window to find Remy offering her a mug. "Thanks." Her hands hugged the steaming cup. "You even added little marshmallows. Pulling out the big guns, huh?"

"Of course," Remy said with a gentle smile. "After the day you've had, you deserve all the marshmallows and chocolate out there." She took a seat next to Kinsley on the couch, tucking herself under the blanket too.

Soft jazz music played through the speaker on the mantel, as Peyton exited the kitchen holding two more mugs. She gave Remy one, then sat in the chair across from them, facing the fire. "Feeling a little bit better?" she asked Kinsley.

"Much. Thanks for letting me come back here," Kinsley said. "Hospitals have got to be the worst place to be ever."

Peyton gave a solemn nod. "They're definitely cold, but I swear it's to motivate people into wanting to get better and leave." And she should know. Before moving to Stoney Creek, she'd worked as an emergency room nurse in Seattle.

"Well, they succeeded," said Kinsley, who then yawned. The day, the emotions, it was all slowly coming down on her like a heavy weighted blanket. She snuggled into the couch and took a tiny sip of her drink, the heat instantly hitting her tongue, and the sweetness following soon after. The warmth of the mug bled into her hands, and she wanted it all. It didn't matter that she had fleece pajamas on, or fuzzy slippers, or the blanket, the coldness that hit her the moment she woke up in the ambulance with a very worried Benji at her side wouldn't quit.

"So…" Remy said, blowing on her drink. "Can we talk about Rhett and who the hell he became today?"

Kinsley smiled softly. There was one thing she needed more than sleep, and that was not to think about the danger she'd been in today. How scary that moment was, and how afraid she was that her attacker might come back. Remy must've known that. "You mean, how sweet he was?"

"Yes." Remy nodded firmly, taking a fast sip then bringing her mug back down to her lap. "I've never in my life seen him like that."

"Definitely attentive," Peyton added. "Even Boone looked a bit shocked by his reaction to seeing you in the hospital bed."

Kinsley gave a little shrug. "He's changing. Little by little. And yes, it surprises me, too, but then it also doesn't. He's always been a good guy. He's just had a hard time readjusting to life here again."

Remy cringed. "Which makes me feel like total shit."

"Why, because you yelled at him at Merlots?" Kinsley asked with a smirk.

Remy's brows rose. "He told you I yelled at him?"

"I saw you drag him away. It's not that hard to put two and two together."

Remy set her mug down, obviously not as desperate for warmth as Kinsley. "Well, first, I didn't exactly yell at him. I simply reminded him that I have hexing abilities, and if he hurt you, I'd hex him so he couldn't get a hard-on."

Peyton burst out laughing. "You did not!"

"Of course I did," Remy said seriously. "I had no idea he was being this sweet, caring guy. I thought I was dealing with tough, emotionally closed off, looking for his next lay Rhett." She hesitated and shrugged. "I thought he was being all for show or something, but today...well, that was different."

Kinsley sipped her hot chocolate, taking in a marshmallow. She didn't really have a response, and she knew Remy was just being a good friend. Kinsley probably would've done far worse by now if the roles had been reversed.

"Wait," Peyton said slowly, her eyes narrowing on Remy. "You can't really hex people, can you?"

Remy rolled her eyes. "I don't know why everyone doubts me all the time."

Kinsley chuckled. She didn't believe in everything Remy believed in, but she'd seen some of her spells literally work magic. Once as a child, Kinsley had poison ivy so bad that nothing would help it. Remy's grandmother whipped up some cream, and within twenty-four hours the poison ivy was gone. When Remy's grandmother passed, she left her *Book of Spells* to Remy, and those spells were what Remy sold at her shop. "You should have seen him later that night after their talk at the bar," Kinsley said to Peyton. "He looked so pale."

Remy's smiled beamed. "Good. I'm glad he took me seriously, but honestly, I didn't know..." Genuine curiosity in her bright eyes. "So this is really how he's been with you?"

Kinsley nodded. "Rhett's wanted everyone for so long to believe that he's this ruthless bastard. But...I don't know...I see him through a different lens. Maybe that's stupid of me and will inevitably get me hurt, but he doesn't scare me."

Peyton picked a marshmallow out of her mug. She blew on it, then tossed it into her mouth. "Maybe all this time he just needed someone who understands him like you do, and maybe that's what you are for him. Maybe he's coming out of his shell."

Kinsley laughed softly. "That's a lot of 'maybes.'"

"It is." Peyton shrugged. "But it also could be true."

Remy watched Kinsley intensely. "I know that look," she said. "You're waiting for the bomb to drop and for this to all fall apart."

"I'm putting all my hopes into that not happening," Kinsley responded. "But it would be stupid of me not to see that Rhett's got a lot of shit to deal with. He's been through a lot, and there is...this part of him that's trying to fit into this world he wasn't expecting to fit into. He saw himself as a soldier. A warrior. He didn't want a wife, a kid, this nine-to-five kind of life. He wanted to protect his country. He picked that as his path. And while there is this huge part of me that wants to believe that this is actually happening, that we can have something beyond sex, there's another part of me that is well aware that no one can change like"—she snapped her fingers—"that."

Peyton frowned. "But you do think it's possible, right?"

"I think he's trying really hard," Kinsley said honestly amid the comfort of the two women she loved and trusted immensely. "But no one can change that drastically, and that's just the reality I'm left with. That one day, while this is going okay right now, I'm going to wake up and want more than he can give me."

Awareness drifted into Remy's eyes, and her voice softened. "That's why you've been okay with this arrangement with him?"

Kinsley nodded. "He's trying, and I want to let him try to see if we can make it work. What else can I possibly ask for? I want our child to have two parents. Happy ones that want to be there." Both friends gave her a look of understanding. "I won't bend on my happiness, but I love Rhett. I've loved him for so damn long. And that means I have to love the parts that aren't totally put together. He's either going to get to where I am, or he won't. But if that happens, we'll have to co-parent, and we need a solid friendship for that to happen. That's what we're working towards right now. Not love. Maybe something deeper than we had before, yeah, but just…figuring this out, you know?"

Peyton's eyebrows slowly drew together. "Yes, I totally understand. He's doing what he should be doing, and even more than I think any of us expected."

A long moment of silence drifted between them as everyone sipped their hot chocolate. Until Remy broke it. "Out of curiosity, do you think he'll ever be the marrying type?" she asked.

Kinsley shrugged and admitted the honest-to-God truth. "I have absolutely no idea."

"Well, one thing is for certain," Remy said. "I've never seen the kind of rage I saw in Rhett today. Whoever did this to you today, whoever wants you to close down, I actually pity them. Rhett is coming for them, and I wouldn't want to be on the receiving end of that wrath."

Peyton gave a firm nod. "That's why Boone thinks it's not someone from town."

"Did he say why?" Kinsley asked.

"Because no one who knows Rhett would be so stupid to come at him like this," Peyton said slowly. "No one."

Kinsley nodded, as that made a lot of sense. Anyone who knew Rhett knew not to mess with him. The United States government had trained him to kill, and he had no qualms about it when he was protecting those he was told to protect.

"All right," Peyton said, setting her mug down on the table.

"We've had hot chocolate, Boone's bringing us dinner soon, and we've got a couple of Hallmark Christmas movies. What else can I get you? What do you need?"

Kinsley took a long sip of her cooled-down hot chocolate, wiggling her toes. She looked between her best friend and her sister-in-law and smiled, the coldness finally fading away to the warmth and love in this room. "Just this. Nothing else but this."

* * *

On the north end of Whitby Falls, anticipation flowed through Rhett's veins as he leaned forward, staring out the front window while Asher pulled his truck into the parking lot of Red Dragon's Saloon, the local biker bar. Resting just off the gravel road in the rural area of the city, the bar was what biker movies were made of, with its worn plank boards for walls and western false front architecture. But the red and blue neon lights were like a beacon calling Rhett forward. There was a time and a place to let a case fall where it fell, and there was a time to push forward and demand answers.

Rhett planned to push. Hard.

From the back seat, Boone let out a long deep sigh. "This could end very badly."

"Yes, it could," Rhett replied, eyeing the rows of motorcycles, his seatbelt the only thing holding him back from rushing in and getting answers.

Asher stopped the truck off to the side of the motorcycles. "My vote is still that this is highly stupid."

"I won't wait for answers anymore." Rhett unbuckled his

seatbelt then turned to the men he trusted as much as his military brothers, if not more. "You both know what to do?"

"Plant the bait," Boone said.

Asher added, "And then we meet at Flannigan Corners." The four-way stop in Whitby Falls had been the location of a terrible accident where seven members of the Flannigan family had all perished in a crash caused by a DUI.

Rhett nodded and grinned. "Keep the truck on, just in case I come running."

Asher snorted, turning off the ignition. "Only you would enjoy this."

Rhett did enjoy this. He lived for the adventure. The rush of adrenaline that followed as Rhett exited the truck was his fuel. That steady excitement kept him sharp and ready as Boone and Asher headed off toward the bar's front door. Rhett reached for his weapon in the holster at his waist and moved to the bar's window. He stayed off to the side and glanced up into it, watching Boone and Asher walk into the bar. Every head turned in their direction, but there was only one person Rhett kept his focus on.

Dalton. He rose from his spot at the bar as Boone and Asher approached him. The bikers went still around them, all looking to Dalton on how to react. Boone spoke, and they had a short conversation. One that had been planned down to each and every word spoken. Boone and Asher were reporting the attack on Kinsley today and asking the questions they needed to ask to plant the seed to get Dalton acting, if Rhett's instincts were right. They usually were.

When Boone and Asher left the bar, the bikers once again looked to Dalton for a reaction. He said something to them, then turned and headed toward the back, past the two strippers dancing around the poles. Rhett moved swiftly, his military training clicking into place, as he became part of the shadows. He slipped through the back door, passing the chef working at the stove, flipping burgers. Loud music came from the front, but Rhett moved hastily, already aware of the layout of the bar that the detectives in Whitby Falls had provided after Rhett left the hospital.

He stalked carefully down the hallway, taking each breath slow and easy while an aroma of grease and bacon lingered in the air. He held his weapon in his hands, aimed at any threat coming his way. When he overheard Dalton's enraged voice, he lowered it slightly.

"I don't know what shit you're pulling," Dalton growled. "But we never signed up for this."

A quick peek into the room revealed Dalton speaking on the phone, his back to the door. Rhett slipped in, then tucked himself behind the door, and Dalton was none the wiser, focused on his conversation.

"You fucking attacked the police chief's daughter. Do you understand the position this puts us in? The heat you've brought on us?"

Rhett slowed his breathing further and counted with each of those breaths. Patience wasn't necessarily his strong suit, but hours of practice had made him better. Stronger.

"You never told us of this plan," Dalton stated. "And if you had, I wouldn't have agreed."

Rhett took in every single word, imprinting the conversation into his memory.

Dalton's back went ramrod straight at whatever the person had said. One hand pressed against the desk. "You've fucking made your point now. Leave it at that." A pause, and Dalton let off a tense laugh. "You're a fool to believe that. She's surrounded by cops and a retired Army Ranger." Another pause, and Dalton snorted. "Yeah, good luck with that. You've given your warnings, now I'll give mine. Do not put heat on me again. You will regret it if you do." And then he hung up, tossing his phone onto his desk. "Fuck," he spat.

Rhett lunged forward, slamming the door closed on his way, and a blink later, had Dalton up against the wall by his neck, Rhett's weapon digging into his chin.

Dalton chuckled, though his nostrils flared. "You are either stupid or want to die."

"I could say the same to you." Rhett pressed the gun harder against Dalton's neck and said through clenched teeth, "Tell me who that was on the phone."

Dalton snorted. "You're not going to shoot me, West. You're a cop."

"You're wrong," Rhett said slowly. "I'm first and always a Ranger. I protect mine. And don't think for a fucking second I won't end you to find out who attacked her."

Dalton's eyes flared. "You'll never walk out of here if you do."

Rhett dropped the veil off the cold-blooded warrior inside him. "Do you honestly believe I give a shit about that?" He dug the weapon deeper into Dalton's jawline. "Give me a name."

Maybe it was the tone of his voice or the look in his eyes, but Dalton's expression shifted, going lax. "I cannot give you a name," he said firmly. "To do so would be to endanger my club."

Rhett felt the racing of Dalton's heart beneath his fingers on his neck. "If you can't give me a name, then give me something to find this person."

Dalton's Adam apple bobbed. "Look into Bernie."

Rhett lightened his fingers on Dalton's neck. "The owner of Merlots?"

"Yes, him," Dalton growled. "Now, get your fucking gun out of my goddamn face." Rhett slowly lowered his gun. He backed away, keeping his gaze on Dalton as the biker said, "I should kill you."

Rhett grinned, a smile he knew promised death. "You won't."

"Why is that?"

"Because I overheard your conversation," Rhett explained. "You want this fucker gone as much as I do, and instead of starting a war, you'll let me end this."

Dalton's eyes blazed and he gestured to the door. "You've got one minute to leave before I send my men after you."

Rhett kept his weapon aimed at Dalton's head. "If you've lied to me—"

Dalton raised his hand, a hardness filling his expression. "I don't touch women or children. A line was crossed today. Fuck off and go deal with it."

And that was as close to peace as Rhett and Dalton were ever going to get. Rhett didn't say anything more; he simply turned and exited the bar the way he'd come in, with no one else aware that he'd even been there. His feet hit the gravel parking lot and Rhett took off running to the east, through the cornfield that was his cover if Dalton indeed sent anyone after him.

But ten minutes into his run, only silence greeted him as the corn stalks that had been used for the pumpkin festival maze brushed across his arms, snow fluttering down.

Another few minutes later, he caught the headlights of the truck, and in seconds, he was back in the passenger seat. Asher hit the gas a second later, and the tires skidded against the gravel road.

From the back seat, Boone asked, "Did you get anything?"

"Bernie," Rhett wheezed, his chest heaving.

"What about Bernie?" Asher asked, taking a quick right turn.

Rhett used the front of his T-shirt to wipe the sweat from his face. "That's who Dalton pointed to."

A pause. Then Boone asked, "What the fuck would Bernie have to do with this?"

Rhett holstered his gun at his hip. "That's exactly what I'm going to find out."

Heavy silence fell as Rhett caught his breath, and Asher made it back out on the country road that would lead them to Stoney Creek. Until Boone broke it, and asked, "Just catch me up to speed here. Are you suggesting that Bernie is the one responsible for the attack on my sister?"

Rhett couldn't believe it either. Bernie was kind and considerate, a family man. "Not directly," he explained. "But whoever did do this is somehow connected to Bernie."

"Unbelievable," Asher muttered.

"Believe it," Rhett said, grabbing his phone and texting Cameron. I need to talk to Bernie Weis. Bring him in.

Cameron replied: Roger that. ETA?

Two hours. Keep him in the interrogation room.

Consider it done.

Rhett wanted Bernie to fret, sweat, and everything in between. "Cameron is bringing in Bernie as we speak."

"Good," Asher said, tapping his thumb against the steering wheel. "Back to the station then."

"I need to make a stop first," Rhett said.

Asher glanced sideways. "To?"

"Kinsley."

Chapter 13

"Run, Kinsley, run," Rhett roared, a dark shadow dancing around his feet until it began swirling up his body.

"No," Kinsley screamed, desperate to reach him. That shadow would swallow him whole, steal him away. He stood in front of a forest, but no matter how fast she ran, she only seemed to get farther away.

The branches of the trees behind Rhett reached out. He tried to fight them off, but the shadows moved faster now up his body until they encased his neck, squeezing tight. Until his eyes went warm, accepting. "You don't belong here," Rhett said softly. "Run."

A click jolted her awake. She gasped and snapped her eyes open, quickly coming to terms with the fact that she had been dreaming. But as she heard footsteps moving closer, she realized she wasn't alone in Boone and Peyton's spare bedroom. Her father was sleeping on the couch for the night while Boone went off with Rhett and Asher somewhere. She jolted up to sitting, spotting a shadowy figure by the closed door.

"It's me," said Rhett, his warm voice washing over her.

"Jesus," she exhaled, dropping back onto the bed, placing a hand over her thundering heart. "You scared the crap out of me."

"Sorry." He moved in next to her, fully clothed, and she knew he wasn't staying long.

He gathered her close, spooning her from behind. "I wasn't expecting you back so soon," she said after a long moment of silence. "Everything okay?"

His breath tickled her neck as he held her close, his arms locked around her. "We're waiting for Bernie to be brought in. I wanted to come check in on you first."

Sweet and all, but…she spun in his arms, turning to face him. "Bernie?" She couldn't see Rhett's face in the dark room, except for the outline of his chiseled jaw. But the coffee on his breath indicated he'd planned for a long night ahead. "Why in the hell are you bringing in him?"

Rhett tightened his arms around her. "Intel dug up his name."

"What intel?"

"You know I can't tell you that."

None of this made any sense. *Bernie?* She'd known him since she was a kid. When she'd bought the bar, he hadn't seen her as competition and, instead, offered her advice. Suddenly, she was wide awake. "The intel has got to be wrong. He'd never be a part of my attack today. You saw him the other night; he didn't act like someone who wants to hurt me."

"Never say never, Kinsley," Rhett said, his voice a low rumble. "People do terrible things in the right circumstances."

Sure, she knew that was true, but not Bernie. He'd never do this to her. But the tightness in Rhett's voice told her one thing for certain. "You actually think he's involved?"

Rhett hesitated then sighed heavily. "That's what I'm going to find out when I leave here and question him." A pause. "I admit I'm finding it hard to believe that he'd have any part in hurting you, but I don't doubt the source."

She didn't have to see his face clearly to grasp his mood. Today hadn't been long only for her. She wiggled closer, running her toes against his leg. "I guess every question I've got right now, you won't have an answer to."

He gathered her closer and kissed her forehead. "Believe me, when I know something worth telling, you'll know it."

She nuzzled into his neck, embracing his strength, letting go of her answerless questions, and the nightmare that had woken her. All day the same thought had haunted her. Now even more so. "I've been thinking about something."

"What's that?"

"I'm going to close the bar until this is all over."

His sigh tickled her forehead. "As much as I don't like yielding to this prick's force, until we understand what's going on, I agree that's a wise choice. It's not safe for you or your employees to be at the bar." He hesitated, his arms tightening around her. "But let's figure that out in the morning after we talk with Bernie."

Her mind raced. "Should I—"

"Kinsley," Rhett interjected, his voice tired.

She shut her mouth. That was a tone she'd heard growing up with her father. He needed normalcy and quiet, not questions. And her heart fluttered with the knowledge that Rhett had come to her, not a bar for a drink, and not another bed. *Her.* She pressed a soft kiss to his neck, shutting her eyes and leaning into him.

Silence drifted between them, and right as she began to doze off, he asked, "Are you afraid of becoming a mother?"

It took her a minute to truly believe he'd asked that. Rhett wasn't deep. He didn't do emotions. "Deathly afraid," she admitted, wondering where he was going with this.

"Why?" he asked.

She leaned away and caught the shadowy outline of his cheekbone. "I don't want to become my mother."

He snorted. "Impossible. You're nothing like her, Kinsley. You're loyal to your bones."

"I know that I'm nothing like her," she said. "But I also know that what happened with my mom shaped me. It made me love those who love me harder and deeper. It made me be honest about love, because life can drown you otherwise."

A heaviness filled the space between them. Normally she'd fill it, but she wanted—no, *needed*—to hear what was on his mind. She hoped that by her opening up, he'd realize sharing personal thoughts wasn't so hard after all.

He eventually asked, "If you know that, then what are you afraid of?"

"That I'll think of my happiness first like she did."

"You *should* think of your happiness first," he said after a moment of consideration. "You deserve to be happy, as much as our baby deserves that too." He slid his hand over her hip beneath her nightgown. "The difference is, your mother didn't care who she hurt to be happy. You don't have that in you."

She hoped that was true. "Are you afraid of becoming a father?" she asked, pushing on, taking advantage of his openness.

"Today"—his voice tightened—"today was new for me. I have never felt fear like that." She reached out with her other foot and rubbed her toe against his sock-covered foot as he went on, "But as for being a father, I'm more concerned than afraid."

Her foot halted its strokes. "Concerned about what?"

"That I'm going to get this all wrong."

She wasn't sure what she could say or do to break through this hard wall around him, where he felt incapable when it came to the straight and narrow. She just hoped she could...eventually. "Just be you, and you'll get this right."

A pause. "Being me is what's concerning."

"You know, one day, Rhett, you're going to look back and realize that you're not nearly as scary as you think you are."

"And how will I realize that?"

She snuggled into him, feeling like she belonged there. "When a little toddler looks at you with all the love in the world and wants only one thing."

"What's that?"

"You."

Something shifted in the air between them then. Heat and things unexplored between them lay heavily in the space separating them. He shifted slightly until she was lying on her back again, and he placed his hand on her belly. "You need to tell me if I'm getting anything wrong, all right? I need you clear and open, always up front."

She swallowed against the sudden emotions that rose up within her. "Have you ever known me to withhold my thoughts?"

He didn't answer her question; he simply went on. "If I hurt you, tell me. If I say something wrong, tell me. If I disappoint you, tell me. I need to hear these things. I don't want to fuck this up. Promise me you'll be honest. Always."

Sudden tears welled in her eyes. "That's an easy promise, Rhett." She placed her hand over his, feeling his slight tremble. She understood. Today had rattled her too. But this felt like even more, like a line had been crossed today, and he couldn't uncross it anymore. "We're in this together," she told him, lacing her fingers through his. "I'll be honest. Promise."

"Good," he whispered, gathering her in his arms and bringing her up against the hard lines of his body. "Go back to sleep. I'll stay here until you do."

And there, in the tightness of his hold, she began to believe that maybe…*just maybe*…those walls of his were falling.

* * *

By the time Rhett got back to the station, his mood had soured. He'd wanted to stay in bed with Kinsley, ease her worries and his, not deal with the reality that the reason Kinsley had been attacked was because of someone in his town. Especially if that person was Bernie, a man that Rhett knew personally. He'd spent many nights at Bernie's club. Mostly because when he'd looked for women to warm his bed and keep him afloat when he'd been drowning, he hadn't wanted to shove it in Kinsley's face, not when he knew she had feelings for him.

As he headed down the hallway toward the interrogation room, the station was quiet around him. At a little after three in the morning, Stoney Creek was a ghost town. The bar rush had already gone home to sleep off the booze, and Main Street had been empty when Rhett had parked his truck in the station's lot.

He skipped the door to the interrogation room and walked into the one next to it. Boone was leaning a shoulder against the wall, arms crossed, gazing through the two-way mirror at Bernie and Asher in the interrogation room.

"Good. You're here," Boone said, picking up his phone and firing off a text.

Asher glanced at his phone, receiving Boone's text, then flipped it over, setting it next to the file folder on the table.

"All right, Bernie," Asher said. "I know you're curious about why we brought you in here today."

Yeah, so was Rhett.

Bernie nodded frantically. "You're right, I am curious, and concerned, for that matter. Why won't anyone tell me what's happened?"

Rhett stepped closer to the two-way mirror. There was a good reason both he and Boone weren't in that room. Rhett most definitely did not trust himself not to flatten Bernie if he'd had any part in Kinsley's attack.

"Before I tell you what's happened, I want you to understand that I know you, Bernie." Asher kept his hands laced on top of the table, a poster of calm. "I know the type of man you are and what you're not."

Rhett didn't know how Asher did it. He was so cool and collected with men that Rhett would've punched first and talked to later.

"Okay," said Bernie, a bead of sweat running down the side of his face.

Asher drew in a long deep breath and then said softly, "Earlier today, Kinsley was attacked outside her bar."

Bernie's eyes went huge, the shock palpable in their depths. "Dear God, is she okay?"

Rhett cocked his head at that. Unless Bernie was a very good actor, and he doubted he was, his concern looked genuine.

"Not quite the reaction I was expecting," Boone said, obviously thinking along the same lines.

Rhett crossed his arms, widening his stance. "No kidding."

"Kinsley and the baby are fine." Asher's voice grew gentler now. "Our problem here is that, through our investigation, your name came up."

Bernie blinked. "My name?" He shook his head, shifting in his seat. "No. No. No. Whatever you've heard is wrong. I would never be a part of that. I've known the Knight family for years."

"And yet, we got your name, Bernie," Asher stated more firmly now.

The color drained from Bernie's face. "I don't know why." He blinked rapidly, his mind obviously working a mile a minute. "It's...it's just wrong," he said. "I would never do that to her. To anyone."

Asher's gaze flicked to the mirror.

Boone sighed. "This doesn't make sense." He pointed at Bernie through the window. "That is not a man who orchestrated what happened to Kinsley. I don't believe it for a second."

"Neither do I," Rhett stated. He reached for his phone and texted Asher: Not seeing anything on our end.

Asher looked at his phone again and then flipped it back over. "Here's the thing, Bernie. The manner by which we got your name leaves no misunderstanding that you're connected to this in some way. I don't want to arrest you. But you need to tell me now, if you were not the one responsible for Kinsley's attack, then who do you know that would do something like this? You need to explain why we got your name. If you don't, I cannot help you."

Any remainder of color in Bernie's face drained out, leaving him ghostly white. He bowed his head. His fingers trembled on top of the table as he wrung them together.

"He's afraid," Rhett commented.

"But why?" Boone said, taking a step closer to the window.

A long moment of heavy silence followed, with Bernie keeping his head down. Then he finally said, "I had no idea any of this would happen." Everything got real slow after that, as Bernie went on, "I only just learned about what happened the other night, but even then, I still wouldn't have believed anyone would hurt her." He lifted his head, tears rimming in his eyes. "I would have come forward if I'd known."

Asher reached out and placed a comforting hand on Bernie's arm. "I know that, Bernie. Like I said, I know what kind of man you are."

Bernie visibly swallowed, a single tear trailing down his cheek. "It's Josh."

"Your son, Josh?" Asher asked. At Bernie's nod, Asher pressed, "What about him?"

Bernie's voice cracked. "He gambled all his money away. He lost everything, including the bar, and owes even more."

Asher sat quietly, letting Bernie talk in his own time.

Bernie added, "Josh didn't know, you know. He's just a stupid kid. Didn't know what he was getting himself involved in."

Rhett would've been in there shaking him to hurry up.

Asher stayed perfectly still. "What didn't Josh know, Bernie?" he asked.

"What…what owing money to the wrong people would cost him. That'd they take the bar. That'd they take everything."

"Who are these people?"

Bernie's face got even paler now. "I…I didn't know…who…I didn't know."

"Bernie," Asher said with a snap to his voice. "Who are they?"

"The Wild Dogs," he said. "I've seen the symbol on their leather jackets. It's one of those motorcycle clubs."

Boone shot Rhett a look. "Do you know them?"

"Never heard of them," Rhett said, grabbing his phone from his pocket to search the name on the Internet.

And right as the browser found the name, Bernie added, "I only found out when they came to the bar that they're a biker gang from New York City that's expanding, and that Josh had taken a loan from them. He didn't realize that the loan gave the biker gang ownership of the club." His voice blistered. "It's not even ours anymore. The bar. They've taken over. I'm there to ensure the bar's success or Josh's life…it's over. They came to the house with guns…my wife…she was so afraid…"

"You should have come to us with this, Bernie," Asher said. "We could have helped you."

"I didn't know…I just didn't know…" He began sobbing.

Asher's heavy sigh was visible when he turned toward Boone and Rhett in the window.

"It makes sense," Boone finally said. "They now own a bar that is losing to Kinsley's. From what she's told me, she's been having her best year yet. While that wasn't a problem with Bernie, that would be a problem to this gang."

Rhett thrust his fingers through his hair. "The force…the warning…fuck, it does make sense." But now that he knew the answer, he realized the danger. "If this gang is infiltrating Maine, expanding across state lines, it's powerful."

Boone sighed his frustration. He rubbed his face. "Fuck, I'd rather it be King. At least I'd know what we were up against."

Rhett felt things he couldn't explain even to himself. He'd faced threats before and he'd hunted high-valued targets. And he'd bring hellfire down on this gang for touching Kinsley.

The door opened then, and Asher walked into the room, a frown marring his face. "Well, that was quite a lot to take in."

"No shit," Boone grumbled. "But at least we've got a way to move forward now."

Asher gestured toward the interrogation room. "What do you want to do about him?"

Rhett glanced at Bernie, still weeping, and for the first time in his life, he understood the man in a way he never thought he would. What would Rhett do to protect his child? Things far worse than what Bernie had done. "Cut him loose."

Boone and Asher balked at him.

"The guilt over what happened to Kinsley will be a punishment that far exceeds not coming to us," Rhett said. "And as for Josh, bring him in. Let's press him about the Wild Dogs location." Someone needed to answer for what had happened to her. First, Josh. Then these Wild Dogs. Rhett wouldn't stop hunting until Kinsley, their child, and her bar were safe. "And let's put some surveillance on Merlots in case those bastards come back."

"Good plan, but…ah…" Boone cocked his head. "Excuse me, but who are you and what have you done with the cutthroat Rhett we know, who would *never* let Bernie walk?"

"Don't blame me, blame your sister's influence." Rhett spun on his heel and headed for the door.

"Where are you going?" Asher called.

Rhett swung the door open. "To learn all I can about these fuckers before I hunt them down."

Chapter 14

The next morning, while sitting in her father's old Ford truck as he drove, Kinsley took her phone out of her purse and texted Rhett: I've got a midwife appointment this morning. Sorry, I forgot to tell you before you left. Don't worry about coming to this one, but if you want to next time, it's at 197 Cherry Hill Lane. She hit Send and shoved her phone back into the purse on her lap. The plan this morning had been to meet up with her staff and go over closing the bar until all this got resolved, only she'd suddenly remembered about the appointment. The fact that she'd forgotten only told her that maybe she wasn't dealing with all of this well; maybe she was feeling a bit more lost than what she'd thought.

"Ready?" Dad asked after he'd parked the truck at the curb.

"Ready." She noted the tight lines around Dad's eyes. "Okay, what gives? Something is definitely wrong. Out with it."

"It's nothing you need to worry about."

Kinsley frowned, releasing the door handle. "Dad. What is it?"

Dad sighed and turned to face her. "The boys went to bring in Josh?"

"And?"

"He's gone," Dad explained.

"Gone where?"

"He drained his bank account and left," Dad said solemnly. "First, to even think that Bernie's family could have any hand in this, to now knowing that Josh is on the run. It's just…"

Dad had updated her on all the gritty details about Josh's involvement earlier this morning. "Terrible," she offered.

Dad nodded. "Very terrible." He blew out a long, deep breath then opened the door. "All right, kid, let's go see about some good news."

Kinsley let go of every other thought too. She couldn't control this situation, and she had enough on her plate; she didn't need to add worrying about Bernie and his family to it. When this was all over, she'd go and talk to the poor man. He had to feel terrible, and she truly liked him. Josh, on the other hand. Well, she hoped the guys got those cold cuffs on him sooner rather than later.

She hurried out to greet the blisteringly cold day with dark, gloomy skies hovering overhead. She didn't remember Rhett leaving last night after she'd obviously fallen asleep, but neither he nor Boone was at the lake house when she'd woken up. It wasn't until just before Kinsley was in the shower that she remembered her midwife appointment this morning.

Dad followed her up the steps of the old two-story stone house that had been converted into an office space a few years back. The town had marked the house as a historic site, and the property was dripping with old charm. She yanked the door handle hard, then shut it quickly after she and her dad hurried through. God, it wasn't even December yet and the winter was already cruel. She didn't want to think about how January would be.

She unzipped her boots, leaving them at the front door, and hung up her coat, as did her father. She led the way into the waiting room on the left, likely once a living room when the Phillips family, the original owners, built the house. The seats in the waiting room were all empty as Dad took the one next to the lit gas fireplace.

"Hi, Sally, how's things?" Kinsley asked, approaching the receptionist. Sally had gone to Whitby Falls High School like Kinsley, but she was two years ahead of her. Every Stoney Creek teenager was shipped off to Whitby Falls. The town simply didn't have enough teenagers for its own high school.

"Same old, same old." Sally smiled, sitting behind her desk, twirling her blond hair around her finger. "Samantha's pregnant again."

Samantha had been in Kinsley's grade. "What's this, her third child now?"

Sally nodded. "She'll have her hands full for sure."

Kinsley was still coming to terms with having just one child. She didn't know how any woman handled three. "Is Sam still loving it out there in Texas?"

Sally's mouth twitched. "I sent her a picture of the weather today and she told me she's never coming back."

Kinsley laughed. "I can't blame her there one bit."

"Me neither," Sally said, gesturing back to the waiting room. "Go on and take a seat. Maria will be right out."

"Thanks." Kinsley grabbed a mint from the tin on the counter and unwrapped it, tossing it into her mouth and stuffing the plastic wrapper into her purse.

Before she could even sit down, her attractive middle-aged midwife, Maria, stepped into the room, reading through a file folder in her hands. "Kinsley, hi." When Maria looked up from the file, her warm dark brown eyes weren't on Kinsley; they were fixated on her father, who suddenly rose and offered his hand.

"Hank Knight," her father said with his low gravelly voice. "You must be new to town."

Maria blushed and shook his hand, then tucked her shoulder-length brown hair behind her ear. "Yes, I've only lived here now about a month or so. It's nice to meet you, Hank."

Her father smiled at Maria. All bright. Cheery, even. "I hope the town's been kind to you," he said.

"Very kind," Maria said softly. "Thank you."

Kinsley glanced between them repeatedly. She'd only known her dad to date twice after her mom had left. One was a teacher from Kinsley's elementary school, and another was a woman who'd once owned a coffee shop in town. Both women eventually moved away, one after her father stopped seeing her, and the other before. Maybe this would be the third time she'd see him get some happiness in his life.

Kinsley smiled at them both, but gently intervened since she did have things to do today. "I won't be long, Dad," she told her father, who was still making eyes at Maria. And Maria was making them right back.

The front door suddenly flew open and snow whirled through it before Rhett appeared in the doorway. He shut the door quickly, stomped his feet, and shook the snow out of his hair. "Sorry, I couldn't get here sooner," he said, stepping out of his boots. "The roads are terrible."

Kinsley's heart squeezed and then turned to mush. *He*

came… "Considering I *just* told you about the appointment, you got here really fast. Thanks for coming."

Sally's eyebrows rose as Rhett approached, obvious surprise washing over her face that Rhett had shown up to the appointment. And there was something in that surprise that bothered Kinsley. Like, really bothered her. She wished everyone saw Rhett the way she saw him. The good there.

Her stomach filled with butterflies when Rhett stopped beside her to kiss her cheek before addressing Maria. "I'm the father," Rhett told her, offering his hand.

Maria blinked then finally looked away from Dad. "I'm the midwife," she said with a laugh before shaking Rhett's hand. "Come on, let's take a look and see how things are going."

As Maria strode away, with Rhett right behind her, Kinsley leaned into her father and said quietly, "Might want to wipe your mouth, old man. You're drooling."

Dad snorted and gestured her forward with a flick of his chin. "Better not keep her waiting, kid."

Kinsley laughed, noticing him wiping his mouth as he returned to his seat.

She quickly headed for the door. When she reached Rhett, he said, "Dare I ask?"

"I think Dad just met a possible new romance." She passed him and entered the hallway.

Rhett sidled up to her. "The midwife?" At Kinsley's nod, he smiled. "Good for him."

Kinsley returned the smile and nudged her shoulder into his. "I've got no doubt you want everyone to forget, but"—she grabbed his hand and stopped him to place a butterfly kiss on his mouth—"Happy Birthday."

Rhett shifted on his feet. "Thank you."

He sounded as tense as he looked, and Kinsley laughed as she continued on down the hallway. Rhett had always hated his birthday. He hated any fuss being made over him. But when Kinsley woke up this morning, she knew she'd make a fuss. This year, she had the right to. Just later.

She entered the examination room, and in minutes, she was up on the table, her pants pulled down past her hips, and her top lifted to just below her bra. Maria began measuring Kinsley's belly, making notes and asking questions.

Rhett stayed off to the side, and out of the way, until Maria asked him, "Would you like to hear the heartbeat?"

He glanced at Kinsley. She nodded. "I've heard it. You should too."

"Then absolutely yes," Rhett said. He stepped up to the table, placing his hand on Kinsley's ankle. "Please do."

While Maria took out the Doppler, Kinsley caught the excitement on Rhett's face. An expression she couldn't remember ever seeing on him. Truth was, in all her teenage dreams she'd imagined moments just like this with him, only they also involved walking down the aisle to him, and other wild dreams belonging to a young girl. A small part of her still couldn't believe she was having his child. But the stronger part of her felt like this was exactly where they were meant to be.

"All right," Maria said, adding some gel to Kinsley's belly before turning the Doppler on. "Let's take a listen." She moved it along the gel twice and then settled it lower on Kinsley's belly. Seconds clicked by...and then, there it was...*thump...thump...thump.* A steady, strong beat that made Kinsley smile.

Maria said, "Aw, baby wanted to let its daddy hear too."

Kinsley took in what Maria said, but the world faded away

to Rhett. His head tilted toward the monitor, and he listened carefully, his eyes on her belly. "That's the heartbeat there?" he asked roughly.

"Yeah," Kinsley barely managed. "That's our baby."

Her breath caught when he slowly reached out and placed both hands on her belly. And when he lifted his gaze to hers, she couldn't hold back the tears at the raw happiness there. "You're happy?" she asked.

"Yes, Kinsley," he murmured. "I've never been as happy as I am right now."

* * *

Six hours. Three hundred and sixty minutes. That's all Rhett had to get through before he could end this day. He'd brought donuts to the station for everyone this morning, the one requirement they had at the station for a birthday. He'd endured listening to everyone wish him a Happy Birthday all day. Soon, it would be over. He'd shut his office door the moment he got inside, where most days he left it slightly opened. He'd spent the better part of the day after the midwife appointment learning all he could about the Wild Dogs, but his mind kept drifting to that soft sound. *His child...* Something changed in him at that sound, something he couldn't quite put a finger on.

The ringing of his cell phone snapped him out of his thoughts. He saw it was his mom calling on the screen. "Hi, Mom," he said after he'd raised the phone to his ear.

"Happy Birthday to you. Happy Birthday to you. Happy Birthday, my dear Rhett. Happy Birthday to you."

"Thank you," he said for the hundredth time today.

"How has your birthday been so far?" Mom asked, her voice a sweet comfort. "Anything exciting going on?"

That was the biggest understatement of the year. He'd been putting this off, but now, after today, he didn't want to anymore. "Listen, is Dad there too?"

"Of course, he's watching the game."

Dad loved sports. If he wasn't working, he was sitting in his recliner, with a bag of chips and a beer, watching whatever game was on. "Could you put me on speaker for a sec?"

Mom paused. "Sure. Is everything okay?"

"Everything's great."

"Derek, mute that," Mom said. Some shuffling came across the phone line before she added, "Okay, you're on speaker."

Rhett didn't know the right way of sharing this news to lessen the shock, so he simply laid it all out there. "Kinsley and I have been seeing each other and she's pregnant."

The longest pause of his life filled the phone line.

His father spoke first. "The baby is yours?"

"It is."

"Okay, wait. Hold on," his mother said. "Are we talking about Boone's sister, Kinsley?"

"That's the one," Rhett said.

Another long pause. Rhett didn't try to fill it. But then his mother surprised him.

"Oh, my goodness, we're going to be grandparents!" Her squeal nearly deafened Rhett. He leaned the phone away as she screamed words Rhett couldn't understand.

"Madeline," his father said calmly.

"I can't help it, Derek," she exclaimed. "Rhett, this is so very exciting. I never thought you'd have children."

He and she both. "It was a surprise, but a good one." And he was beginning to realize just how good after this morning.

"Are you two serious?" his father asked.

A valid question since Rhett had never mentioned Kinsley at any of the times his mother had asked if he was dating. "More serious than I've been with anyone." Which was the stone-cold truth. He'd never slept with a woman more than once, but Kinsley...yeah, this was different. "We're...figuring how all this is going to work."

"Sounds like a good way forward," Dad said.

"Can I call her?" Mom asked.

That request was not unexpected. She knew Kinsley very well. They'd all grown up around each other. "Are you going to harass her, obsess over this, or in any way drive her nuts?"

"Rhett West, of course I won't," his mother rebuked him.

"Then I'm sure she'd love to hear from you."

"Okay, well, let me call her then. Bye, honey. We're so excited for you. Love you, and Happy Birthday."

The phone line went dead. Rhett laughed and shook his head. His mother was a force, much like Kinsley. Truth was, she wanted details. Details she knew Rhett wouldn't have. He placed his cell back on his desk and sighed. That went better than he thought it would. Rhett smiled at the joy in his mother's voice. He didn't know this kind of life. One he began wanting to hold on to.

A knock on his door erased his smile. Asher opened the door and said, "You can't hide in here until your birthday is over."

"Watch me," Rhett countered.

Asher gave a dry laugh then dropped down into the client chair. "I hate to do this on your birthday, but I don't have good news."

"It's fine." Rhett waved him on. "Out with it."

Asher's expression turned grave. "The Wild Dogs are terror-izing towns up and down the East Coast."

Rhett nodded, having found those same conclusions himself when he scoured the Internet and reached out to other police forces throughout day. "Let me guess, similar incidents are happening elsewhere?"

"Yes. The gang is taking over night clubs, strip bars, and everything in between, and the outcomes are not good."

"Meaning?"

"Fires. Murders. Intimidation. Whenever they acquire a prop-erty, another similar property suddenly goes out of business. Either by fire, or because the owners walk away. These bikers make the Red Dragons look like a bunch of preschoolers."

"Any arrests ever made?"

"When there are arrests, someone steps up and claims the crime, but the person who does is typically either a first-time offender or has crimes as a juvenile that get overlooked during prosecution."

"This is not what we want." Rhett scrubbed at his face, almost wishing they were dealing with King. At least they knew how King worked. Rhett had no idea who he was up against, and he didn't like it, not with Kinsley involved. "Kinsley told me last night that she's closing the bar until we get this squared away. That should give us time to get this solved without placing her in further danger."

Asher inclined his head. "That's really for the best. The game has changed now. These aren't some punks. These bikers use lethal force to ensure their competition is taken out."

Rhett leaned back against his chair, stretching. "Did you get any good leads on them?"

"That's the part that's concerning," Asher said, rubbing the back of his neck. "They're clever, clean, and smart. They don't leave evidence. Police reports all point to them, but there's just not enough evidence to ever indict them."

"Terrific," Rhett grumbled. "We've got bikers that are out-smarting cops up and down the East Coast, and we've got no ammo to stop them. That's what you're telling me?"

Asher frowned. "Right now, that's what I'm telling you. We've got Bernie's word about the bikers, but that's not going to hold anyone. Bernie isn't the most credible of witnesses now, considering he kept this information from us. How about on your end?"

"The rookies are still making calls to identify the perp with the tattoo," Rhett explained. "Nothing's come from that yet. I'm not seeing a headquarters for the Wild Dogs, though it looks like they hail from New York City. I've got a call with the NYPD, and I'm sure I'll have more to go on after that."

"When's the call?"

"Tomorrow. The lead in the gang unit was away sick today. He'll be back in the morning. We've got a call scheduled for nine."

"Good," Asher said.

A cop walked by the door, eating one of the donuts Rhett had brought in today. "I spent the last couple hours scour-ing the Internet," he said, turning his focus back on Asher. "From what I read, the leader of the Wild Dogs is Rocco Martinez. He's as smart as King, but far more dangerous. Any charge that comes his way never sticks. His estimated net worth is a few hundred mill, and he owns properties all along the coast."

"Which, let me guess, are all incredibly successful?"

Rhett nodded. "When you take out the competition, what else could happen?"

"Dirty bastards," Asher growled.

Rhett rubbed at his eyes again. At the moment, he had no way forward, and he hated that, feeling the exhaustion settle in deep. He'd slept only four hours on the break room's couch after Bernie left this morning, until the shift change woke him up. "Where's Boone?" He should be there. This was his sister's case, and ever since this afternoon, he'd vanished.

"Had to go somewhere," Asher said.

"That somewhere has nothing to do with the Wild Dogs, right?" Rhett was on edge. He could only imagine how Boone felt.

Asher shook his head. "He had to do something with Peyton. Not sure what, but for right now, things are stable. Go be with Kinsley, and we can start fresh in the morning. We don't have a jumping gun to work off of. Everything's in the works. We need to go home. We need to sleep."

Rhett agreed with a nod, feeling the heaviness of his eyelids. "Good plan."

He flicked off his monitor and rose, shoving his chair underneath his desk, as Asher said, "Besides, there's something wrong about someone spending this much time working on their birthday."

"You know I hate my birthday," Rhett commented.

Asher snorted, rising. "Yeah, I know. Where's Kinsley?"

"Back at her place with Hank," Rhett reported. "He's waiting for me to pick her up."

"Better hurry," Asher said with a sly smile. "We all know how much the chief likes waiting."

Asher headed for the door, and before Rhett could decide

if he was making a mistake, he said, "I heard the baby's heartbeat today."

Slowly, Asher turned around, eyebrows raised. "Did you?"

"Yeah."

A long pause. "And how was that?"

Rhett hesitated, trying to put into words what that moment had been like for him. He never thought he'd have children. He never wanted them. But something shifted at the sound of that steady heartbeat, a realization that maybe what Rhett had been missing were things he didn't know existed. That strong, regular rhythm belonged to *his* child, a part of him. And when he looked at Kinsley, lying there, smiling so brightly, he hadn't felt edgy; he'd felt completely solid and secure.

At Rhett's silence, Asher gave him a warm smile and offered, "The best birthday gift you ever could have got?"

Of course, Asher had the words. "Yeah, buddy, exactly that."

Chapter 15

A few minutes past seven that night, Kinsley slid the curtain aside and glanced out the window, finding her driveway still empty. If growing up around cops had taught her anything, it was not to let the job or the danger or anything else get in the way of important days. Because if you did, there would be no celebrations. Ever. Even when a case needed to be investigated and became top priority, it had to be put aside for a couple hours on special days. Family mattered. And Kinsley had learned a long time ago after her mother left, that no matter what, family, at times, had to come first.

After her midwife appointment, she'd spent all day on the telephone, calling people she'd never met before. And all those people now stood in her living room. Out of any in their inner circle, she had the biggest space for parties, which was why they usually held them at her place. Rhett had a lot of military buddies, she'd come to discover. Boone told her about the guy who fixed her bar, and then she got more names after that. And even more names as the calls continued. Until suddenly her house was full of men.

While she finished up preparing some food, she'd spent a good hour on the phone with Rhett's mom. Obviously, he'd sprung the news on them today, and somehow that didn't surprise her. Something had changed in him today. Some dark part lightened, became less heavy. Rhett's mom wanted all the details, and by the end of the call, Kinsley was smiling ear to ear. His parents were excited. Rhett was happy. Maybe all this was actually going to work out.

A light flashed by the window and she hurried to peek out again, finding Rhett's truck now in the driveway. "Ooh, he's here. Quiet."

The loud chatter behind her went silent.

Sure, Rhett was going to hate this. He hated every birthday, but no one ever listened to his broodiness; they celebrated his birthday anyway. But this year was different, and she wanted it to feel different too. For him.

The door suddenly swung open and Rhett walked in.

"Surprise!" rang out in the room.

Rhett dropped his head and shook it, but when he lifted his gaze again, it locked on Kinsley. The smile he gave her made her heart skip.

"You're lucky I didn't shoot anyone," he said to her, igniting laughter from his friends. He shoved his keys into his pocket and walked right up to her, grabbing her hand and tugging her close. "You behind this?"

Those dark eyes were full of a warmth she never thought she'd reach. "Of course I am," she said, leaning up and giving him a quick kiss. "But before you give me trouble, just know that I asked everyone to donate whatever they could to Sailor's instead of buying you a present since I knew you'd prefer that."

Surprise widened his eyes. He glanced over her shoulder, probably at Theo before looking at her again. Warmth spiraled through her, touching places that she never really thought could be touched with Rhett around. "Thank you for that, Kinsley," he said.

"You're welcome." She smiled.

He dropped his chin and kissed her again before backing away, but he kept her hand in his. She gave him a little shove toward his friends. "Now go have fun. I've got your favorite kind of whiskey."

He headed toward his friends, including Boone and Asher, and she glimpsed a different side of Rhett than the one she usually saw most days. He seemed lighter, freer, more comfortable, while they all congratulated him about the baby. It occurred to her then that this was Rhett not just surviving but living. The soldier. The friend. And a little part of her heart hurt, wishing he always felt this at ease.

She sensed someone watching her and looked around to find Remy staring right at her. Kinsley smiled, trying to hide her emotions. Remy didn't smile back. Instead, she came over as the guys around Rhett began razzing him with jokes and manly hugs.

Remy said, "Men are so…"

"Loud?" Kinsley offered.

"Yeah, loud," Remy agreed with a smile.

Peyton brought her cake in from the kitchen and set it down on the table next to the cooler full of beers. Kinsley was sure that she'd tried to make a gun cake, but hilariously, it looked like a penis. "And rough," Peyton added. "Why do they hug like that? It looks painful."

Kinsley fought her laughter. She couldn't wait until Rhett saw the cake.

Before she could think up a reply, there was a knock on the door. Kinsley answered it, expecting more of Rhett's military buddies. Instead, she found six women, all of whom looked like they'd left a strip club to come there. None of them had winter coats on, holding them in their arms instead, showing off their perfect bodies, perfect breasts, perfect *everything* in their skintight minidresses.

"Hey," a stunning brunette with big blue eyes surrounded by dark makeup said. "Is this Rhett's party?"

"Um, yes," Kinsley said. "Sorry, but who invited you?"

"Hey, Suz," one of Rhett's military buddies called.

Dammit. Not strippers. She had no reason to shut the door in their face.

The woman gave Kinsley a quick grin, and then hastily ignored her, sauntering into the house with her friends in tow. Kinsley became their coat rack as the women handed her their outer garments. Then they were gone, on their gorgeous high heels, strutting toward the men.

"Geeze, that was rude," Peyton said, taking the coats from Kinsley. "I'll put them in the kitchen."

"Okay, thanks." Kinsley forced a smile.

But that smile died as the brunette threw her arms around Rhett from behind and hugged him very intimately. In such a way that it became very clear they had been together before. She followed that woman's hand as she slowly ran it down his arm in a familiar way like she'd traced those muscles before. The lust-filled smile she gave him. The way her breast pressed against him when Rhett turned, his hand sliding over her back before dropping. Kinsley stared at his face as he realized Kinsley wasn't the one hugging him.

"You okay?"

Kinsley's stomach churned with hot jealousy. The same jealousy that she had felt every time she saw Rhett leaving with a woman. One that broke her every damn time. She forced another smile at Remy. "Yup, totally fine. You?"

Remy gave her a lopsided smile. "I'm great, but I'm also not the one swallowing my emotions."

"It's okay." She glanced in Rhett's direction again as he maneuvered his way out of the woman's hold and stepped back. And yet the woman only looked more determined. It occurred to Kinsley in that moment that Rhett could, in fact, be with that woman if he wanted to. They weren't exclusive. She actually didn't know what they were doing. All of which seemed fine until she was presented with the reality that Rhett was gorgeous, and women wanted him. "I'm okay," she repeated, not even believing herself.

Remy's eyes turned sad. "Okay, well, what can I help you with?"

Kinsley needed to get out there. Just to breathe and not cry in front of everyone. Damn these pregnancy emotions. She forced her voice out from her tight throat. "Wanna start bringing out the food? I need to pee."

"Kinsley," Remy said softly.

She couldn't reply. Her chin trembled as she turned away and booked it upstairs to the bathroom. She shut the door and locked it, dropping her head back against the wood, unable to stop the tears.

A sudden knock came at the door. "Just a minute."

The knock came again. Remy could be persistent when she knew Kinsley was sad. She unlocked the door and opened it. "Remy, I—"

Rhett arched an eyebrow. "No one should look that sad at a birthday party."

"I'm fine. I'm just pregnant and emotional." She moved to the sink and turned on the tap, dabbing cold water onto her hot cheeks.

Rhett shut and locked the bathroom door behind him then closed in at her back. He pressed his hands against the sink, trapping her. His chin rested on her shoulder. "Are you threatened by that woman downstairs?" he asked.

"No," Kinsley lied, staring at him through the mirror. "I'm just holding in my vomit from watching Ms. Perfect hanging off you."

His mouth twitched. "What would you rather I had done when she hugged me?"

"Drop-kicked her," Kinsley said. "You're good at that. I've seen you."

He chuckled. "I'd go to jail for drop-kicking her."

Well, she didn't want that. She drew in a long, deep breath, staring at him through the mirror. Hard. "Have you slept with her?"

His expression went flat. He had his emotions very much in check. "Yes."

"Do you still want her?"

"No." His gaze fell to her lips through the mirror. "I want you."

She rolled her eyes. "You have to say that."

"Why?"

"Because my knee is primed and ready to take you down to the ground, and you know it."

He laughed aloud now and took her by the hips, turning her toward him. He gave her a leveled look. "I guess I'll have to show you then that you're all I'm thinking about now. The only woman I want." He thrust his fingers into her hair and his mouth sealed hers in a kiss that turned her head to mush.

But then the kiss went to an entirely different place. His lips slid to her neck and he nipped at her flesh, proving he was only getting started. When he reached for the top of her stretchy maternity jeggings, she broke the kiss with a loud gasp. "Everyone is out there."

"You had better be quiet then," he murmured against her nape, grabbing the jeggings and yanking. As he pulled them down, he went onto one knee.

She looked down at him. "But—"

"I want *you*, Kinsley." He kissed the top of her thigh then grinned pure sex up at her. "Stop talking and let me have you."

Oh, dear Lord… her mind went blank to anything but the pleasure of the first stroke of his tongue against her hot flesh. The tickle he gave there, followed by the deep press against her clit. She shuddered, threading her hands into his hair, not caring about anything but having *more*. She tried to spread her legs, bringing him in deeper, but her jeggings held her ankles together, allowing only a little space between them. But in that space, Rhett had managed to slide a finger up inside her that began moving with his perfect licks against her sensitive skin.

He flicked, swirled, nibbled, and sucked, and soon, she was gripping the edge of the sink, mindless to anything but him and the way he touched her so perfectly. Like he knew just how to make her body *his*. She was all but putty in his hands when she began moaning softly, grinding her hips into the pleasure.

His finger moved faster, harder. His teeth gently hugged her clit while he sucked deeply, sending her up on her tiptoes. And with a final look down at Rhett between her legs, a fantasy she'd imagined for years, she dropped her head back and came against his mouth with a quiet shudder, only a soft moan spilling from her lips.

When the shuddering eased, he slowly withdrew his fingers. She finally opened her eyes, finding Rhett's wild with desire. "Just you, Kinsley," he said, giving her inner thigh a kiss, then he pulled her jeggings up over her hips. "Only you."

* * *

The screaming deafened Rhett's ears. Fear and horror, the sound was one he'd never heard before. One he didn't believe anyone should hear. Rhett moved swiftly through the warehouse and bodies dropped as he fired off rounds. "Clear to the south," he said.

"Clear to the west," Matthews added.

"Move east," Elliott roared. "We're under heavy fire." The gunfire echoed through the warehouse that the CIA had discovered housed a chemical weapon.

Rhett and the three men behind him turned, heading down the hallway. They'd studied this building. He knew in a few short minutes he'd get to Elliott's location. A door to the right opened and an enemy appeared. Rhett squeezed the trigger of his assault weapon and the person fell. Rhett kept his breath steady, his stride quick but guarded. Two shots sounded behind him. Lester or Michaelson had handled the threats behind them.

When they rounded the corner, Rhett spotted Elliott and his three-man team set up behind a wall, keeping safe from the rapid

gunfire coming their way. Rhett shot out the window and then
pulled the trigger, removing the danger to his men.

"Breathe."

Rhett bolted upright, his heart hammering. Kinsley was on her knees next to him, gently placing her hand on his trembling shoulder.

"Breathe, Rhett," she repeated softly.

Slowly, he exhaled, realizing that she'd turned on the lamp on the night table. Judging by the concern on her face, he must have been yelling in his dream.

"Fuck," he exclaimed, running his hands through his hair. He shifted to sit on the side of the bed, pressing his feet against the worn floor, grounding himself.

Kinsley moved in closer and kissed his shoulder. Once…then again…and he felt the sweat slicking his flesh.

Many minutes went by. Rhett's heart was still beating fast, thundering in his ears. A run or a shower helped usually, but he couldn't find the strength to get up and leave her.

Apparently, she'd realized that. "Come lie with me," she eventually said.

He had to force himself to glance back at her over his shoulder. Why would anyone sign up for this? Men were supposed to be strong, not haunted with nightmares that woke them up in the middle of the night, obviously scaring those around them. And yet…*and yet*, there she was offering him a place to land.

She pulled on his arm a little, her warmth calling to him. "Come. Please."

Needing her, he went then, and lay down on his back. She snuggled into him, resting her cheek against his heaving, sweaty chest, and he wrapped his arms around her tight. She pressed her hand to his heart, obviously feeling the thundering beat of his. He exhaled slowly, trying to calm down. Show her that he was fine. That she didn't need to worry.

"Can you tell me about the dream?"

He shut his eyes. "You don't want to hear about this shit."

Heady warmth filled the space, invading all his cold spots, and yet her voice firmed. "I'm strong enough to take this on. Please don't insult me by thinking otherwise."

He shut his eyes, battling his way back from the dream. "It's not about you being strong enough. It's that I don't want you to know this shit, Kinsley."

"But it's you," she said in an instant. "It's what you went through." She snuggled even closer, bringing all that warmth up against him, and said, "It won't make me think different of you."

"It will," he told her straight.

She pushed up. "No, Rhett, it won't."

He could feel her hard stare on him and was unsurprised when he opened his eyes to find the sternness in hers. Christ, her strength blew his mind. He gave her a little smile and tucked her hair behind her ear. "Always such a fierce warrior ready to take on any fight."

"Not any fight," she countered. "*This* fight."

He felt her sweet affection sweep around him and settle into spots he thought long dead. He drew in a deep breath and blew it out slowly before he addressed her again. "You think my nightmares are the problem here, don't you?"

She cocked her head. "Aren't they?"

He waited for his chest to tighten, for his throat to squeeze, leaving him unable to voice his thoughts. But that's not what happened. The words fell easily from his lips. "It's when I wake up that I find hard." She was frozen, unnaturally still, clearly absorbing each of his words as he went on. "When I dream, life is familiar. The rush. The missions I'm given. The hunt and the chase. I know that life. I live and breathe it. But when I wake up, in a comfortable bed, in warmth and safety, I don't even know what I'm looking at anymore, and it's jarring."

She hesitated then her voice softened. "You're looking at home."

He slid his fingers down the strands of her hair. "When I came home, everything looked different." He took another deep breath. "It's like I'm looking through a filter. Almost like I'm looking through someone else's eyes. And that filter doesn't only affect me, it affects those who care about me."

"What do you mean?"

He glanced into those pure eyes. "Why do you think my parents moved away?"

She didn't even hesitate. "Because your dad got a new job."

"Partly, yes," he explained. "But the bigger reason was they couldn't handle seeing me. Seeing what I had become."

"Which was what exactly?" Her voice tightened with anger.

He gave her hair a little tug and smiled, oddly liking her protecting him. "Don't be too hard on them about that. It was different when I first came back…I was different then. I'm better now." Although the continuing dreams suggested otherwise. They should have been behind him. He should be more settled; even he knew that.

"You were just fine when you came back," she said, snuggling back into him, her arm wrapped around his chest. "I cannot believe your parents left because you were struggling. That's really shitty."

"It's not their fault, Kinsley," he countered. "I could barely talk to them back then. When they visited, I got too edgy and had to leave. I spent all my time either on the job or at the gym with Theo. Things were very hard for them. They didn't know how to help me. Then Dad's job offer came up. I told them if they really wanted to help me, they should leave, so they did."

"Bullshit," she growled. "So things get tough. That's life. They never should have left, and they should have told you to shove it right up your bossy butt!"

A low chuckle passed through his lips. He flipped their positions, leaning over her while on his knees. "But then there is you. This woman who seems to not listen to a damn thing I say and is somehow fighting like hell to make me happy." Untouched things in his chest warmed as he dropped his mouth close to hers. "Why is that, Kinsley?"

"You know why, Rhett," she said simply. "You've known why for a very long time. The thing is, do you really want to hear it?"

Those three little words were hanging there between them. Words that he simply could not let her say. Not yet. Emotion clawed at his throat; an odd feeling that made him want to crawl out of his skin and yet stay in that warmth too. It felt like a tidal wave of uneasiness flooding him, threatening to drown him, and that was a feeling he knew and understood. "I need you, Kinsley," he murmured, bringing his mouth within a whisper of hers. "Spread your legs for me."

He heard the hitch of her breath, felt her body shudder when he dropped his mouth to hers and kissed her with all the intensity between them. She widened her legs, and he slid between them, keeping his weight on his arms, careful of her belly. The tip of his cock touched her soft, warm folds, and then she was arching her hips up to him in a slight demand. One he didn't ignore. He pushed forward, sliding into her, inch by inch, until he groaned against the pleasure of her sweet body hugging his. He took it slow, feeling all of her, letting her feel all of him.

He drank in every soft moan, loving the way she gave in to him so easily, so open and honest with him, like he deserved all of it. And he took everything she offered, needing it, claiming all that perfection as his own.

Soon, they were moving together. Thrusts meeting thrusts. Skin slapping against skin, the scent of their sex only intensifying the pleasure. Her moans brushing against all his senses. With every rock of his hips, he became more and more amazed at how perfectly they fit together.

Her breath hitched first, then her body responded to the pleasure, clamping down against him tight. And with a few long, slow, intimate thrusts, they soon came together, tangled in each other's arms, sweaty and breathless in their pleasure. And he wondered, in the quiet moments after his release, if that's what Kinsley was to him. *Home.*

Chapter 16

The next morning, Rhett dropped Kinsley off at Remy's magic shop. As she was getting out of the truck, he said, "Listen, we've taken protective detail off your bar, not on your person. For now, just stay clear of it. All right?"

Cold bit into her that had nothing to do with the freezing temperatures outside. "You think they're coming back?"

"We don't know the answer to that"—his gaze flickered to his rearview mirror—"but I'm only thinking about keeping you safe. If you want to go anywhere, Cameron goes with you, all right?"

"Okay." She smiled and was unsurprised to find Cameron sitting in his cruiser behind Rhett's truck. She glanced back at Rhett through the window. "I'll see ya later then."

He winked. "You will."

She leaned away and waved at Cameron, who was drinking his coffee, while Rhett drove toward the station. She was not at all surprised that the guys in her life were going into full protective mode. She entered Remy's store but stopped short when she saw that Remy was with a customer. "I'll go see Peyton for a bit," she said quickly.

Remy gave her a quick nod and a wave then turned back to the customer, who was looking at a love potion. Kinsley smiled, thinking maybe that love potion had some merit now as she shut the door, chiming the bell.

Cameron opened his car door and got out. Kinsley assured him quickly, "Just going to see Peyton."

"All right." Cameron got back in his car.

Okay, the babysitting might end up annoying her, but being safe mattered more. Truth was, that attacker's eyes still rattled her. She'd never seen eyes so dead before.

She strode past her bar, missing it like crazy. Whiskey Blues had been her whole life for so long, but maybe the break wasn't terrible either. Her current plate wasn't only full but overflowing now.

When she entered Peyton's shop, she found her behind the counter, scrolling through her phone. "You look happy this morning," Peyton said by way of greeting.

Kinsley shrugged, letting her mind wander to where it had gone after Rhett's nightmare last night. "I am happy, but I'm also…" She hesitated. "Actually, I don't know what I am."

Peyton's brows lifted. "Damn, girl, that sounds complicated. Come have a seat." She pulled the stool around from behind the counter then patted the top. "You're usually the town's therapist at the bar, but I'm a really good listener too, so spill the beans."

Kinsley plopped her butt up onto the chair, resting her elbow on the counter and her head on her hand. "Where to start?" she muttered.

"At the beginning is usually a good place." Peyton leaned a

hip against the counter, one arm folded, the other hand holding her coffee mug.

Kinsley missed coffee something fierce. She inhaled the nutty aroma while drawing in a long breath, pulling all her thoughts together. She finally looked up at her sister-in-law and spoke the truth. "I don't know how to help him."

Peyton's brows rose. "Help Rhett, you mean?"

Kinsley nodded. "He has nightmares." She hated admitting that truth to anyone, but she needed to talk this out. Her head felt heavy this morning. Her heart even more so. She wanted to break through those nightmares, keep him here in the present, and save him from his past. Emotion clawed at her throat and she fought the tears. "I hate watching him struggle."

Peyton's eyes saddened. "No one wants to watch anyone struggle, but that's the thing, Rhett needs to want to come out of whatever is haunting him for himself. No one can help him do that."

And that was exactly why Kinsley wanted—no, *needed*—to talk to Peyton about this. "You came out of what haunted you." Peyton lost her first husband in what she thought was a car accident, but later turned out to be a murder. Sometimes Kinsley didn't know how Peyton survived that, but then, she was just so happy now that she'd found Boone. "What you went through is unimaginable. Sometimes when I think about it, I can't believe you had the strength to not only wake up every day, but to start this brand-new life."

Peyton sipped her coffee, then returned her mug to the counter. She sighed very, *very* heavily, her eyes going distant, far away from there. "I did get through my past, but let me be honest with you, it was hard. Unbelievably hard. And I had to do it myself. Nothing anyone said or did would have helped me."

Kinsley figured that, but part of her was hoping for a magic answer. Something that she could give to Rhett to make him...*better*. "Do you think it's possible...you know, for him..."

"To be happy again?" Peyton offered.

Kinsley nodded. "Yeah, exactly."

"Of course." Peyton took Kinsley into her arms, and Kinsley settled into the warmth of her embrace, as she went on. "Anything is possible, Kinsley, especially when love is involved." She leaned away, keeping her hands braced on Kinsley's shoulders. "You're bringing Rhett out of his shell. Everyone is seeing it. Especially Boone. And believe me when I tell you that no one expected him to act like this. So if this is possible so far, then yes, I think that love can help Rhett. Especially the way you love him, so fiercely, so loyally."

Kinsley hoped so. "I know Remy thinks deep down giving Rhett a chance is a big mistake, but what do you think?"

Peyton regarded Kinsley intently. "Remy is protective of you, and Rhett's past screams danger. I'm sure, out of anyone, Rhett is not the guy anyone would choose for you. He's got his issues. But I know that sometimes one life ends, and another begins. Rhett's becoming this guy that is surprising everyone. He hasn't fallen down yet. And you know what?"

"What?"

"The fact that through all of this, the danger around you, the stuff with your bar, and that you're pregnant too, you're still thinking about him and how to love him better...that has to stand for something."

Kinsley smiled, warmth spreading down into her chest. "Maybe."

Peyton returned the smile then patted Kinsley's hand. "All I know is, I never thought I'd be happy again after Adam passed away. It seemed inconceivable to me. But look, here I am in this amazing town, surrounded by the best people." She lifted her chin, grabbed her mug again, and said, "So to answer your question, no, I don't think this is a big mistake. Rhett will either find his way closer to you or he won't. And it sure looks like he's trying very hard to follow you. Fate made you strong, Kinsley. And maybe that's because fate knew you needed to love Rhett."

Kinsley shot off the stool and wrapped her arms around Peyton, spilling the coffee from her mug onto the counter. "See, this is why I come to talk to you," Kinsley said, not caring about the coffee. "You always make me feel so much better."

"What else are sister-in-laws for?"

Kinsley leaned away to grab some tissues from the box and clean up the spilled coffee before tossing the tissues into the garbage. When she rose up, the same gorgeous cherry red lingerie nighty that she'd admired a few days ago once again caught her eye on the hanger. The loose fit in the front would surely accommodate a growing belly. "So, you know, with Christmas around the corner, if you're going to be making a list for Santa anytime soon, that"—she said, pointing to the nighty—"would make this girl a very happy one."

Peyton laughed. "I'll make sure to send Santa a note."

Kinsley stopped at the door and glanced back over her shoulder. "Seriously, Peyton, thank you. I really needed this talk. Love you."

Peyton's smile warmed. "Love you back. I'm here. Always."

Kinsley left through the door, all loved up. She peeked into Remy's window again, and she was busy with two different customers now. Today would obviously be long, and Kinsley was useless when it came to explaining Remy's magical items. She'd offered to work the cash register today and help Remy out while the bar was closed, but she realized she needed something to do as well or else the day would take forever to end. She figured if she was sitting at the counter, she might as well grab her books and get caught up on all the things that she'd been putting off. Especially because right now she'd rather be in bed with Rhett, not worrying about anything or thinking about life's realities, just enjoying the hard lines of his amazing body.

She caught Cameron getting out of his car again. Poor guy. "I just want to grab my books from my office. Is that all right?"

"Yeah, of course," Cameron said.

After she unlocked the door, she headed inside, and Cameron followed her in. Silence surrounded her as she walked through the main room. Which was both depressing and nice too. She missed the bar, but her head had too much in it to really process anything right now, including this mess her bar found itself in.

Cameron entered the back room first, but he'd taken only two steps inside when he yelled, "Run!"

Time slowed. And yet everything happened so fast. Cameron drew his weapon, only to be grabbed around the neck. He was disarmed in mere seconds. Kinsley's purse fell to the ground as a group of men wearing ski masks all turned to her. Two things occurred to her at the same time.

The first, her alarm was disabled. She hadn't entered a code when she walked into her bar.

The second, the man who attacked her stood only a few feet away. He turned those cruel, dead eyes to her.

Run…Kinsley…run…

The words came as clear as she'd heard them in her dream. She turned and sprinted for the door. She begged her legs to run faster. The door was right there; all she had to do was get there. Masculine yells erupted behind her, igniting a fear that hit her straight into her soul. She'd only begun to taste happiness. This surely couldn't be it. Her baby needed her. Rhett needed her.

Faster.

Run…

She screamed and pushed harder, her muscles burning. The door was *so* close. She reached out to grab the handle, but her fingers slipped away as a hard body slammed into her, taking her down to the ground. She forcibly shifted onto her side, desperate not to land on her stomach. Her hip took the brunt of the fall. But that pain seething through her was nothing compared to the fear she felt staring down the barrel of a gun.

Her attacker growled, "Time's up."

* * *

The morning had been long and exhausting, and last night with Kinsley occupied Rhett's mind. He felt torn between finding the bastards threatening her and keeping her safe and close to him. Rhett never felt torn, and it was beginning to eat away at him. He wanted to see that smile, feel that warmth she offered him, listen to her talk. Instead, he spent most of his time on the phone with the NYPD discussing the Wild Dogs, who they were and what Rhett and the guys were facing. The news was grim, and still, Rhett had no idea how to even find the men who'd attacked Kinsley. He had no leads. Nothing. Josh was still MIA; no hits had come on the APB that Rhett had put out. And he hoped that when Boone and Asher came back from wherever or whatever they were doing, they had a better answer for him.

With a curse, he grabbed his mug to refill his coffee, but when he stepped out into the cubicle area, he was met by a flurry of activity. "What's wrong?" he asked one of the rookies who rushed by.

"Whiskey Blues is on fire."

It took Rhett a few seconds to process what that meant. His coffee mug smashed to the floor and he charged for the door. He was vaguely aware that people were yelling at him when he ran out of the station. *Get there*, his instincts roared at him. He listened. Regardless of the fact that his head told him everything was all right, he sprinted down Main Street, spotting the dark, thick smoke billowing up to the sky, as well as Cameron's empty cruiser. Peyton and Remy stood at the curb, matching looks of horror on their faces.

Rhett took note of the pedestrians on the street, and one person was missing. "Where's Kinsley?" he asked the women.

"She was going to Remy's last time I saw her," Peyton said.

Remy shook her head. "She never came back after this morning."

Peyton's face went ashen. "But she left my shop this morning and said she was going to yours. She never came?"

"No," Remy said, reaching out for Rhett's arm, fright shaking her voice. "No, she never came."

Rhett snapped his head back to the bar as a window burst and flames licked out. He charged forward while the women yelled for him to stop. When he reached the door in the back parking lot, he spotted that it was ajar. Rhett grabbed his gun from his holster, then pulled up the front of his shirt and held it to his face while he got down on all fours and crawled beneath the thick smoke through the back room. *Kinsley...*

His heart thundered, the worst thoughts filling his mind.

He'd been in the most dangerous missions of his life, but this shook his hands now. A cold sweat washed over him, a stark contrast to the heat at his flesh. A rawness rocked him to his very core. The fire roared, a sound that reminded Rhett to move swiftly. He crawled through the back, clearing Kinsley's office and the kitchen, but then he met a body.

Cameron.

He checked for a pulse and found one. Rhett grabbed Cameron and yanked him out the door before he charged back inside. Desperate to find Kinsley, he touched the door to the main bar and was relieved to find that his skin wasn't scorched. He lay flat on his stomach and opened the door. The fire had been set at the front of the bar, and currently the only thing not on fire was the floor. Rhett's training clicked into place. His objective to search for a victim was the only thing on his mind.

He cleared the bathrooms, behind the bar, the stage, and when he knew for certain Kinsley wasn't lying injured in the bar anywhere, he crawled his way back out. The moment he cleared the outside door, he was greeted by sirens and lights as the fire department arrived. He burst into a coughing fit and was pulled away by a fireman, an oxygen mask shoved on his face. The world spun slightly, and for a moment he couldn't quite piece together why he was there or what had happened. Until Boone grabbed his shoulders, and with the oxygen returning to his body, he said beneath the mask, "She's not in there."

"Thank God," Boone said, holding Rhett steady.

Rhett tried to get his bearings. The paramedics were working on Cameron, who began coughing; obviously he'd been knocked out. Peyton and Remy stood just behind Boone, tears in their eyes as they held each other. No, no sadness. Rhett couldn't take it. He grabbed his phone and called her. The call went straight to voicemail. "Does she ever turn her phone off?"

Boone shook his head. "No. Never."

Rhett took in another long, deep breath then tore the mask off and dropped it on the ground. He grabbed Boone's arm. "The security cameras." He took off running, with Boone hot on his heels, and the firefighters yelling at them to come back.

Every step burned his lungs a little bit more. He stormed back into the station, glancing at the chief's empty desk. Rhett had failed to keep his promise. He shoved the shame aside. He'd find her...*and the baby*...his chest constricted tightly, but he shoved that thought aside too, desperate to stay sharp. By the time he was sitting behind his desk and powering up his computer, he was still coughing. He logged into Kinsley's security system and fast-forwarded through the morning. Nothing.

"Stop there," Boone snapped, glancing at the monitor over Rhett's shoulder. "There."

Rhett hit Play again but now in slow motion. A black van drove up to the back door and half a dozen men wearing ski masks got out, reaching for gas canisters. They gained entry by picking the lock. One man stayed by the door, an obvious lookout.

One minute went by...then two...and then two men charged forward out of the door. One held Kinsley by the waist, the other held her feet.

Life for Rhett stopped then.

Rhett knew pain. He knew what it felt like to have a bullet rip through his flesh. He knew what it felt like to lose people, to watch them bleed out and for the life to fade from their eyes. *This*...watching helplessly as men shoved Kinsley into a van was something he had no idea how to deal with. Pride filled him as she fought. Kicked and squirmed and punched, but the truth remained. They were physically stronger. And in a minute, they had her shoved into the van with the doors slammed shut. She didn't come back out.

Kinsley. His child.

They were…*gone*…

Something inside him cracked and then broke, shattering until he could barely get air in his tight lungs. He couldn't think. He couldn't move. *Kinsley…*

Boone was on the phone, snapping at the person on the other line, "I need an Ashanti Alert issued." Much like the Amber Alert, this act helped find endangered adults. "Victim is five-foot-five, brunette, twenty-nine years old, wearing a black jacket and dark jeans. Numerous suspects driving a black van. License plate unknown." He ended the call abruptly, shoving his hand into his hair. "Why the fuck would they take her? Why? Where?" He frantically paced by Rhett's desk, looking for all the answers that Rhett couldn't find either.

Rhett rose on shaky legs. He placed his hands flat on his desk and breathed deep. Kinsley needed him sharp and strong. There would be no finding where they'd taken her fast enough. Unless they found the van, but judging by the timestamp, they were a good hour ahead of them.

Boone loosened a breath. "If they hurt her, I'm going to kill them."

"No, you won't," Rhett said, finally looking up. Boone was too good. Too clean. Rhett…*wasn't*. "But I will." Planning to do whatever it took to find those men, he pushed away from his desk.

"I have—"

Rhett stopped dead, finding Asher in the doorway, looking

like he'd seen a ghost. "Fuck," Asher finally spat. He thrust his hands into his hair, his eyes fraught with worry. "I have no idea how to fucking say this."

"Talk now," Rhett ordered, feeling dread seeping into his bones.

Asher glanced at Boone and then back at Rhett, pity in his eyes. "A body was found twenty minutes ago on the 102 near Whitby Falls." Rhett flopped back in his chair, all the strength gone from his legs, every bit of air squeezed from his lungs as Asher added, "She's a brunette."

Chapter 17

Roars echoed across the coastline and small beach area off the main road as Boone fought to make his way past the cop from the Whitby Falls PD. Rhett stood motionless, time ticking by and yet it felt like it hardly moved. They'd roped off the beach area, and from what they'd learned from Asher on the drive to the scene, the body had been dumped over the cliff. Rhett felt like he moved in a fog. He needed to find out if this new life he'd tasted was over. If the one woman who'd touched something deep in his soul was gone. If his unborn child was stolen away.

"Get fucking control of yourself," the cop yelled, grabbing Boone by the jacket and shoving him back. "You don't want to see this."

Boone wasn't muttering words anymore, just screams, veins popping out of his forehead and neck. His eyes wild with fear.

Where Boone had morals, Rhett did not. He couldn't wait. Everything around him felt slow and unstable, and if he didn't act soon, he wasn't sure what he would do. When it became clear they were never going to let them on the scene, Rhett stepped forward and slammed his hand into the cop's ribs. The guy dropped, gasping for breath. Rhett raced under the tape, dodging every cop who charged at him.

He had to know…

He had to see…

Another cop went to tackle him, but Rhett turned and maneuvered out of his reach. The cliff was right there…he was so close…

But then arms locked on to him, and Rhett roared, "She's pregnant with my child. Let me fucking identify her."

Those arms, whoever they belonged to, released him. Maybe at the raw agony in his voice that even he heard and barely recognized. He rushed forward, stumbling over his own feet as he reached the edge of the cliff. There, on the rocks, as the water sloshed up around the ice, he saw the body dressed in a black jacket and jeans, the dark hair. He couldn't remember…was this what Kinsley was wearing?

A bitter east wind cut across the cliff, lifting the woman's dark hair away from her face. Rhett's world slowly turned on its axis. Everything he thought he knew altered as he realized he couldn't survive without her. Kinsley had been there, every day for years, making him smile, laugh, showering him with her warm affection, pulling him back when he'd been so lost. Something deep inside him shifted as he dropped to his knees, pressing his hands into the cold hard ground. He knew Kinsley's mouth. He knew her eyes. The lines of her jaw that he'd kissed. The curves of her body. He knew everything about her.

Boone suddenly dropped next to Rhett, and Rhett reached out, grabbing his shoulder. "It's not her," he barely managed. "It's not her."

"Jesus," Boone wheezed, staring down at the deceased stranger.

"Jesus, Lord. Thank you." He planted his hands on the ground, bowed his head, and breathed deep.

"I planned to call you."

Rhett glanced over his shoulder to find Detective Anderson behind them, his dark gray eyes weary. His black cap was pulled down low on his head, only the ends of his dark brown hair showing. "I only learned of Kinsley's abduction on the drive over. I hadn't had a chance to identify her." He stepped closer to the edge. "A couple of guys told me that we've got the woman's husband already in custody. He drove to the station right after and confessed to pushing her and she fell over the edge."

Rhett turned back to the woman, staring at her. He could survive war, loneliness, and even a gunshot wound. But he couldn't live without Kinsley and this new life she offered him. One that was hot at night and warm in the morning. A life of laughter and love.

Love.

Fuck, he loved Kinsley, madly, deeply. That's why he'd spent years trying to protect her, because that's what he did. He protected those he loved. And he wanted to protect her from the damage he could have caused her. But Rhett knew now that he'd changed, these past months more than ever. He'd touched her once, then everything changed.

This last push, though, that belonged to Kinsley. Her love did that. Every time she smiled at him, he saw that love. Every time those sweet eyes met his, he felt that love. She loved him wildly, and he'd never told her that he loved her back.

Why didn't he tell her? Why did it take so long for him to realize it?

"I'm sorry about your sister," Anderson said to Boone, offering him a hand. Boone took his hand and rose, looking slightly wobbly, as Anderson went on, "Whatever I can do to help in finding her, I'll do."

"Thank you." Boone shoved his hands through his hair and glanced at Rhett. "We need to find her."

Rhett rubbed his face, shedding the emotions dripping off him. He needed to think, to get a plan going. He couldn't lose Kinsley and their baby. Helplessness trembled in his muscles. They had nothing. No one had spotted the van. There were no tips. No leads. Even Whitby Falls PD didn't know much about this new biker gang. But Rhett knew that going the good way, the right way, sometimes didn't work. "Go to Dalton," Rhett said to Boone. "Shake him and get whatever else you can. He very well might know where they've taken her."

Boone gave a firm nod, the horror beginning to fade from his eyes. "Yeah, all right."

Rhett turned, and was immediately faced with the cop he'd taken down. He was still on his knees, wheezing. Asher stood next to him, offering a bottle of water. "It wasn't personal," Rhett said to the cop as he strode by. "You were in my way."

"Remind me never to do that again," the cop grumbled. Rhett offered his hand, and the guy took it, rising to his feet.

The cop patted Rhett's shoulder. "I get it. We're all good, West."

Rhett nodded in acknowledgment before heading toward his truck. "Get Anderson to drive you back," he called over his shoulder. When they'd arrived, he had left his door open and the truck running.

"What are you gonna do?" Boone called after him.

Rhett bellowed back, "Whatever I have to do to find her." He hopped in his truck, the tires squealing as he sped off.

The engine roared beneath him, the adrenaline waking him

up, making him feel alive. His mission in life was to protect. To hunt, if need be, and destroy threats, whatever the cost. As he turned down the first road on the right, his cell phone rang. "What?" he answered with the click of a button on his steering wheel.

Asher asked, "You're not about to do something stupid, are you?"

"I am." Rhett hung up and tossed his phone on the passenger seat, ignoring it when it rang again and again.

Kinsley was his. His to protect. His to love, as fiercely as she had loved him. The baby was theirs. He wanted those moments, with both of them. He'd been trained for exactly this mission. And ten minutes later, when he pulled his truck off to the side of the road, he felt primed and ready. He grabbed his gun, and took the safety off to confirm he had a full magazine clip. Then he got out, and every thought vanished from his mind. He met the tall stone fence, then raced toward it, climbing up the side and scaling over the top, landing hard on the other side. He breathed steadily, slowly, keeping his heart rate quiet and out of his head. He moved swiftly through the trees, spotting two security guards standing in the circular driveway. Rhett waited for them to turn away, then he sprinted toward the house. He hid behind a tree then slipped through the first door he found and was immediately greeted by a guard.

In an instant, he had the guy in his arms, squeezing his neck tight, while the guard pounded on Rhett's arms and kicked out. When he finally fell unconscious, Rhett moved swiftly, remembering the layout.

It felt like a lifetime before he reached the door to the office. With silence around him, the guards unaware that one of theirs was knocked out cold, Rhett opened the door.

Joaquin King lifted his head, surprise filling his dark eyes.

Rhett raised his gun, aiming it at King's head.

King slowly arched an eyebrow. "Are my men alive?"

"One is taking a nap."

King chuckled. "A nap, huh?" He leaned back in his chair, calm as any other time Rhett had seen him. "I'm surprised you got past them. They're skilled men."

"Today I was better," Rhett said.

King's eyes darkened. His mouth pressed into a firm line before he addressed Rhett again. "You've got one minute tops before my team storms in here. If you're here to kill me, I'd do so now."

"I can't kill you," Rhett retorted. "You have information I need."

"What information is that?"

"The headquarters of the Wild Dogs here in town."

King's mouth twitched. "Now why would you think I'd have this information, when you and the police do not?"

Rhett knew men like King. He'd studied them for years. He'd hunted them. Men who held a territory didn't like others in it. "Because they will become a threat to you. Maybe not now. But eventually. And I'm certain you're already aware of that threat and keeping eyes on them. They have something that is mine. Something I will use hellfire to get back."

The door suddenly burst open and Rhett sensed, more than saw, three men circle in behind him, weapons drawn.

King held up his hand, freezing the guards in place. "What if I do have what you need, how will it benefit me to assist you?"

"I'll remove the threat," Rhett promised. "We both know that no one will come out of there alive. The threat to your territory will be erased without you lifting a damn finger."

King cocked his head, a smile crossing his face. "It's a damn shame you won't work for me, West. I could use a guy like you."

"You could never trust me, King," Rhett countered. "I'd kill you the first chance I got."

King's men inched their way closer to Rhett, as King grinned darkly and said, "Ah, but that's what would make it so much fun."

* * *

The van went over a bump and Kinsley banged her back against something hard, darkness engulfing her because of the blindfold tight against her face. A gun, she grimly realized. The men surrounding her talked to each other and laughed at each other's jokes, like they hadn't abducted her. She tuned out their voices and instead listened intently to the outside sounds, counting the minutes since they'd shoved her in the van to establish a time frame. They passed the train on the right. Later, the highway on the left, telling her they had driven past Whitby Falls. A half an hour must have gone by, and she listened for every little detail in case she got hold of a phone. Anything that could help Rhett and Boone narrow down her location. Because undoubtedly, they were ripping apart both towns trying to find her.

She tried to piece together everything that had gone wrong. Had she not gone into her bar, she would never have even been in this situation. From what she saw, Cameron had only been knocked out, and she hoped he got out before they set the blaze. She slid her hand over her belly, worry engulfing her. She had to keep the baby safe, no matter what. She had to be smarter than these men around her. Men who apparently weren't happy with her just closing temporarily but wanted the bar shut down. Permanently. But the bigger question remained: Why was she still alive? They could have killed her right there in the bar.

Why didn't they?

The van suddenly slowed, then it turned right, and soon after they'd stopped, her blindfold was torn away. The two guys in the front got out first and then the back door opened. She kept her head down, hoping they wouldn't feel threatened, not wanting them to act. As long as she didn't see them, she couldn't identify them, and hopefully, they'd let her go. She was none too gently tossed onto a concrete floor. She scanned the area, discovering that they were inside a chop shop. She noted the Lamborghini across from her, being repainted, and ten more luxury cars, all being altered.

"Get in that corner," her attacker ordered.

She scrambled into the corner, unable to look away from him as he used a piece of rope to tie her to a post. He was too rough ever to be handsome. Everything about his face was hard angles and cruel lines, but his eyes were far scarier than anything else. They weren't only dead; they were evil. Those eyes told her that he liked to hurt people. Got off on it. Once he was done, he warned harshly, "Move and you're dead."

She took the threat seriously and remained still. The men got beers and cheered each other on, obviously proud they'd destroyed every single thing she'd ever worked hard for. Her dreams. Her everything. But now she realized all of that was nothing compared to the baby she was desperate to keep safe. To keep far away from the evil creeping into this room.

Rhett...

He'd come. He had to find her.

Minutes turned into hours. And soon, she didn't even know how much time had gone by. The men were waiting. That much she could tell. Waiting and restless, and all the while, she remained in the corner, sitting there like a target ready to die. She drew in a long, deep breath and shut her eyes. This couldn't be happening. This couldn't be real. She was finally tasting happiness with Rhett, but maybe that's all fate would give her. She could hear the men still talking, planning what to do with her. She opened her eyes and scanned her surroundings, looking for any way out.

With a sinking stomach, she realized there simply wasn't one. They'd shoot her the second she stood up.

"What the fuck is this?"

She jerked at the nearness of the frigid low voice. She kept her head down as roughed-up boots with dirty jeans came into view.

Her attacker responded from his spot on the couch in the sitting area of the garage. "She came up on us at the bar. Wasn't sure what the boss wanted to do with her. Figure it best to bring her back here."

"Wrong," the guy snapped. "You should have left her to burn in the bar. Why the fuck would you bring her here?"

"We didn't have time to think it through," her attacker growled. "We acted and grabbed her. There are security cameras there. Killing her was too risky."

There was a long pause. Then, "The boss isn't gonna like this."

The men around Kinsley shifted on their feet.

Kinsley's hand went straight to her belly. She knew she had to run, get away. Because, suddenly, it wasn't *if* she was going to die, but *when*. A cold sweat washed over her, fear pumping her heart until her head swam.

Rhett…

Her hand pressed tighter against her belly… *Oh, little one…*

Her family, her friends, her life, it was all flashing through her mind. She wasn't ready to say goodbye. Nowhere near ready.

A pair of shoes clicked against the cement floor. Each *click* deepened her breath a little bit more. Until the man stopped in front of her. The power emanating off him had her lifting her head even though she told herself that she shouldn't look. Her eyes met the dark stormy depths of his, and she knew there was no getting out of there. The coldness there, the lack of humanity, made her shiver.

Tears welled up in her eyes before she forced herself to blink them away, not wanting to show weakness. Never. Not in front of this killer.

The man finally looked at her attacker with his gun aimed at her. "Do you realize who this is?"

Her captor shifted nervously on his feet. "We had no choice but to bring her."

"You most definitely did have a choice," he countered. "You should have put a bullet through her head and left her there."

Kinsley froze at the sheer callousness that dripped from his voice. She'd never really believed in evil people. She'd always thought that people just made bad choices. But here, with these men, who knew she was pregnant and yet were still speaking about killing her like she was some spider on the wall, she believed evil was very real and present in this room.

She stared into his cold, dark eyes that made her want to flee. Everything about him from his worn black leather vest with the WILD DOGS logo on it, to the way his thin lips dipped down, screamed of danger. "Please don't do this. I'm pregnant." That had to make someone stop.

The man didn't even flinch. Nothing showed on his face, except pure boredom.

Two men strode up and stopped behind him, assault rifles in their hands. They were like soldiers ready to go to war, but this wasn't war, she wanted to scream at them.

She'd never wanted any part of this. She wanted to go home to Rhett and her family and friends. To her life. A life that was not perfect and was full of flaws, but it was most certainly hers. She wanted more time…

The leader eventually broke the heavy silence. "Bringing her here was fucking stupid." He shoved his hand into his pocket. "Did you not think about how they will move the earth to find her?"

They meaning Rhett, Boone, and her father. And they would. They would stop at nothing. But she knew there was more at stake here than just her own life and the life of her child's. Rhett would never forgive himself. He'd never recover. So many lives ruined, all because of the greed of these scumbags.

"They've got the security cameras," the guy on her right said. "We couldn't kill her there."

"Again, you could have, and you should have." The leader turned around and Kinsley heard a telling *click*. "I'm growing very tired of fixing your sloppy mistakes." He turned around and fired two shots, killing both her attacker and the guy on her other side.

Kinsley threw her hands over her ears, the *bang* near deafening, as she stared into her attacker's dead eyes while blood poured out of his wound. The click of a gun being cocked again lifted her eyes. She scrambled back, the wall stopping her from getting anywhere. "No," she barely managed. "No. Please." She'd nearly had it all. Everything she ever wanted.

Love, happiness, family, it'd all been right there, ready for her to grab it.

No, it couldn't end this way. She wanted the husband, the family home filled with memories, the big dinners celebrating people and achievements. She wanted to grow old with someone. There was so much more she wanted to do.

And yet...*and yet*...the man squared his shoulders and took aim. Kinsley shut her eyes, holding on to her belly. *I love you.*

Chapter 18

Rhett sat next to Boone in the van, with Asher on the other side, wearing full tactical gear. They'd joined the Whitby Falls SWAT team after getting a location from King. This was their fight, and luckily the Whitby Falls chief understood that and allowed them to assist. Rhett had to give it to the Whitby Falls PD—they got their SWAT team assembled and in the van in thirty minutes. But those thirty minutes had felt like hours, and every minute was more daunting than the last. He needed Kinsley safe in his arms, nothing but that. And while the address that King gave Rhett could still have been fictitious, Rhett oddly believed him. The last thing King needed was word that he'd taken out a biker gang to clear away the competition. King appeared to want money, not a war, and Rhett hoped his instincts to push King had set them on the right path.

"We're going to get her back."

Rhett glanced up, finding Boone's determined gaze on him.

"And when we do," Boone added, "I think you're gonna need this." He offered him a card in a brown envelope.

Rhett took the card. "What is it?"

Boone gave a soft smile. "To be honest, I don't really know. It wasn't mine to open when I received it. You'll have to tell me once you open it."

Rhett glanced down at the envelope, which was slightly weighted. The van hit a pothole, and Rhett hurried to slip the envelope into his cargo pants, zipping up the pocket.

The men across from Rhett suddenly sat up a little straighter, shifting their clothes and bulletproof vests and righting their helmets. They were close.

Not even a second later, the van pulled up to a large square warehouse. On the outside, there were no distinguishing features, nothing telling anyone what lay inside. Probably just how the Wild Dogs wanted it. Rhett let the Whitby team exit first and lead the way inside. They moved as a highly trained unit, and Rhett didn't want to interfere with that.

In seconds, they blew out the door and triggered the alarm. The team rushed forward, and mere moments after that, the flash grenades were launched and immediately followed by rapid gunfire. With Boone behind Rhett and Asher at the rear, guarding the back, Rhett took the hallway on the left lined with offices. Each one he passed was empty. They'd studied the building's layout, and Rhett wanted this hallway. Logic told him they'd keep Kinsley as far away from the main entrance as possible.

The gunfire got louder and closer together as Rhett closed in on a doorway at the end of the hall, which led into the open space at the back of the warehouse. Rhett burst into the room, his assault weapon trained forward. He scanned the room in a quick sweep. No one noticed their arrival, every man there focused on the SWAT team putting them under heavy fire.

Rhett moved then and said a silent prayer for their safety as he looked for Kinsley. A pulsating energy filled the room, like a beacon, calling him forward. She was there; all he had to do was find her.

A man suddenly jumped out from behind a cement post, and Rhett fired, the threat immediately removed. The gunfire became nearly deafening, but he kept on, needing to get to her. To keep her safe—to keep them both safe—like he'd promised.

Two more men stormed from the back, their guns spitting bullets. Rhett stayed behind the beam, keeping cover. He caught sight of Boone, hiding behind a large metal barrel. He held up his fingers and counted down: 3, 2, 1. Rhett spun and fired, taking out the first threat while Boone took out the other.

Rhett moved quickly, his gaze trained ahead of him, knowing that he had Boone and Asher at his back.

As he passed a sports car, his gaze flicked left. There, in the corner, Kinsley sat with her head down, her hands covering her ears. Everything stopped for him then. Rhett wasn't thinking at that point. He sprinted for her then slid on his knees until he had his hands on her. Alive…She was alive.

She jerked her head up, teary eyes wide with surprise and fear.

"Hold on to me," he told her.

"I can't," she gasped.

He began to pull her away when he caught sight of the rope binding her wrists. He grabbed his knife from his leg and cut her free then helped her to her feet. "Stay close."

"Yes, yes," she cried, her legs barely supporting her.

Boone was there a second later. Once he was by their side, Boone spun around quickly, taking the front, his weapon ready to keep her safe. Rhett positioned himself beside Kinsley, keeping his attention on their left, and Asher closed in and took the back. He fired off two rounds, and Rhett knew that whatever threat was coming for them was now gone.

With a quick look ahead, Rhett saw three SWAT officers taking up position near the door they'd entered, clearing a path out. With a guy now on Rhett's other side providing cover, Rhett grabbed Kinsley's arm, keeping her close, and placed a hand on her head, covering her body with his as much as possible. Bullets rained down, and the noise ricocheted, making it impossible to identify where the gunfire came from.

On the way to the door, his foot slipped on blood, and he held Kinsley tighter, hoping she hadn't seen the river of death on the floor. Boone went out the door first, with a SWAT officer in front. The door was right there, so damn close. Gunfire burst into the hallway. Instinctively, Rhett pushed Kinsley down and shielded her with his body.

When the noise silenced, he had her up again and moving swiftly toward the door. She didn't belong in the middle of a gunfight. She was too pure. And this was too raw. Too real. His two worlds were meshing, and he fought to pull them apart.

Once outside, Rhett squinted against the sunny day, quickly guiding Kinsley toward safety. The van doors were still open. Boone stopped just before the doors, providing more cover. Rhett picked her up by the hips and hoisted her into the van, blocking her body with his. He lay over her until Asher and Boone jumped in the van, and the SWAT officer yelled, "Go!" He slammed the doors shut.

The van took off, squealing out of the parking lot. Rhett knew another van would arrive any minute to replace this one. But nothing else mattered except the woman lying next to him.

"Kinsley," he said, helping her to sit. Her ashen face and dull eyes made his chest ache, and she shook violently. "Blanket," he said to no one in particular, rubbing her arms, knowing exactly what she needed right now.

He wasn't even sure who handed him the blanket. He simply wrapped it around her and brought her into his arms, holding her against his chest. Shock was a very real thing that happened to a body. Rhett had seen people take hours to come out of it. Boone's hand came down on her shoulder, and Rhett dropped his head into her neck on the other side.

Safe. He'd almost lost her. He held on tighter, feeling her trembles get harder as a sob broke free.

"That's it. Don't hold it in," he told her.

"Rhett," she finally cried.

He dropped a kiss on her neck, feeling her fierce shudders beneath his mouth. "Yeah, darlin', I'm here."

"Don't let go."

He locked his arms around her. "I never will."

* * *

Four hours later, Kinsley felt a little more like herself again. She had given her report, cried enough not to have any tears left, and hugged everyone as much as she could. All her family and friends had been at Rhett's house, and no one left until she finally believed she was safe. Her captor, their leader, and everyone else was dead. The SWAT team came out a little bloodied, a couple with gunshot wounds, but alive, and they'd all go home tonight, and from what she learned, so would Cameron.

She thought she should feel happy now, but she couldn't find happiness anywhere, only sadness that any of this had happened at all. She had seen her life flash before her eyes. Had Rhett,

Boone, and the others stormed the warehouse even two seconds later, she would have been dead. Now, with life giving her this second chance, she realized she couldn't waste it. She couldn't simply wait and wait and wait, because in a snap, it could all be over, just like that.

She had to live. Fully. Authentically.

And that's why when Rhett asked her if she wanted to go home, she asked him to bring her somewhere else instead. Now, in her favorite place on top of the summit, staring up at the stars above, with a blanket resting on her lap, she couldn't hold off any longer. "Rhett, I…"

He glanced sideways and took her hand. "Can't keep loving me the way you've been loving me."

Surprised he got that so right, she drew in a long breath, emotion tightening her throat. "No, I can't, and I'm sorry for that." She wanted a commitment, and she wanted forever with someone.

"Damn, Kinsley, never be sorry. Not for anything." He slowly shook his head, his mouth thinning before he addressed her. "You've been so loyal and good to me. More than anyone ever has."

Her heart leapt up in her throat; tears welled in her eyes. "No matter what, even if there isn't an *us*, we're going to be okay. Our baby will be okay. We're going to make all this work."

He hesitated then leveled those warm eyes at her. "What do you need for there to be an *us*?"

"I need to hear that I'm loved," she said, a tear slipping down her cheek before she wiped it away with her mitten-covered hand. "I want a house for my family to grow in. I want to grow old with someone. I want a husband. I want forever. I want it all."

Unfamiliar softness reached his expression and his voice. "You deserve all those things. Every single one of them." His gaze bore into hers, the world fading away, the cold wind on her cheeks barely there now. "I don't know why you love me the way you do," he added gently. "Why you see the good in me and reach to bring it out. I never thought I needed anyone, but when I thought I was going to lose you, I realized my world cannot exist without you."

"Rhett," she barely managed.

A long pause. "I think you need to see this." He reached into his jacket pocket then and pulled out a card. She immediately knew what it was, had seen similar ones many times in her life. It was one of her grandmother's handmade cards.

With shaky hands, she opened it, and her breath hitched at the familiar handwriting.

Dear Kinsley's future husband,

I'm guessing you must be a spectacular man if my Kinsley has picked you. But as her grandmother, I thought I should tell you something you should know about her. You'll never meet anyone more loyal, but if you break that loyalty, you'll lose her forever. Don't mess this up! She needs hugs even if she tells you she doesn't want one. Please hug her all the time, real tight. Those are her favorite. She's got really soft spots on her soul, even if she doesn't show them often. Protect those soft spots. Always! Sometimes, she'll need you to love her extra hard when she remembers her mother and gets sad about that. Remind her the best people are here with her, and that's all that matters. Nothing and no one else but that. She loves without restraint, without fear, and is brave enough to fight for what her heart wants. Since you're her guy, the man her heart wants, always remember that she needs that love back.

Take care of my girl,

Margie

Kinsley choked on a sob, blurry eyed. "I had no idea that my grandma wrote this letter."

Rhett took the letter back, setting it beside him. "I'm glad she did. Sometimes"—he chuckled—"most times, it's good to hear it straight. It also only confirmed that this is exactly what I should do…"

She felt something in her hand and she looked down, slowly opening it. Her vision suddenly became even blurrier as she stared at her grandmother's engagement ring. "Is this…"

"Your grandmother's ring."

She blinked. "I don't understand. I thought the ring was buried with her." Only now that she thought about it, she hadn't seen her grandmother wear the ring in her later years.

"Your grandmother gave the ring and the card to Boone for safekeeping." Rhett hesitated then added, "Well, I'm not exactly sure he even knew what was in the envelope. Only that he was supposed to give it to the man who wanted to marry you."

"Wait…are you…" Her heart exploding, words just *gone*.

He took the ring then turned her hand around. "Yes, Kinsley. I want us. A family. I want you forever."

Her breath hitched, tears falling.

"I love you, Kinsley. Will you marry me?"

She stared at him, her fingers and feet tingling, her voice absent.

Silence settled in for so long that his mouth twitched. "I know I'm not great at all of this," he said, "but usually there's a response at this point, isn't there?"

She forced her voice to work. "I have envisioned this moment so many times. Dreamed of it, really. But now I'm actually wondering if maybe I died in that chop shop and I've gone to heaven. Everything you just said is too good, too perfect. It can't be real."

He took her finger and slid the ring on. It was a perfect fit. Whenever her grandmother let her try on this ring, it hung off her finger. She both laughed and cried when the ring settled into place. "Does that feel real?" he asked.

"Yes, but still too perfect," she said. "I need something…something *more* to show me this is real." She wanted him—no, *needed* him—but Rhett had been worried and scared, and she knew he'd be too gentle, too soft. She didn't want that. Not now. Not when she needed to believe that all this was actually happening.

A frown tugged on his mouth. "You're hurt."

She shook her head. "My hip is tender from landing on it, but otherwise, I'm fine."

He pulled back. "Today was traumatic." He jumped off the truck, reaching for her waist. "I'll take you home, and we can discuss this more there."

She grabbed his arms, stopping him. "Rhett. Today was traumatic. Horrible for the both of us, but I won't let myself change because of what they did." She cupped his face. "I want this. I want you. Show me that what you're telling me, that I have all of you, is real. I don't want to be sad. Make me feel better in the way that only you do."

His warm smile was like a hot bath washing over her. "All right, Kinsley." He stroked her tears away. "And this, does this feel real?"

"Definitely too sweet for Rhett West," she whispered. "I'm still not convinced."

A sexy smile crossed his face. "Hmm, is that so? Then how about this?" He closed the distance between them, and with his hands on her face, he sealed his mouth across hers in a kiss that seemed to never end. "Does that feel real?" he asked when he broke away.

She saw the glint in his eyes. "Too damn good…I've got to still be dreaming, better keep trying."

"I better do better then." He scooped her up in his arms. In seconds, he had them in his truck, sliding her against the bench seating in the back. Standing by the door, he grabbed her boots and yanked them off, careful of her hip and the bruise already there. In the next moment, her maternity jeggings were also off. His coat followed, and he quickly unzipped his jeans. With that sexy grin in place, he climbed in while she scooted to the other side. He shut the door behind him and locked it before hovering over her. "How about now? You're half naked in the back seat with your teenage crush. Real enough?"

"No," she managed, wildfire spreading through her veins. "You're far too hot. I must be dreaming."

He chuckled then dropped his head to hers. He kissed her long and slow, savoring every part of her mouth. Nothing lay between them; she felt that now. The barriers separating them had blown apart. Something had changed when she was missing. Something in Rhett. The very thing she'd hoped would happen...he let her in, past the guarded soldier to the young guy she remembered. And for the very first time, Rhett kissed her without restraint and with pure love. His hand slowly dipped between her legs and he groaned when he found her wet and ready for him.

His head lifted to watch her as the tip of his cock found her slick heat. "How about now, Kinsley?" he asked huskily, his pupils dark with lust.

Before she could answer him, he entered her in one swift stroke. Her chin angled as hot pleasure swept over her. "Real," she rasped. "God, yes, so real." She slid her hands over his corded neck as he began pumping his hips, slow and long, just how she liked it.

"Look at me."

She hadn't realized she'd shut her eyes. When she opened them and gazed into his eyes, she instantly lost herself in their depths. Once dark and guarded, his eyes were now soft and welcoming, showing her something he'd never shown anyone. His vulnerable spots.

His hand slid down to her uninjured hip, pinning her, while he rocked harder into her, never looking away. He gave her something he hadn't given anyone—intimacy—and she felt every wall she'd put up to protect herself suddenly fall.

She loved him. He loved her. End of story.

But their story *would* continue, and she relished that knowledge. Dreams came true with Rhett, and as his throaty moans brushed over her, with every thrust, the pleasure grew higher and higher until there was no controlling where he took her.

She came in a powerful hot rush of pleasure, and he followed her.

A long moment passed while she slowly returned to her

body and her mind, feeling like, tonight, they'd won. When she opened her eyes, she found Rhett staring at her openly, adoringly. "I love you, Kinsley. Will you marry me?"

"I love you, too." The words she'd longed to say left her mouth in a hurried whisper. She cupped his face, breathless. "Yes, I'll marry you."

And the smile he gave her, that smile right there, so blinding and true, was better than any fantasy she'd ever had.

Chapter 19

A week later, Rhett held Kinsley's mitten-covered hand as they strolled down Main Street, the snow blessedly giving the town a break. The last three days they'd gotten more than three feet, and most businesses had been closed, with everything reopening only today. Except for one. Kinsley's hand tightened around his as they walked toward her bar, where wood boarded up the door and the windows. While Josh had been located yesterday a couple towns over and arrested, with no one having any doubt the charges would stick, Rhett knew that news wouldn't give Kinsley closure. She needed her bar to reopen to put all this behind her. He'd seen the reports. Fortunately, the fire department had managed get the fire under control quickly. The only damage had been to the interior of the main bar. The building had been deemed structurally sound, allowing for Remy's magic shop and Peyton's lingerie store to reopen. "We'll rebuild," he said to her.

Kinsley offered him a warm smile, her big blue eyes standing out against her white beanie and dark hair. "We will." She stopped by the door and glanced up at the half-burned sign. "Do you believe in fate?"

"You know I don't," he said. "I make my own fate."

"I wondered if your opinion on that changed after all this," she said, finally setting those gorgeous eyes on him.

"Because we're together, you mean?"

She slowly nodded her head, stepping closer until her sweet belly pressed against him. "It's like the universe gave us absolutely no choice but to be together." Her smile warmed her eyes further and melted something hard in his chest. "Have a one-night stand? No, still not together. Okay, here throw in a baby. Still fighting it? Bring danger, make you face what you feel. Do you think we had any choice at all in any of this?"

He brushed his leather-covered finger across her rosy cheek. "Do I think I had any choice in this once you set your sights on me?" His mouth twitched. "No. You are a force, Kinsley, warm as you are bold. If you really wanted me, I don't think there was a damn thing I could have done to stop that or you."

She laughed, leaning into his touch. "You think I have more control over my life than fate?"

"Absolutely," he said immediately. "Fate would look you in the eye and run away with its tail tucked between its legs."

"I'm that powerful, huh?"

Cars drove by on the road, splashing up slush. Luckily the snowbanks kept them clean. "Your soul is your superpower." He dipped his chin and brushed his mouth across hers. "And I'd die to protect it."

She reached up to finish the kiss, and he cupped her face, knowing that whatever life was before Kinsley told him she was pregnant, it wouldn't be the same life going forward now. It'd be better. She had even brought him back closer to his family. Mom called every day now to check in. Somehow, she'd broken through those walls Rhett didn't even know were there. And most important, she reminded him what happiness felt like.

He liked it. He refused to ever let her go.

With a final press of his lips, he backed away, "Thank you for being here with me today."

"I wouldn't be anywhere else." She smiled. "And say it again, you know…those three little words."

He chuckled. "I love you."

"Yep, that's them." She laughed and he took her hand again as they continued walking down the road, away from the past and moving into the future. One he'd get right. No more excuses. No more uncertainty.

When they reached the white-steepled church, he looked up the steps and exhaled deeply.

"Oh, there's the girls."

Rhett glanced across the street at the coffee shop, finding Peyton and Remy waving at them from the doorway. He turned to Kinsley again as she said, "I'm going to go stuff my face with hot chocolate and cookies." She leaned in to give him a quick kiss. "Meet me there, okay?"

He nodded.

She took a couple of steps before he snatched her hand again, pulling her back to him. "Hey!" she squealed. "Missing me already?"

"Always." He placed a harder kiss on her lips, and he knew it would be his life's mission to put that smile she gave him on her face every day. "I'll see you soon," he told her.

"You will." She walked away, finding a space in the snow-banks, then quickly crossing the street between cars. She hugged

Remy and Peyton before she gave Rhett a final wave and entered the coffee shop.

Rhett turned to the church and trotted up the steps. When he went inside, he found the sanctuary quiet, all the pews empty except for one woman sitting in the front row. He turned left, heading down the stairs and into the basement, where he stopped in front of the first door.

"Dr. Adams? I'm Rhett West."

Standing in the doorway of the small meeting room, Rhett took in the group of five men and two women sitting in chairs in a circle. A man with salt-and-pepper hair nodded and waved him forward. "Rhett, we're glad to have you." Dr. Adams gestured to the one empty chair across from him. "Please, come sit."

His heart thundered as he took his seat, unable to look anyone in the face. Maybe he knew some of them. Maybe he didn't. But right now, he couldn't do more than sit down and keep his gaze fixated on the doctor.

Dr. Adams said, "Everyone, this is Rhett. Let's welcome him."

"Welcome, Rhett," the group said.

Rhett swallowed and his gaze unwillingly shifted around the room to the strangers he found. He looked from face to face, recognizing the unrest he once saw in his own eyes. A pain that slowly had begun to fade. Because of Kinsley. She had made that happen, and he would never forget that. "Good to be here," he told the group.

Dr. Adams smiled, his warm brown eyes creasing. "Listen, Rhett, we're not going to ask anything of you. You don't need to talk, unless you want to and you're ready. You're in good company here with people who aren't great at talking about the shit going on in their heads. Isn't he?" he asked the crowd.

Soft laughter and nods followed.

Dr. Adams turned back to Rhett. "The military gives you the tools to stay alive, to protect and defend, but they don't train you to return to civilian life. And that's what we're all trying to do here. We're figuring out how in the hell we go from being trained killers to people with everyday jobs and family that aren't constantly at the ready for a firefight. All right?"

"Yeah," Rhett said. "Thank you."

He unzipped his coat and took off his gloves as Dr. Adams said, "Gerry, why don't you get us started. Anything new you want to talk about?"

Gerry was a big guy. All muscle. Rhett was pretty sure he'd seen him at Theo's a few times. "The nightmares are back. They're...drowning me." His voice lowered and his shoulders curled, making him look small. "Just so goddamn real."

Dr. Adams smiled gently. "Nightmares are sometimes the brain reliving trauma, trying to heal through that pain."

Gerry nodded, and his voice cracked when he added, "My wife won't sleep with me anymore." He lifted his head, tears in his eyes. "The screaming. She can't take it."

Rhett released a breath and stared at Gerry, feeling like they had once been the same man. He understood that pain in Gerry's face. And for the first time, in a very long time, Rhett felt like he was exactly where he was supposed to be.

One day at a time. And eventually, he'd finally talk about those nightmares, not simply survive them. For Kinsley. For their child. And for himself. Because he had only one mission now—to love her right. Forever.

Epilogue

One year later…

The crowd on the dance floor had their hands up, moving to the beat of the rock song that the live band played. Behind the bar, Kinsley looked around at the new Whiskey Blues. It took two months to get the place reopened, and as much as she missed the old bar, she loved this new one too. Besides, all she had to do was glance over her shoulder at the photograph of her inner circle all sitting at the bar to remember what this placed used to look like. This time, she'd redesigned the bar with more of a rustic sexy feel, with big wooden beams running across the roof, wrought iron fixtures, and soft lighting.

"Ladies and gentlemen," the singer called as the crowd applauded. "Let's get the bride and groom out here for their first dance."

Kinsley smiled, sensing Rhett watching her. She found him near the doorway, looking damn near mouthwatering in his suit and a black tie. Her heart still fluttered when he smiled at her.

After months of therapy, his nightmares had gone away and something else had replaced them...*peace*. An obvious weight had slowly dropped off Rhett's shoulders. And the rest, well most of that had disappeared the moment that both their lives changed forever. Leo, their little boy, bounced in Rhett's arms, waving his chubby arms up and down, smiling from ear to ear. Baby blue noise-canceling headphones covered his ears. He looked nearly identical to his father, same dark hair, same nose, but he had the Knights' signature blue eyes.

The commotion on the dance floor caught her eye as everyone moved off to the side. Her father, dressed in a dark gray suit and smoky blue tie, held his hand out to his new wife, who wore a gorgeous vintage wedding dress. Dad and Maria had just gotten married outside Boone's lake house. Tonight, they were celebrating their love, and Kinsley's heart nearly exploded with happiness.

She replaced the vodka bottle behind the bar then smiled at Benji, touching his arm. "Thanks again for holding down the fort tonight."

He grinned. "You know I wouldn't have missed this celebration."

"Of course he wouldn't have—I'm here," Lola joked, grabbing a couple beers then heading back toward the end of the bar.

Kinsley laughed. Just another day at Whiskey Blues. She made her way around the bar and approached Rhett. He was talking to Boone, but his eyes followed her with every step, warming as she got closer. The rings around her finger were a weight she enjoyed, a reminder that three months before Leo came into his world, they were married on the beach at Rhett's house. The party had been there too. Nothing fancy, but beautiful under a blanket of stars. All the important people were there. Friends, family, everyone who mattered. Her heart warmed as Leo bounced faster, and all but leapt into her arms when she closed in on him. "I missed you too, sweetie," she told him before attacking his little neck with kisses.

His laughter washed over her, the best sound she'd ever heard.

When she leaned away, Rhett caught her chin. "My turn." His smile heated before he dropped his mouth to hers.

"Not only is your kid here, but so are others."

Rhett chuckled against her lips, before pulling away and saying to Boone, "My son is gonna know how to love a woman right."

Boone returned the smile and cupped Rhett's shoulder. "Ah, Rhett West lessons. Never thought that'd actually be a good thing."

Rhett barked a loud laugh. "You and me both, brother."

Peyton and Remy came over then, a wineglass in Peyton's hand. She gave it to Kinsley as Asher offered Rhett a beer. Peyton wobbled into Boone's arms, and his hand went to her round belly. She was due any day now. Asher threw an arm around Remy, kissing her forehead. Remy still had five months to go. Kinsley inhaled deeply, nearly smelling the beauty of all the love in this room. She slid her arm around Rhett's waist, leaning her head into him, watching her father smiling down at his new wife. "I've never seen him look this happy," she said.

"Me neither." Boone smiled. "It's a good day."

"So what now?" Remy asked.

"With what?" Peyton asked.

"With all of us," Remy explained, glancing between everyone. "It's been a wild ride to get us here."

Asher added with a knowing look, "That might be the understatement of the decade."

Rhett chuckled. "I, for one, am good with the current adventure. Less danger. More visits to the park. Quiet days and nights."

Remy barked a laugh and said, "God, look at you, Rhett West, being all domesticated."

Rhett winked at her. "I like it too."

"Well," Remy said. "I guess this should just prove to all of you how much my nana's spells really do work. Look how happy everyone is."

Asher kissed her forehead. "No one doubts you, Remy. Not ever."

Everyone gave her that. Remy's smile spoke of love and happiness, and sometimes that's all that mattered.

Kinsley glanced around at her family, her found family, and everyone in the town that had come out to share in the happiness of her father. "You know what I want?" Everyone looked at her. "Just this. Us. Happy like this forever."

Soft smiles greeted hers.

Rhett's being the gentlest, as he turned her into his arms, keeping Leo between them. "If anyone can make that happen, Kinsley, it's you."

Boone raised his glass. "To this. To us. Forever."

Rhett's eyes bore into hers, his mouth dropping to hers. "To this. To us. Forever."

She reached for the kiss. "To this. To us. Forever."

Did you miss the first book in the Dangerous Love series? Read on to see how it all started with Peyton and Boone's story in *Naughty Stranger*.

Chapter 1

Detective Boone Knight was an ass man.

Or he had been until Peyton Kerr—the woman currently standing by the window of her lingerie shop, Uptown Girl—rolled into town a month ago and kissed the hell out of him. After that, he'd become an entire body man. Every inch of Peyton drew his attention and brought *him* to full attention.

A surprise, even to him.

Ever since his marriage ended two years ago, he'd preferred his relationships be fleeting. He had no intention of getting married again. He'd tried the marriage thing and failed epically, no need for a repeat. But he wanted this five-foot-five woman with the soulful hazel eyes, long blond hair, and perfectly curved body in his bed—and he'd already figured that one time probably wouldn't be enough. But since that one *hot* kiss, she'd done her best to stay clear of him, when all he wanted to do was re-create that moment.

Not that he understood her distance. She *wanted* him close. He saw her responding interest in the way her gaze ate him up. Christ, he swore he could damn near smell her pheromones running wild when he stood next to her.

"Focusing on the dead might be better than the living at the moment."

Boone's brain snapped back to its proper position in his head. He glanced at his lifelong friend and fellow detective, Rhett West. Dark haired and dark eyed, Rhett had always been an imposing guy, even as a kid. "The scenery is distracting," Boone admitted.

Rhett shook his head with a laugh. "You're such a fucking goner."

Yeah, Boone was, and he knew it. Peyton had gotten into his head, and by all appearances, she wasn't even trying. That one kiss had played on his mind constantly. He wanted *more*.

He also became aware of the crowd outside being forced off the sidewalk by the yellow tape. Even from where he stood, he saw the concern on the faces he recognized outside. People he knew growing up. His high school principal was there. The lady who owned the flower shop a few blocks down. Even the receptionist from the doctor's office was in the crowd.

Stoney Creek was a small town. Everyone knew each other. And from experience, Boone knew that as soon as word got out that there was a murder, calls would start coming in about neighbors, old boyfriends, and enemies ratting each other out. But he also knew fear would run rampant in the town he loved and served to protect.

Reminding himself of the job he needed to do, he gave Peyton one last look as she rubbed Kinsley's back. His sister was sitting on the floor next to Peyton. Her head was over a bucket, her long chocolate-brown hair hanging over the sides. All of which didn't surprise him. His baby sister had a weak stomach on the best of days. "Catch me up," he said to Rhett.

"Peyton opened the shop this morning. Kinsley was with her," Rhett reported. "That's when they found the body."

Boone turned his attention to the matter at hand. A few inches away from his boots lay a blond woman in a pool of her own blood. She looked in her mid-twenties, and by her body position, Boone suspected she had no idea the shot was coming. He couldn't see any defensive wounds on her hands. Her clothes were all in place, making him believe the murder wasn't sexually motivated.

Doing what he did best, he surveyed the scene. The lingerie shop was narrow and long and set into one of the historic buildings on Main Street. The walls were painted hot pink, with blood spatter now. In the front of the store was a sales counter and white tables set out with the lacy garments, but the victim lay in the back storage room, where a small desk sat with a computer monitor on top. The back building door was closed, and nothing seemed out of place, except for the deceased woman.

Behind the woman, the crime scene technicians were already processing the murder. "First thoughts?" Boone asked no one in particular.

"I'd say it's a robbery gone wrong," the third member of their rat pack growing up, Detective Asher Sullivan, said as he walked in through the back door from the parking lot with latex gloves on his hands. His blond hair was styled and gelled, and his eyes were a bright green.

They'd all become best friends in grade school—the three troublemakers back then, who all ended up in law enforcement one way or another, and now tended to work together often.

Asher stopped near the body and gestured at the safe not far from the victim. "Broken into and emptied."

Boone squatted down, getting closer to the woman's lifeless body. He kept his hands on his thighs, careful not to touch her, knowing full well if he did even with gloves, the medical examiner would serve him up for dinner. "A shot to the back of the head doesn't shout robbery." No, a shot where the victim wasn't looking at the killer typically meant the shooter felt guilt, not wanting to look at the victim when the life faded from her eyes.

Rhett peered into the safe, then turned around. "Why hit a lingerie shop? The petty cash can't be worth killing someone over."

Boone agreed with a firm nod. He'd moved to New York City in his twenties and worked for the New York City PD for ten years. In those years, he'd seen crimes in the city that would always haunt him. A small, coastal Maine town like Stoney Creek didn't have the gang violence or murders like New York City. Murders were few and far between here, with most being domestic, or resulting from organized crime in surrounding areas. Rapes were even less common. Minor robberies, thefts, and burglaries tended to be what Boone spent his days investigating. Which was a far cry from his time in the NYPD. The blood, the cruelty, the hate—Boone had seen enough death to last him a lifetime. He straightened, shoving his hands into his pockets. "And why hit this shop with a busy club next door?" Kinsley's jazz club, Whiskey Blues, *would* have cash on hand, and a lot of it, compared to what the lingerie shop had.

Asher made a note on his pad, then clicked his pen closed. "I agree. Something about this one feels odd."

Anything *odd* was never a good thing, and the tension spilling out from Rhett and Asher mirrored what Boone felt too.

The back door didn't appear broken into, but the residents in Stoney Creek didn't lock their doors. Boone couldn't pinpoint what bothered him about what he was seeing here, but something made his skin crawl. And *that* sensation he trusted, telling him there was more going on here than first appearances.

He parted his lips to say as such, when a high voice snapped, "Stop right where you are." Marissa, the five-foot-one, short-haired brunette fireball medical examiner entered the back room. "You better not have touched a single thing."

With a smirk, Boone leaned against the doorframe, folding his arms. Marissa believed in protocol with a capital *P*. Her compulsive disorder had served her well and made her one hell of an ME.

"Is this still enough for you?" Rhett mused, grinning from ear to ear.

She studied him, her thin lips pinching tight. "Your mouth is moving, so no."

Rhett laughed softly.

Marissa placed her bag down near Boone, then waved them out of the back room. "Get gone." She believed in spirts, in energies, and she needed quiet when she worked to allow the victims to speak to her.

Boone never questioned her method, no matter that more than once he questioned her sanity. Marissa never missed a damn thing, and he'd seen her attention to detail send criminals to jail. "You'll be in touch when you have your findings?"

"Yeah. Yeah." Marissa flicked her hand at him again, solely focused on the victim now.

Boone went to turn away, when the air in the room shifted

slightly, becoming thicker, harder to inhale. It came as no surprise after a quick look back, he found Peyton staring at him. When they met that first night in the club, he'd been curious about the gorgeous woman who'd walked through the doors looking a little lost and edgy. But lately, for reasons he couldn't figure out, his curiosity had gone from mild to hard-core all too quickly. She had this hold over him he couldn't explain, even to himself.

Needing answers that only she could give him, Boone headed Peyton's way. She wasn't the typical blond bombshell. There was an undeniable softness about her. A sweetness, even. Her long hair resembled the color of honey, and his fingers twitched to tangle in their strands. But the ghosts in the depths of her rich hazel eyes were what held him tight. Heartbreak was a pain he understood. And any sort of sadness on her pretty face made him damn near clamor to make her smile.

When he finally reached her, he studied her calmness, surprised she didn't look more rattled at finding a woman murdered in her shop this morning. "All right?" he asked.

Peyton's pink lips parted.

"Hell no, I'm not all right," his sister snapped, still sitting on the floor, head still in the bucket. "I just barfed my brains out." She finally lifted her head, soft eyes meeting Boone's. Her skin went sheet white and she smacked her hand over her mouth. "Nope. Not ready to talk yet. It'll happen again."

Peyton knelt next to Kinsley, rubbing her back, and said in a soothing voice, "Remember, think about something else—like that funny story you were telling me about earlier."

Boone watched the exchange closely. Every time he saw Peyton, she'd reveal a little more about herself. Which admittedly wasn't much. All he'd gotten out of her was that she lived in Seattle before moving to Stoney Creek. But right now, he'd bet money that in Seattle she'd been in the medical field. She had the *touch*.

A touch he desperately wanted.

When Kinsley gagged, he glanced at his baby sister, and his chest tightened. Last night, Kinsley had been working behind the bar at Whiskey Blues. Far too close to this murder for his liking. "You'll need to give your statements, but feel free to wait outside until then," he said.

"Thank fucking God." Kinsley stood up, white faced, her dark hair a wild mess, and beelined for the door. One foot outside, she looked back at him. "I don't know how you do this as a job. Seriously, Boone, it's gross."

He snorted at his sister. Law enforcement was in his blood. Boone was a cop, so were his father and grandfather. Kinsley seemed to have skipped that gene.

Peyton watched Kinsley leave. She finally turned to Boone and gave him the sweet playful smile she'd given him for a month now. "I guess I'll see you later." She turned.

Yeah, right.

Boone snagged her wrist gently and watched her closely. Like every time he got close, she inhaled sharply, an obvious shiver running down her spine. Her pretty eyes flicked to his. And held.

He was blinded by the heat between them, wanting desperately to give her everything she wanted and more. Because he wanted all those same things.

She finally blinked and those eyes became haunted. Instincts were 90 percent of being a good detective. Boone had honed his instincts through the ten years he'd spent with the NYPD—five as a beat cop and five more as a detective—and the last two years he'd worked in Stoney Creek as a detective. Those instincts told him now that *this* death had brought a memory of another death in her life. "Before you head out," he murmured, unable to let her wrist go, "were there any signs of a break-in when you came in this morning?"

She shook her head and licked her lips, taking a step toward him.

Damn, he ached to close the distance. He stared at that pretty mouth, and he realized he stroked the inside of her wrist, earning him another shiver. He couldn't fight his slight grin. If he could do that by a soft swipe of his finger, he knew he could make her shiver even deeper once he really touched her. Then he'd make her scream. His name, preferably.

But like a vault door slamming shut, she took a step back, all the heat vanishing from her expression. "The front door was locked, nothing seemed out of place. I don't know about the back door."

Boone gently released her wrist and shoved his hands into his pockets to ensure he didn't reach for her again. "Do you know the victim?"

Peyton shook her head. "I don't know her personally. I think she works for DX Industrial Cleaning. They always come after I close up, so I never meet the person they send."

"Do they have a key?" he asked.

She nodded. "Yeah, I gave them a copy when I first hired the company."

"That's good to know." He took a mental note to ensure someone talked with the cleaning agency before moving along. "Have you seen anyone strange hanging around the shop or anything like that?"

"No one. Nothing." She dropped her head and sighed before

addressing him again. "Do you think whoever did this will come back?"

Boone considered. He didn't want her to worry, but he never believed in sugarcoating things either. "Honestly, we won't know anything until we investigate further." Yeah, that was his bullshit standard cop answer, and she knew it, giving him a frown. To ease her worries, he added, "Right now, this looks like a botched robbery. It could very well be that, unless you have enemies—"

"God, of course I don't," she sputtered. "I don't even have people who dislike me. Seriously, my life in Seattle was boring as hell."

He doubted anything about Peyton Kerr was boring. "All right," he said, glancing back at the blood beneath the victim. "The crime techs should wrap up everything by tonight. I'll arrange for a cleaning crew to come in and get you back open tomorrow morning."

"Thank you," she said with clear gratitude and gave him that sexy smile again.

Christ. His cock twitched. What inappropriate timing. But that smile unraveled him. Every damn time.

"Come on, Peyton." Asher suddenly sidled up next to Boone. "Let's go make sure Kinsley isn't puking in your flowerpots. I'll drive you both back to her place and take your statements there."

"Great," Peyton said, all too calmly.

At that, Asher's brows furrowed. Boone understood perfectly. Her calmness wasn't typical and that raised questions that needed answering. While he was pretty sure that Peyton had nothing to do with this murder, there was a dead body in her shop, and her reactions were unusual.

She turned her smile onto Boone again. "Bye."

He nodded his goodbye, watching her carefully as she strode away, leaving a trail of her sugary-scented perfume. That scent. That ass. Those damn pretty eyes had him itching to slide one hand along her back and yank her tight to him, while the other tangled into her hair as he kissed her, until she went all soft against him. *All of which was entirely inappropriate.*

When she reached the door, she turned and gave him a loaded look. Then she was gone, with Asher walking behind her.

Peyton had secrets. Whether those secrets related to the murdered victim on the floor of her shop or not was something he would find out.

Boone hadn't had a cold case for over two years. He didn't intend to break his record now.

Acknowledgments

To my husband, my children, family, friends, and bestie, it's easy to write about love when there is so much love around me. Big thanks to my readers for your friendship and your support; my editor, Junessa, for taking on this book and helping me end this series perfectly; my agent, Jessica, for always being there; the kick-ass authors in my Sprint group for their endless advice and support; the entire Forever Yours team for all their hard work throughout the entire Dangerous Love series. Thank you.

About the Author

Stacey Kennedy is a *USA Today* bestselling author who writes contemporary romances full of heat, heart, and happily ever afters. She has published over fifty titles and her books have hit a number of online retailer bestseller lists.

Stacey lives with her husband and two children in southwestern Ontario—in a city that's just as charming as any of the small towns she creates. Most days, you'll find her enjoying the outdoors with her family or venturing into the forest with her horse, Priya. Stacey's just as happy curled up indoors, where she writes surrounded by her lazy dogs. She believes that sexy books about hot cowboys or alpha heroes can fix any bad day. But wine and chocolate help too.

You can learn more at:
StaceyKennedy.com
Twitter @Stacey_Kennedy
Facebook.com/AuthorStaceyKennedy

Don't miss the other books in the Dangerous Love series!

Now Available from Forever Yours

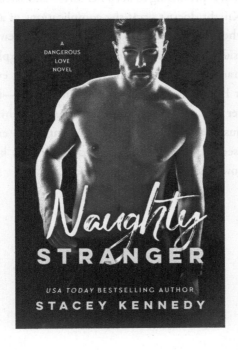

A
DANGEROUS
LOVE
NOVEL

Naughty
STRANGER

USA TODAY BESTSELLING AUTHOR
STACEY KENNEDY

**From *USA Today* bestselling author Stacey Kennedy comes a
thrilling, sexy romance about a woman in danger and a
small-town police detective who will do anything to keep her safe.**

After a sudden tragedy blew her world apart, Peyton Kerr fled her
big-city career and started over in Stoney Creek, Maine. So far,

she's loving small-town life—no one knows about her past, and her easy flirtation with Boone Knight gives her a reason to smile. But then someone is murdered in Peyton's store, and her quiet, anonymous existence is instantly destroyed. To make matters worse, Boone—a police detective—is assigned to the case, and Peyton knows she can't keep him at arm's length any longer. She's resisted the simmering heat between them, but now this gorgeous man is promising to keep her safe—and satisfied...

Boone Knight doesn't want the complications of a relationship. But when he volunteers to protect his town's newest—and sexiest—resident, he finally admits he'd like to explore their sizzling attraction. And after one incredible night, everything changes for Boone. Peyton is sweeter—and braver—than anyone he's ever met, and with her in his arms, everything makes sense. He just needs to convince her to trust him enough to reveal her secrets, or risk losing her to a merciless killer who seems to grow bolder with each passing day.

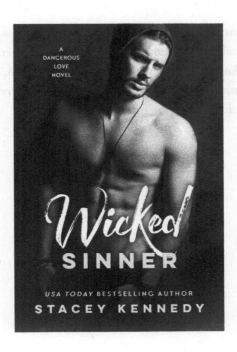

A DANGEROUS LOVE NOVEL

Wicked
SINNER

USA TODAY BESTSELLING AUTHOR
STACEY KENNEDY

A gripping, heart-pounding romance from *USA Today* bestselling author Stacey Kennedy about a former FBI agent who will do anything it takes to protect his ex, or risk losing her for good...

Asher Sullivan was once Remy Brennan's entire world—until he broke her heart into a million pieces. So when Asher crashes her wedding, Remy is certain he's come to claim her. *To make her his again.* Instead, it turns out Remy's groom is a con man scheming for her inheritance. Now all she's left with is an empty bank account, a serious case of lust for her gorgeous ex...and a duffel bag of cold, hard cash that might just fix *all* her problems.

Detective Asher Sullivan has always protected Remy. So when dangerous criminals start threatening her, Asher's most primitive instincts take over. Sticking by Remy's side means Asher is finally able to make amends for leaving her all those years ago. And soon they're giving in to their wicked, insatiable need. But just as Asher gets his second chance, a secret Remy is keeping could rip her away from him...forever.